A Postcard from PARIS

Alex Brown is the author of eight books and three novellas including the No. 1 bestsellers *Cupcakes at Carrington's* and *The Secret of Orchard Cottage*. Her books are loved worldwide and have been translated into twelve languages. Before becoming a full-time author, Alex worked in financial services and wrote the hugely popular, satirical *City Girl* column for *The London Paper*. Alex lives by the sea in Kent on the south coast of England with her husband, daughter and two glossy black labradors. When she isn't writing, she can be found singing in her soul choir, walking on the beach or enjoying a pornstar martini cocktail.

For more about Alex visit her website www.alex-brownauthor.com, and sign up to her newsletter to receive *The Beach Walk*, a free short story. She also loves chatting to readers on Facebook at www.facebook.com/alexandrabrownauthor, Twitter and Instagram @alexbrownbooks.

Also by Alex Brown

The Carrington's series

Cupcakes at Carrington's
Christmas at Carrington's
Ice Creams at Carrington's

The Tindledale series

The Great Christmas Knit Off
The Great Village Show
The Secret of Orchard Cottage
The Wish

The Postcard . . . series

A Postcard from Italy

Short Stories

Me and Mr Carrington
Not Just for Christmas
The Great Summer Sewing Bee

A Postcard from PARIS

ALEX BROWN

HarperCollins*Publishers*

HarperCollins*Publishers* Ltd
The News Building
1 London Bridge Street
London SE1 9GF

www.harpercollins.co.uk

HarperCollins*Publishers*
1st Floor, Watermarque Building, Ringsend Road
Dublin 4, Ireland

A Paperback Original 2021
1

A catalogue record for this book
is available from the British Library

ISBN: 978-0-00-842198-4

Set in Birka by Palimpsest Book Production Limited,
Falkirk, Stirlingshire

Printed and bound by
CPI Group (UK) Ltd, Croydon CR0 4YY

For Caroline, Tracey, and Rachel for continuously lifting me and being the best friends I could have. I'm truly grateful to have found you xxx

'Friendships between women, as any woman will tell you, are built of a thousand small kindnesses . . . swapped back and forth and over again'

Michelle Obama

1

Tindledale, in rural England, 1916

Beatrice Crawford craved adventure. Yearning to escape the confines of her provincial young ladyhood and find her purpose, to be a positive influence in the world. A woman of substance, just like Lady Dorothy Fields, the inimitable, flame-haired woman who had ignited the dimly lit village hall earlier this evening with a very rousing speech. Beatrice had listened intently as Lady Dorothy had talked about her nursing work with the Voluntary Aid Detachment, or VAD, carrying out her patriotic duty to look after the brave soldiers fighting in fields far away for King and Country in the Great War.

After buttoning up her cotton nightie, Beatrice sat at her dressing table and brushed out her ebony curls then, securing them away from her face with a tortoise-shell clip, she pressed cold cream over her cheeks and neck, sweeping down and across her collar bones. Going over in her mind the events of such an extraordinary evening, she recalled with wonder the atmosphere in the village hall. It had been quite thrilling. An audience of young women just like her, suffragettes too, with little tricolour brooches pinned to their lapels, sat shoulder-to-shoulder, all united in their desire to do so much more for the war effort than endure a stifling life made up of endless tedious occupations such as light domestic work or embroidering samplers in silent drawing rooms. Her younger companion, Queenie, the housekeeper's niece, who was already doing her bit by working in an ammunitions factory in the nearby town of Market Briar, had almost missed out on hearing Lady Dorothy's speech. Queenie had arrived late and in a fluster, discreetly brushing a sheen of fine raindrops from her wool beret and gloves, whispering a grateful, 'Thank you, Trixie,' before sliding onto the chair that Beatrice had saved for her at the end of the row. Exchanging a clandestine glance, Beatrice had pressed her friend's hand in reply, both of them knowing and secretly delighting in their small act of defiance. For Beatrice's stepmother, Iris, had forbidden Queenie from using 'Trixie' as a suitable pet name for her stepdaughter, citing it 'undignified, and quite common!' But Beatrice liked being Trixie:

it made her feel more alive, jolly and without constraint, and so the two friends had continued with it whenever Iris was out of earshot.

Beatrice and Queenie had forged an unlikely friendship five years ago when Iris had insisted that the then 13-year-old Beatrice 'must be perfectly fluent in at least two languages if she were to be a refined debutante and catch a suitable husband.' Eight-year- old Queenie, known to be a quick-witted and fast-learning young girl, with a tumble of auburn curls and sparkling, impish green eyes, was brought in from the village each day to be taught French and High German, in order that Beatrice might practise her own conversational skills. As for Beatrice's rudimentary French and German writing skills, they had been deemed beyond hope and were to be forgotten about forthwith. Even though Beatrice's stepmother was French, she was far too engaged in a hectic social life – which frequently took her to glamorous parties in London, Paris, Monte Carlo and beyond – to idle away her time on academia, especially when, according to Iris, Beatrice hadn't 'shown enough flair in her younger years'. Iris had also declared that revision was a tedious waste of time, and that Beatrice should show humility and recompense for her shortcomings by learning alongside an uneducated and much younger village girl, who would most likely pick it all up in half the time that it had taken Beatrice. 'So that ought to keep you on your toes!'

So, together with her French and German conversational skills, thanks to her insistent stepmother and Swiss governess, Miss Paulette, there were now only ten lectures and ten lessons in first aid and nursing standing between Beatrice and her ambition to help the soldiers fighting on the front line in France. Not that it was imperative to have language skills, but Beatrice thought it might give her a little something extra to offer, and Lady Dorothy had explained that it wasn't only English-speaking soldiers who required nursing. There were Frenchmen too. Some German soldiers, prisoners of war, as well. Of course, she would need practical first-aid training. A hospital in London perhaps, that's what Lady Dorothy had recommended, to get a foot in the door and to show her mettle. And they really were rather keen to recruit volunteers.

Drawing her knees up to her chest and placing her slippered feet on the edge of the velvet cushioned chair, Beatrice wrapped her arms around her legs and hugged the feeling of possibility into her, for she could see a way forward now. It was as if a light had been switched on deep within her, sparking a frisson of hope that she felt barely able to contain. Not that the bleak battlefields of France were a cause for elation. Certainly not. No, it was very much more than that. She had to do something. The newspapers were full of lists. The names of soldiers killed in the trenches. Pages and pages of men, some only mere boys. Thousands on the very first day of the war in 1914 and it had been relentless ever since. Fathers. Sons. Cousins. Uncles. Nephews. Her own dear brother, Edward, having enlisted at the start of the war, had mercifully been missing from the lists so far. But for how much longer? Beatrice carried a perpetual sense of foreboding that seemed impossible to shake off. Although, for the first time in her life, she felt that she also had an opportunity, a sense of purpose.

Of course, Father would protest, preferring she marry Clement Forsyth, the odious son of his banker in London, but how could she when her heart was with another? A secret love. Because Bobby worked in the stables, mucking out and tending to the horses, and so would never be suitable husband material as far as Father was concerned. Beatrice's heart had almost broken in two when Bobby had gone away to fight for his country, and not a moment went by when she didn't think of him, wrapping an imaginary shield of safety around his beautiful body so he would return to her arms once more. The only comfort being that

Bobby and Edward were together in the same PALS battalion. Queenie's older brother, Stanley, too, along with many of the other men from the village, with their camaraderie to keep their spirits up until they could return home. Beatrice treasured the photograph of Bobby that she kept hidden inside her diary, alongside the pages where she had written about her endless love for him.

Instead there was Clement, who had pursued Beatrice from first seeing her at 17 years old in the exquisite gown of white satin with lace trim that Iris had shipped over from Paris especially for the Queen Charlotte's Ball, the pinnacle event of the debutante season. He had been relentless from then on, constantly calling on Beatrice at home and always appearing by her side at society events – Royal Ascot, Henley Regatta, King George's coronation gala, not to mention all the other balls at various grand estates and castles that she had been wheeled out to by her overbearing stepmother. And woe betide if another 'debs' delight' so much as glanced in Beatrice's direction, for Clement had become insufferable in warning them off with one of his supercilious glares and a territorial hand on her arm. Fortunately, all talk of marriage had been suspended for now since conscription had started on 2 March and Clement had reluctantly taken a commission in the army. And Beatrice's stepmother would protest even more to her going to France, branding her desire to volunteer as a nonsensical notion that should be stopped at once, of that Beatrice was certain.

'It's not becoming for a young lady of your standing to take up such menial work. Mopping floors and changing soiled bed linen. Whatever next! Your poor father, having to shoulder such embarrassment from his own flesh and blood is quite unforgivable. And if you refuse to give up such whimsical ideas and continue to rebuff a perfectly suitable marriage proposition, then I fear you will become too old and contrary for any respectable gentleman to consider taking as a wife. You will spend the rest of your days as a spinster!' is what Iris had spluttered in outrage over supper one evening when Beatrice had first mooted the possibility, some months ago, of her helping out at the Red Cross auxiliary hospital set up in the Stanway Rectory on the outskirts of the village. Beatrice remembered the evening vividly, because later, in the privacy of her bedroom suite, she had written down her stepmother's hurtful words in the diary which she kept locked in a burr-walnut wood writing slope that had belonged to her darling mother, and now to her. Spinster! Beatrice had even underlined the word several times and had then spent a great deal of time pondering on whether being a spinster might not be the curse that Iris perceived it to be. Especially if she couldn't be with Bobby and the alternative was to be the reluctant wife of Clement Forsyth.

Beatrice was only 18 years old and a young lady should be 23 to be accepted for an overseas voluntary nursing post, Lady Dorothy had explained. But with her nineteenth birthday next month, Beatrice was determined to find a way around the rule and would increase her age if required to do so. She wasn't usually one for lying but if that is what it took, then so be it. And the other women in the hall had spoken about this after the meeting with such nonchalance, declaring it impolite to ask a lady her age. It was a minor detail to be disregarded for the greater good of the country. So there really was no time to waste. Beatrice was resolute. With her whole life ahead of her, which was far too precious to fritter away in a suitable but none-theless loveless marriage, she wondered about romance. And love. True love, like the love she had with Bobby and the love that her mother had shared with her father before her life had been cruelly cut short.

Beatrice had only been 4 years old when it had happened, Edward 7 and away at boarding school. Their mother had died giving birth to another daughter who hadn't survived either, and from then on Beatrice had felt terribly alone, with long hours spent gazing from her bedroom window, hoping to find a fragment of comfort in the view, out and across the undulating, sun-drenched fields and faraway into the distance, past the wooden water mill that powered through the river, over and over, its melodic rhythm like balm to her grieving young soul. Beatrice had seen a rainbow one time and wondered if over the glistening arc of the petroleum-coloured streaks was where heaven lay, and if she might go there to be reunited with her beautiful mother.

She missed her dreadfully. Baking and sketching together, Beatrice had adored sharing these activities with her mother, along with perfume making and flower pressing, where they would wander through the fields to pick wild flowers and mix them into a scented potion, keeping the brightest blooms to slot into the press for drying and applying to scrapbooks. Beatrice still had the scrapbooks but couldn't bear to look through them after her mother had died.

As time had ticked on and Beatrice's memory of her mother, radiant and enthused with the sweet scent of rose perfume, always with a smile and a kiss for her adoring husband, had faded, Beatrice had grown up and managed to forge a slice of happiness for herself. Immersing herself in her diary-writing and reading books, *Little Women* being her favourite. Beatrice had drawn strength from the vibrant and strident March sisters, developing a passion for gaiety and curiosity about the *joie de vivre* that Miss Paulette had spoken of in those French lessons she'd had as a child.

Where was all of that now? Beatrice knew there was a shortage of suitable men, thanks to this dreadful war; not that she wanted another man when her true love was Bobby, but she also knew her own mind and that she would most likely go mad if she didn't take this opportunity to escape. If she were to remain a spinster for the rest of her life then so be it, but at least she would be in charge of steering her own destiny. There really was no other option, for surely she would suffocate into oblivion if she were to end up leading a very insignificant life as the demure wife of a bombastic banker. Besides, there were only so many samplers one could possibly endure embroidering day after day, with just piano recitals and letter writing to break the monotony. She needed more. Much more. And she had very much more to give in return.

Yes, the decision was made. Beatrice was going to join the VAD. She would volunteer at the rectory hospital first, progress on to a London hospital while completing her training, and then she would broaden her horizons further and travel to France where she would make beds, change dressings and bathe injured soldiers. And she would feel honoured to do so. She would wear a blue uniform with a pristine white apron and linen cap secured with a safety pin at the nape of her neck and feel extremely efficient, knowing that her work there was worthwhile and of the utmost importance. She nodded her head as if to underline the biggest decision she had ever made in her life.

Lady Dorothy had captured Beatrice's imagination with photographs of herself in her own uniform. In one photograph, Lady Dorothy was even wearing khaki trousers tucked inside long leather boots, just like a man. In another, she was driving a motor ambulance and giving the photographer a rousing wave from the open window. And in that moment, Beatrice knew that she would very much like to have this experience too. She could already drive, having driven Father's motor car in the grounds around the house. Sidney, the gamekeeper, had shown her the ropes, and she had mastered the steering wheel and brake in no time at all. So, it was settled, Beatrice was to become a woman of substance and make a positive difference at last . . . just as soon as she had Father and Iris onboard with her marvellous escape plan.

2

London, England, 2019

Annie Lovell momentarily closed her eyes and resisted a sigh as she listened to her daughter, 22-year-old Phoebe, lecture her on FaceTime.

'Oh Mum, why didn't you wait? I would have helped you pack the boxes and put them up into the loft. You only had to ask . . . It's really no trouble at all.'

Silence followed.

'Mum! Are you listening?' Phoebe barked, startling Annie and almost making her spill the generous measure of rosé from the wine glass in her hand. 'Are you OK? You seem distracted. Did you bump your head in the fall?'

'No, darling. Honestly, I'm fine,' Annie said, now wishing she hadn't mentioned falling off the loft ladder.

'And why are you drinking? At this time of the day! It's only six p.m. You know, it's really not a good idea to chug down loads of alcohol every evening. I listened to a podcast during my run this morning and learnt all about the perils of midweek drinking. How middle-aged people, women predominantly, are putting away a whole bottle a night, easily. And then not even real-izing when alcohol becomes an issue for them—'

'Sweetheart! Alcohol is not an issue for me,' Annie jumped in as Phoebe gave herself a smidgen of a second to draw breath, 'plus, I am not middle-aged. I've only just had my forty-ninth birthday. People live to a hundred these days, easily, so I have a good year or so to go before I'm technically middle-aged and you need to worry about me. Not that you ever will need to – worry, that is,' she added gently, pushing a chunk of blonde hair behind an ear and surreptitiously taking another quick sip of the wine off camera. She then placed the glass on the coffee table beside her and carefully angled the laptop away from the wine box that her best friend, Beth, had sent to her.

'For restorative purposes, darling. Put your feet up and take a load off that poor foot of yours,' Beth had instructed when Annie had called her to say thank you for the luxury care package consisting of the wine box, a gloriously scented candle, a box of Annie's favourite chocolate truffles, a stack of glossy home interiors magazines and a Netflix gift card, all wrapped up in pink tissue paper inside a little wicker hamper with leather straps.

Beth had always been kind and thoughtful, and always supportive, especially during the tough times. And there had been a few. From when Annie's ex-husband, Mark, had left back when the children were very young and her heart had broken. Shattered beyond repair. It had been an extremely difficult time for Annie after she had put aside her own career and travel aspirations to marry Mark when they discovered she was pregnant with Phoebe only a year after leaving university. After the wedding, Annie had focused on looking after their young family and home, whereas Mark had carried on pretty much as he always had, building his career and going out with his mates and away for golfing weekends. But he had always come home, and had been loving and attentive when he was there. Until one day when he didn't come home! Then, ignoring her calls and messages for a further two days, until Annie, in desperation, had started calling the local hospitals and eventually his parents, Mark had eventually showed himself to be the coward he was by sending her an email explaining that he wasn't actually ready to settle down and so was moving in with a younger woman he had met at work. It took him a week to actually talk face to face with Annie and explain that Carly didn't have children and loved travelling and going to festivals. A free spirit. Much like Annie had been before she met Mark. And this had made him realize that he wasn't actually cut out for family life after all.

It had been Beth who had got Annie through the harrowing years that followed. A single mum with shattered dreams that had sapped all her confidence. Various lukewarm relationships had followed. Then there had been that time when Annie had found an ominous lump in her left breast, which, after the biopsy, had turned out to be nothing to worry about at all, but she would have crumbled for sure if she hadn't had Beth to wrap her into one of her trademark big bear hugs. And Annie had always been there for Beth too, when her wonderful, kind-hearted dad had died, through to accompanying her to the various gigs and auditions she had done over the years to forge her singing career. Which was why it was such a wrench now that Beth had left for Australia.

Annie knew she mustn't begrudge her best friend the once-in-a-lifetime opportunity of a twelve-month residency singing soprano at the Sydney Opera House – it had been Beth's dream since childhood – but Annie was already missing her so much. Talking and texting on the phone just wasn't the same. With the time difference, there never seemed to be enough hours to gossip and practically laugh themselves into a hernia at a shared joke or a hilarious memory from their joint history. Just like they always had done, almost every day for near on forty years or so. And the last time Beth had tried to FaceTime Annie, the connection had been so slow and terrible that she had disconnected the call after just a few seconds, leaving Annie feeling extremely deflated. Apart from elderly Joanie, who lived next door, Beth was Annie's only close friend, and Phoebe's godmother too.

Having met at primary school, Beth was more like a sister. They had done everything together – sleepovers when schoolgirls, then gigs and parties as teenagers – before sharing a tiny flat in Edinburgh during their university years, and so Annie had never really thought about socializing in other ways, with the people at work, for example. Not that after-work drinks or office parties were her kind of thing, to be honest. Then after the split with Mark, Annie had become very insular, staying at home and only socializing with Beth. But Beth had been gone for three months now and Annie was feeling very lonely. She had found herself retreating back into the familiar cosy cocoon of comfort – sewing, embroidery, knitting, making things for her home – just as she had when Mark had abandoned her. It felt safe. And Annie knew where she was at when she stayed at home. Putting herself out there, socializing, dating, and all that entailed, was fraught with the possibility of getting hurt again.

'I'm not *worried*, Mum . . . well, of course I am worried, but I'm also very concerned,' Phoebe said, bringing Annie's thoughts back to the FaceTime call and the screen on her laptop. 'What were you thinking of, climbing up a ladder with a big pile of stuff in your arms?' she added, her forehead creasing.

'I was storing my decorating supplies – wallpaper books and paint colour charts, that kind of thing,' Annie started, knowing she was a hoarder when it came to her interior design paraphernalia. She also knew that Phoebe cared, worried about her, overly so, but she had also always been clingy and a bit controlling too, and her need for control had intensified in recent years. It had started a year or so after Mark left and his promised weekly visits turned into fortnightly and then monthly, until sometimes he didn't turn up at all. Phoebe would be waiting by the window, looking out for her daddy, who cancelled at the last minute, often because Carly wasn't well, or needed him for some obscure reason or another, and Mark had taken the path of least resistance and done what she wanted. And this had created an insecurity in

Phoebe. Losing a parent, effectively, would do that to a child, because although Mark hadn't died, he hadn't much bothered trying to be a part of Phoebe's life either. And then not long after, or so it seemed, he was married again with two new children. Twins! And Mark's visits to Phoebe fizzled out altogether, even though Annie had tried so hard to persuade him to be more involved, begged him too, on a couple of occasions, even though she knew she shouldn't have to. It was heartbreaking though, seeing her child feeling so abandoned like that. Annie had felt quite helpless at times, especially as she had been trying to cope with her own feelings of loss for the life she thought she was going to have with Mark, the love of her life, or so she had thought when she was married to him.

'Ah, I might have known it would be something to do with your hobby.' Phoebe sighed and shook her head, as if she were a frustrated mother talking to her accident-prone child. 'You do know that you could have fallen down the stairs when the ladder toppled over. You could have actually broken your neck! In fact, it's a bloody miracle that you didn't kill yourself, or worse still, end up paralysed with only the power of your blinking eyelids to communicate.' Annie had to stifle a smile, not because it was funny to think of being paralysed, but because Phoebe genuinely looked absolutely flabbergasted, as she often did in situations like this, which in turn somehow always managed to make her perpetual exasperation seem comical. 'Imagine that! I couldn't think of anything more awful than being caged up inside your own lifeless body. And another thing, falling down the stairs is one of the most common accidents within the home. Statistics show tha—'

'Well there you go, darling,' Annie leapt in again, keen to end the lecture. 'Lots of people must climb up ladders in their hallways every day. It's really not that uncommon,' she pointed out. Annie loved her daughter with all her heart, but Phoebe really could be very pedantic and dramatic at times. And Annie already felt foolish for falling off the ladder, having misjudged the distance from the loft-hatch opening to where the light switch was on the wall inside the roof. So when she had overextended her arm to flick the light on, she had inadvertently pushed her left leg outwards, wobbled before dropping the wallpaper books and paint colour charts and grasping the ladder in an attempt to save herself, but the ladder had toppled over and taken her with it. The fall had happened so quickly and Annie had felt fine after it happened, pulling herself upright and pottering downstairs to have a restorative cup of tea with a couple of chunks of chocolate. It was only when she woke up the following morning with a swollen, painful foot that she took herself off to the minor injury clinic for an X-ray and discovered that one of the small metatarsal bones had fractured, and so she had been instructed to elevate her leg and use cold packs to reduce the swelling. It really wasn't a massive deal, and certainly not the catastrophe that Phoebe was making it out to be.

And in any case, Annie was very pleased that she had been up in the loft as she'd had a little sort-out of the boxes stored up there and had come across one of her old childhood scrapbooks crammed full of colourful postcards from around the globe. So when she had finished comforting herself with the chocolate chunks, she had enjoyed a marvellous half-hour going through her old postcard collection and looking at all the exotic locations that family and friends had visited and, knowing that she collected postcards, had sent one to her especially. It had been Annie's ambition to travel, but she hadn't been able to afford to as a single parent when the children were young.

Annie glanced at the clock on the mantelpiece above the log burner, seeing that it was almost time for the interior design challenge programme she loved; it was her favourite TV show. And it was the semi-final this week which she had been looking forward to, so she really didn't want to miss it.

'Did you call for anything in particular, darling? Or just for a chat?' Annie asked as a preliminary to wrapping up the call as quickly and as politely as she could.

'Yes, I did, Mum, I called to ask you something very important. I've been thinking about this for a while now, since you had that nasty chest infection last winter that went on for weeks, do you remember?'

'Um, yes, vaguely,' Annie replied slowly, wondering where this was going.

'And, well . . .' Phoebe paused and flicked her eyes away, as if searching for the right words. '. . . I've spoken to Johnny about it too.'

'Oh, how is he?' Annie asked, always keen for snippets of information about her youngest child. Johnny, two years younger than Phoebe, had just started his third year at university, and the last time she'd had a proper conversation with him was when he turned up at Christmas, three months ago. Aside from the odd text message on her birthday or Mother's Day, contact from Johnny was extremely rare indeed. That was OK, though, and Annie didn't begrudge him his independence, even if she did miss him dreadfully, but she would never cajole or guilt-trip him into coming home to see her. Especially when he was most likely having the time of his life with his new friends as he travelled to obscure locations to dig up the ground as part of his geology degree course.

'Um, he's good. Busy doing whatever it is he does, most likely sitting up all night playing Fortnite, eating yesterday's pizza and being fascinated by a pile of rocks with all the other nerds,' Phoebe said, uninterestedly. 'Anyway, he agrees that you must come and live with me!'

'Live with you! Whatever for?' Annie sat upright.

'So that I can look after you, of course. Just until your broken foot is better. And then I thought we could find you a bungalow nearby. Somewhere close so I can pop in a few times a day to check on you. It makes perfect sense, Mum. With Aunty Beth gone and you being all on your own now. And I know you love all that amateur interior design stuff that you do, but you're not getting any younger so you really shouldn't be up ladders changing your wallpaper and trying out different paint effects any more, and you don't need a three-bedroom house either. You could sell it and buy a little bungalow, or a garden flat . . . you know, somewhere without any steps. Or a loft hatch for you to fall from! Think of your future. Property up here is way cheaper than down there, so you would have a nice big lump sum left over to save as a nest egg for the future. For your retireme—'

'Retirement!' Annie laughed. 'Don't be silly. That's a long way off. Nearly two decades away. And I have a job. Here, in London. It would take hours to commute every day from where you live, in Yorkshire.'

'Yes, I know, but it's only a boring office job. And you hate it. You've always said so. Mum, you're a work-aholic. And it's not healthy. So it's about time you did something else. Besides, lots of people retire at fifty these days so you're practically there. Think of all the interest that nest egg could earn for you. Plus, who wants to work in an office their whole life?'

'But it's my job! And I've worked hard for it,' Annie said, recalling the late nights of studying she had done when Phoebe and Johnny were little, in order to gain the necessary qualifications to work as a bookkeeper in the accounts department of a big firm of solicitors in London. It wasn't her intended career; that had been interior design and she had studied hard for it at university to gain an honours degree. But she had found it impossible to forge a sustainable career in interior design straight from university, with a young family to care for and Mark often away on his various trips, so she'd eventually given up on trying to set up her own interior design company. Fast forward a few years to when she found herself a single parent with two school-age children, she took a series of part-time jobs that fitted in around school hours and then studied at night when they were asleep. Mark had never contributed enough financially, and so when Annie had managed to eventually find her first full-time role in the law firm in the City of London, life had become a whole lot easier without the worry of debt for the three of them. Even if she had been completely exhausted for much of that decade.

'I know you've worked hard, Mum. You always have,' Phoebe said, seeming to soften, 'so then even more reason to slow down a bit. You don't need to be a workaholic these days. It's not like you've got a mortgage any more, thanks to Granddad leaving you that money to pay it off—'

'Darling, please, I don't want to retire at fifty. Yes, my job is boring at times . . . and it's not that I wouldn't love for us to be a bit closer to each other, but . . .' Annie let her voice trail off as she tried to get her head around what Phoebe was really saying. That she was past it, with no real life of her own, and so should retreat gracefully to become a husk of the woman that she once was! Or so it seemed in that moment.

'Well, just think about it for now,' Phoebe persisted. 'That's the beauty of having a basic life, you can just pack it all in without too much trouble. It's not as if you have loads going on down there anyway, especially now that Aunty Beth has gone away. And you haven't got a boyfriend or any pets or whatever to worry about.'

A long, ominous silence followed.

Did her daughter really think that she was incapable of looking after herself? That her life was *basic*? Practically over with. And 'pop in to check on you'! Annie felt affronted. Embarrassed even. 'Popping in to check' was what friends and family did for properly old people. People in their eighties or nineties with mobility issues or in the early stages of dementia. People like Joanie next door with her halo of white curls and collection of hand-knitted cardies. Not that Joanie had dementia, far from it, she was vibrant and whip-smart and Annie loved spending time with her playing rummy and putting the world to rights. But since slipping on some ice and fracturing her hip last Christmas, Joanie did struggle to get upstairs these days and so was mostly living downstairs now, having converted her dining room in to a bedroom. Whereas, Annie was a perfectly healthy 49-year-old, albeit with a surgical boot on her left foot, but she wouldn't need to wear it for much longer in any case. She had an appointment at the fracture clinic in a week or so and then there would be no stopping her. She already had her eye on a gorgeous pair of new wedge sandals to treat herself with once the ugly boot was no longer needed.

'You could give up your job!' Phoebe kept on. 'Or how about you help me out at the gym? You know, only if you really wanted to keep busy that is. I could do with a part-time receptionist to cover the phones when I'm teaching classes or with my personal training clients. But it's not vital. You could join some clubs, the WI, or there's bound to be a committee of some sort at the parish council, that sort of thing, just to keep your hand in. You could even sign up for a course at the local college, they're sure to have some-thing to interest you. Upholstery or curtain-making, for example. It would get you out socializing and meeting new friends. And then when you do retire you'll have a ready-made friendship group. Staying active, that's the key to a successful old age. As soon as you give in and sit around all day doing nothing but watch the telly, that's when the dementia sets in.' It seemed Phoebe had the next twenty years or so all planned out for Annie. 'Why don't I drive down and pick you up?'

'Phoebe,' Annie started, coughing discreetly and reaching for the remote control to pause the start of the interior design programme. She suddenly felt slightly disconcerted as she had been watching rather a lot of TV recently; the Netflix gift card had been a genius idea from Beth. And her focus hadn't been as sharp as it usually was; the intricate knitting project she was attempting had been a struggle and she had even given up on the file that she had been working on from home today. But, hang on! She inhaled and let out a long breath to clear her head. She wasn't old. Yes, she was tired and jaded and missing her best friend, plus she hadn't had any time off work in ages. They had been extra busy over the last few months; it was the same every year, with all the divorce cases coming in after the Christmas break, and so she hadn't managed to book a holiday. In fact, she couldn't remember the last time she had been away, and if she was really honest with herself then, it was probably true . . . she had become a workaholic.

'Phoebe, it's lovely of you to offer to look after me, but really there's no need. And besides, you're busy with the gym. Plus I'll be off to Paris soon—'

'Paris!' Phoebe's face froze on the laptop screen. 'What on earth do you mean? Mum, you can't go to Paris,' she puffed, incredulous.

'Of course I can. I'm looking forward to it actually,' Annie told her, remembering the bubble of excitement mingled with anticipation when Joanie had asked if she'd 'be a dear and go and take a look for me? I don't like flying, and sitting on a train that goes under the sea really isn't for me. Not with my hip. I dread to think what would happen if the train broke down in the middle of the tunnel. I'd never make it out of there if we had to be evacuated on foot. And if you don't mind me saying so, dear, you could do with a break. You've been looking very pasty these past few weeks.' Joanie had never been one to mince her words.

Annie had been round at Joanie's house a few Saturdays ago, sharing a morning coffee and a slice of her homemade Victoria sponge, when the postman had knocked on the door with a letter that had needed signing for. After reading through all the details, Joanie had called the firm of solicitors in London where the letter had come from and discovered that she had inherited an apartment in Paris! The will also included a boarded-up dilapidated old shop, or *boutique* as they said in France, directly underneath the apartment. But whatever the state of it was, it was now Joanie's. To do with whatever she pleased.

Reading between the lines, Annie had taken this to potentially mean that Joanie could have inherited a serious financial burden that the executor wanted to offload. But after verifying her identity and signing a pile of paperwork, Joanie found she was now the legal owner of a one-bedroom apartment in an eighteenth-century stone building located on a cobble-stoned private pedestrian street off the Place de la Bastille, accessed through a grand archway, and she wanted her neighbour and good friend, Annie, to go and check it all out for her. Joanie had offered to pay for travel and a hotel, but Annie knew she needed to step out of her comfort zone and try to put the spark back into her life and so was more than happy to fund her own trip. She would make a holiday of it, and so had booked herself into an Airbnb place with an English-speaking host called Marguerite. From there, she could visit the apartment and report back to Joanie with her findings and recommendations before doing all the wonderful Parisian sights.

'Looking forward to it! What do you mean, Mum?' Phoebe reiterated, leaning closer to the camera so that Annie could see the frown lines on her daughter's alarmed face. 'And why do you look all glowy and perky all of a sudden?' Silence followed. 'Ah, hang on! Don't tell me you're going to Paris with a man! Is that it? Mum, have you met a man? Why didn't you say?' Phoebe's eyes lit up momentarily, before she added, 'Oh, please say you didn't meet him online. You do know those dating sites are riddled with con artists. Catfishing and all sorts goes on. They are only after your money, you know. If you're feeling lonely, then why don't you let me set you up with a proper profile, a nice picture and all that. I could help you find the perfect partner. Or better still, if you move up here then I could introduce you to some of the men who come to my gym. Geoff! Yes, Geoff is very nice. He's divorced, fifty-something so a bit older than you. But still in pretty good shape and he's not bad looking for an older bloke. And he likes cooking, fishing and doing crosswords. How exciting! Mum, you could have a wonderful romance and a partner to hook up with and do fun things like . . . go to the cinema, or to a nice restaurant, afternoon tea at the garden centre—'

'Phoebe! Stop it! Please. Darling, there is no man. I'm not looking to meet a man. Well, not unless the right one came along . . .' And certainly not one like Geoff, Annie thought to herself. Sitting around doing crosswords wasn't her thing. Fishing definitely wasn't. Plus afternoon tea at a garden centre was something she was looking forward to doing when she actually retired, in about twenty years' time. Mind you, the cooking might come in handy as Annie wasn't a keen cook, preferring to pierce a cellophane lid and wait for the ping of the microwave, or to try out a lovely café or restaurant whenever she could. 'I'm going to Paris on my own.'

'Then I'll come with you. If you really want to see

Paris. But you can't go on your own . . .' Annie thought Phoebe looked genuinely concerned now.

'I'll be fine. Please try not to worry, sweetheart. I'm only going for a fortnight and I can call you while I'm there,' Annie assured her, trying to sound light about it, even though inside she was starting to wonder if two whole weeks away from home, her comfort zone, was a good idea after all.

'A fortnight! But what if something happens to you?'

'I'm sure it won't. And I'll send you a postcard. A postcard from Paris, you'd like that. Do you remember when you were little—'

'No, Mum. That was years ago. I don't collect postcards any more. And nobody sends postcards these days.' Annie was sure Phoebe actually looked aghast at the idea, and suddenly she felt foolish, behind the times. Maybe she had become too insular, past it, on account of her 'basic life'! 'Even Aunty Beth knows that – did you know she emailed me a gorgeous film of her doing all the sights in Australia, so I could see them too. How cool is that?'

'Wow!' Annie said, impressed and delighted for Phoebe, but then cross with herself for feeling a little put out that Beth hadn't sent her a film too. 'Very cool,' she confirmed, 'I'd love to see the sights of Australia . . .'

'Oh, um . . . sure, I'll send it on,' Phoebe said

nonchalantly, clearly not realizing that Annie felt left out. She inhaled and let out a long breath. It was ridiculous to feel jealous; she wasn't 12 years old and in a school playground any more, yet still . . . she missed her best friend so much.

'So why are you going to Paris then?'

'To check out Joanie's new apartment and then have a look around Paris. I've always wanted to travel and so now is my chance.' Annie explained about Joanie's inheritance, trying to sound much more confident than she felt about travelling on her own, while Phoebe stared very solemnly at the screen, taking it all in.

'Well, it sounds very clandestine to me,' Phoebe said, eventually. 'And why doesn't Joanie go there herself?'

'You know she's getting on and her mobility isn't what it used to be. Besides, she has no intention of living in the apartment in Paris – she has other plans.'

'Then doesn't she have a relative who could go?' Phoebe squinted, as if interrogating Annie. 'It seems weird that she wants a neighbour to go for her.'

'No. There's nobody else. She doesn't have any children or relatives and her friends are all elderly too. Anyway, I'm happy to go for her; she trusts me and we are friends after all. And have been for a very long time. I want to help her out. Isn't that what friends do for each other?'

'Hmm, she's always put upon you. Do you remember when she had that fall and you ended up at her house practically every night doing everything for her.'

'And I was happy to do that too,' Annie said, thinking how mean her daughter could be sometimes. Joanie had been a godsend back in the day when Phoebe and Johnny had been young, often babysitting at short notice and never accepting payment, always happy to step in when Annie had a rare evening out or had to work late. So it was the least Annie could do now to go and take a look at an apartment in Paris. It was hardly a hardship; in fact it was exciting and she felt delighted to have the opportunity. She loved nosing around properties and had spent many a happy Sunday afternoon, cosy by the log burner, searching through Rightmove looking for her dream 'doer upper'.

'But what about the person who left her the apartment? Beatrice Archambeau, did you say?'

'Yes, that's right,' Annie nodded.

'Who even is she? Surely she must have had some family, and by the sounds of it Joanie knows nothing at all about the woman. What if it's some kind of elaborate hoax to make Joanie pay to refurbish a Parisian apartment which they then steal from her?'

'It's not a hoax, Phoebe,' Annie said, firmly. 'The solicitor here in London has been very thorough and

I'm to collect the keys and paperwork to the apartment from a Monsieur Aumont, an *avocat* – that's the French word for solicitor. He's the executor in Paris dealing with Beatrice's will. I'm making lunch for Joanie next week so we can discuss it all before I go to Paris, so I guess I'll find out more about the apartment and how Joanie has come to inherit it then. And no doubt the *avocat* will tell us more about Beatrice Archambeau when I get there.'

'Hmm,' Phoebe pondered, then, 'ah, but what about your foot? I'm not sure you can fly with a fracture.' And Annie was sure she spotted a fleeting flicker of triumph on her daughter's face, and if she was perfectly honest with herself, it irked her. Why couldn't Phoebe be happy for her? Yes, she understood Phoebe's insecurities with having a distant dad, and Annie felt that she had done everything she could to ease them for her – organizing and paying for courses of expensive therapy sessions over the years and giving her as much love and attention as she possibly could to make up for her missing father. As children, Phoebe had always had the biggest chunk of Annie's time over Johnny, with her numerous cheerleading lessons and tournaments. Phoebe had become fascinated with cheerleading at a young age, after watching a reality TV show about a squad of impossibly athletic girls and boys in an American high school.

From then on, the three of them had spent practically every weekend travelling around the country so Phoebe could compete and add another trophy to her impressive collection that was now housed in a display cabinet in the reception area of her gym. But Phoebe was an adult now, and with a boyfriend who adored her, a successful business of her own, a lovely home and busy social life. So she really did need to try to be happy, instead of always looking for a reason not to be, or so it seemed to Annie.

'Then I'll take the train.' Annie sneaked a quick sip of the wine, feeling ridiculous at the subterfuge, but she didn't want to antagonize her daughter even further.

'Mum, what's got into you? Next you'll be telling me you're going on that train, the *Orient Express*, like you're Miss Marple in one of those Agatha Christie films or something.'

'Oh, what a good idea. I might just do that!' Annie couldn't resist, perking up even more at the prospect of travelling in style as she embarked on an adventure. Yes, she was nervous about going to Paris on her own – she had never travelled solo; in fact, she hadn't really done much at all on her own. Her life had revolved around the children, and then when they had left home, it had been her safe bubble indoors or at work, especially since Beth had left. But what better way to escape her 'boring job' and 'basic life' as Phoebe said, than by spending a fortnight in the most romantic city in the world?

The city of light. Paris. Where she would check out the apartment for Joanie and then spend the rest of the time visiting all the iconic sights – the Eiffel Tower, the Arc de Triomphe, the Champs-Élysées and Notre-Dame. Followed by plenty of shopping. Sephora! She couldn't wait to visit the popular cosmetics emporium, and they had three stores in Paris. How exiting! And meander along pretty cobbled boulevards where she would choose a chic café by the river Seine to sit and watch the people of Paris go by as she sipped sweet *chocolat chaud* and ate a deliciously buttery, flaky croissant. *Oui. Très bon*, she mused to herself in schoolgirl French. And if she pushed aside her reservations about travelling on her own, then she found that she was actually looking forward to venturing out of her comfort zone to put the sparkle back into her 'basic life' in one of *les plus belles villes* in the world . . .

3

The following week, after her appointment at the fracture clinic, Annie was relieved to be free of the surgical boot and was now cocooned in Joanie's sumptuously saggy, but extremely comfy sofa with a large slice of her homemade Victoria sponge cake and a steaming mug of tea.

'Well, thank you, dear, for a marvellous lunch,' Joanie twinkled, her rheumy blue eyes crinkling at the corners. 'That steak and ale pie was the very best I've tasted,' she nodded, smoothing down her floral skirt before getting comfortable in the armchair opposite Annie.

'Ah, well, I can't take all the credit,' Annie admitted. 'You know I'm not much of a cook, so we have Marks and Spencer to thank.' She tilted her head to one side before taking a bite of cake, using the linen napkin that Joanie had given her to wipe the gooey, sweet strawberry jam from her fingertips. 'Mmm, this is delicious, Joanie.' They had polished off a scrumptious lunch of the pie, a medley of vegetables and a big bowl of creamy, cheese-topped mash which Annie had cooked in her own kitchen and then wheeled round on Joanie's lovely vintage gold-and-rose-patterned hostess trolley.

'I've had lots of practice, not only baking it, but eating it too!' Joanie chuckled, her halo of white curls bobbing around for a bit as she patted her ample middle. 'And that reminds me, I've boxed up a wedge of cake for you to take on the journey to Paris tomorrow. The train might have one of those buffet carriages on board but you'll pay a fortune for a tiny little slice of their cake,' she puffed disapprovingly. Then, with her eyebrows knitting, added, 'Are you really sure you are up for going all that way on your own?'

'Oh, Joanie, you didn't need to do that, but thank you, your cake will make the journey even more pleasurable,' Annie smiled. 'And yes, I'm definitely up for going on my own. I'm thrilled that I can do this for you – you've helped me out so much over the years so it's the least I can do.'

'Well, we've helped each other out, dear, to be fair. But I wouldn't want you to be worried about travelling on your own. If you don't mind me saying so, Annie, you've seemed a bit withdrawn lately, not your usual chatty self. Is it because you are missing Beth?'

Silence followed as Annie busied herself by picking at the corner of the cake as she contemplated how she had felt over the past few months. It was true, she had felt dull, as if a light had dimmed within her.

'Yes, she has left a big gap in my life, but I didn't realize my missing her was that obvious,' Annie eventually said.

'Maybe not to others, but I've known you a long time, Annie, and I've noticed a change in you,' Joanie started softly, a look of concern on her lined face. 'Of course, Beth is bound to have left a big gap and I know how much she means to you, but don't take this the wrong way, love, because we can't all be the bold, upfront one, but maybe this is an opportunity for you to step out of her shadow now.' Joanie paused to take a bite of her slice of cake while Annie thought about what her elderly friend had said. Joanie was right, of course . . . Beth was a larger-than-life character and it had been very easy to float along through life as her sidekick. Easy. Especially through the years after Mark left. As a single parent with limited opportunity to go out or travel, Annie had to admit that she had lived vicariously through Beth. She had looked forward to a lovely long chat of a Sunday evening, as Beth regaled her with tales of her riotous Saturday nights out full of blind dates in cocktail bars, after whatever show she had been singing in that evening, often in the West End of London, as her career took off. And it was exciting. And a world away from Annie's quiet nights in and days spent doing the school run before commuting to the office. But Beth had also been a considerate friend, and had always made an effort to pop round whenever she had an evening off so they could watch a film and eat pizza and drink prosecco when the children were in bed. Then, in recent years, they had enjoyed cinema trips and meals in new restaurants, even the odd spa weekend away when Beth hadn't been working. But it was impossible to do any of those things now with her on the other side of the world.

'So, what do you reckon?' Joanie asked, interrupting Annie's reverie. 'Could this be a chance to put the *joie de vivre* . . . as they say in French, back into your life? Now could be a good time to do a bit more for yourself. Not that you aren't capable, my love, I know you are, but it's good to venture out. It will help you gain your confidence back. Put a spring in your step. You don't want to slip back to how you were when Mark left! And with Johnny and Phoebe having flown the nest . . . well, you're not having to dash around as much as you used to, and trust me, I've learnt the hard way that inactivity is the worst thing, especially as we get older. Sitting indoors isn't good for the mind, or the old joints!' she said, echoing Phoebe's warning.

'I know, and I reckon you're right,' Annie agreed quietly. She certainly wasn't ready to pack up her life and live in perpetual anonymity in a bungalow with only a WI meeting each week and a blind date with Geoff from Phoebe's gym to look forward to. 'So, tell me more about the apartment, what would you like me to do when I get there?' Annie asked, to move the conversation on.

'Right you are,' Joanie said, taking the hint and nodding resolutely. 'Well, apparently, the apartment is small and in need of considerable updating, the solicitor has warned,' she started, reaching over to the coffee table to put down her plate and pick up a big folder full of paperwork. 'I think he doesn't want to raise my hopes as it hasn't been lived in for a long time. Beatrice, she's the woman who owned it, reached the impressive age of one hundred and four, and spent the last decade of her life in a *village retraite*, or retirement village, in the South of France, before she died in 2002. There was a caveat in the will requiring the inheritance to be given to me only on the death of another tenant, or when notice was given by that tenant of their voluntary intention to move, and that happened a year ago.'

Joanie took a breath as she opened the folder, took out a pad and thumbed through the papers before pulling out a couple of sheets that looked like letters from the solicitor.

'It sounds very intriguing,' Annie said, polishing off the last of her cake. 'And you really have no information about Beatrice, or know who she is?' She lifted her eyebrows.

'No, none at all! It's a complete mystery to me. I don't know who she is, other than she was one hundred and four when she died and – before moving to the retirement village – had lived in the apartment since the 1920s. And we only know this because of the paperwork linked to the apartment.'

'Well, somebody must know of her,' Annie said.

'I hope so. It's one thing having dates and facts on pieces of paper, but I want to know who Beatrice really was. The woman. What was she like? What did she do? What was her life like? And if she is a long-lost relative, then it would be very nice to see a picture of her. I'm wondering if I look like her.'

'I'll do my very best,' Annie assured her. 'I could ask around – see if there's a neighbour perhaps . . .'

'Yes please,' Joanie said. 'You know, it's taken all this time for the executor, a French solicitor called Monsieur Aumont, to find me, apparently. And he hasn't been forthcoming at all. Cagey, in fact! I did ask the solicitor here in England to see if he could find out more about Beatrice, but he's not had any luck.'

'Oh,' Annie sat upright. 'Why is that?'

'Well, this is the very intriguing bit . . . Beatrice's will only noted a Joan Smith, born in 1944. No more details, other than an address in London's East End that had been bombed in the war.'

'And did you ever live in the East End?'

'Oh yes, dear. I was born there. But I grew up in a children's home far away in Suffolk. You see, both my parents were killed during the Second World War – my father, a soldier in France, never made it back home, and my mother died when our home in Mile End took a direct hit from a German V2 bomber. I was left an orphan. I have no family of my own and so have never heard of Beatrice Archambeau. I can only assume that she must be a distant relative.'

'I'm so sorry, Joanie,' Annie said as her friend glanced away before pursing her lips in a small, tight smile.

'Me too, dear. But it was a long time ago.' Joanie's smile softened. 'Fortunately, I was in one of those big, sturdy Silver Cross prams in the back garden and miraculously survived unharmed.'

'Oh, Joanie,' Annie said, remembering her friend

having mentioned it years ago and what a sad story it was. 'It must have been so hard for you, growing up without any family of your own . . .'

'Yes . . .' She paused, seemingly lost in thought for a moment. 'Not marrying was harder though . . . in hindsight. I had the chance many years ago but I declined as he was stepping out with another girl and I had only found out a few days prior to the proposal, and so I was still too angry with him to say yes. I used to think that was a mistake as I would have liked to have had children,' Joanie sighed. 'But then I was delighted when you and the children moved in next door and became like the surrogate family that I never had.' And she leant across and clasped Annie's hand.

'And I'm so glad we did move here as it's been wonderful having you as a neighbour and a surrogate granny to the children over the years,' Annie beamed.

They both sat in silence with their own thoughts for a moment or two until Annie remembered a conversation they'd had a while back about Joanie wondering if it was time to move into an assisted living place. She would miss her terribly.

As if reading Annie's thoughts, Joanie said, 'I'd really like you to take a look at the apartment and the shop and cast your expert interior design eye over it. Would you make a list of everything that needs doing to make it look its best for prospective buyers? And if you can ask the neighbours if they knew Beatrice, that would be marvellous too. I'd love to know more about her and how she fits into my family. Any little snippet would be helpful, and then I could always get one of those ancestry buffs to do my family tree. It might be nice to find out where my parents came from.'

'Sure, I can do that for you,' Annie said, her mind working overtime as a bubble of excitement fizzed within her. She secretly hoped there might be a bit of renovation and styling required. Nothing too costly – a fresh lick of paint and some small touches. She would be in her element. 'Are you definitely planning to sell the apartment then?'

'I think so, dear. It's time. I'm rattling around in this house and I don't need all the space – I only really use the downstairs rooms. You'll come and visit though?'

'Of course I will,' Annie said. It wouldn't be the same as having Joanie next door though.

'Wouldn't it be marvellous if the apartment was worth a few bob?'

'It certainly would be,' Annie laughed. 'And it's bound to be – doesn't everyone love Paris?'

'Let's hope so. Then I can sell it to buy myself a de-luxe en-suite room at that plush assisted-living place for old people,' Joanie mused, her eyes lighting up at the prospect of luxury living. She'd had a notion for it ever since she embarked on her first cruise around the Caribbean a few years ago. 'It's ever so grand and it overlooks the river. You know, they do all your laundry and they have a proper chef to cater for all tastes, even the vegans!' she nodded, clearly very impressed.

'Wow! Can I come too?' Annie laughed. 'It sounds amazing . . . fancy having your laundry taken care of and a chef to cook all your meals – I could sure do with that.'

'Oh, don't be daft, love. You're a smashing little cook when you put your mind to it. But that's the thing, isn't it? I mostly can't be bothered cooking a meal from scratch just for me. Apart from cake, that is.' And both women chuckled as Annie polished off the last of her slice of Victoria sponge.

'This is true.' Annie licked her lips.

'And they even have a chauffeured minibus with swirly gold lettering on the side, which drives you into town whenever you fancy a bit of retail therapy or one of those posh afternoon teas at a swanky hotel. My pal, Sandra, is having the time of her life in that place and I could sure get used to the luxury life too,' Joanie marvelled, clicking her biro into action as she pulled out a pad on which to start writing her master plan for moving out of her tired old terrace house and into a plush double room with an en-suite next door to Sandra.

4

It was the most glorious sight to see. Lush green fields dotted with sheep, their newborn lambs nestled next to them. Thatched cottages. Even a magnificent old wooden water mill beside a river as the train escaped the grey tinge of London and travelled on through the vibrant English countryside. Annie had decided to take a slow train from London so she could savour the scenery and then transfer to the Eurostar train at Ashford in Kent for the Channel crossing and on to Paris. They had just passed through a rural village called Tindledale, which Annie thought was probably the prettiest place she had ever seen. She made a mental note to visit one day and have a proper look around. The scene as the train had slowed had been like something out of a Constable painting: golden sunshine peeping through puffs of cloud in a perfect blue sky, framing fluffy white lambs in the fields, a couple of lumbering cows meandering along the river bank. Seemingly untouched by time, the station had a level crossing and an old green and white wooden weatherboard signal box; in the car park an abandoned old caravan had an array of colourful wild flowers sprouting from the open roof. The journey was feeling like a real indulgence. A few hours in which to do nothing except read a book and watch the world go by was a rare treat indeed. It seemed like years since Annie had last slowed down enough to actually notice the beauty in her surroundings; her life had been a constant tread-mill for such a long time now.

She sank back into her seat and let her shoulders drop down a good couple of centimetres on realizing that she had been hunching with tension for what also felt like forever. Her fractured foot had almost healed and she was able to wear loose trainers now. The wedge sandals would have to wait a little longer, though, so she had treated herself to a pair of white leather pumps with silver stars on and teamed them with a floaty leopard-print maxi-dress and a cropped black leather biker-style jacket. It wasn't her usual style, which to be honest had kind of morphed into a bland jeans and T-shirt affair this last year, so as soon as the boot had come off she had taken herself off shopping for a brand-new wardrobe for her Parisian trip. She had checked the weather app on her phone and seen that Paris was forecast to be bright and sunny, so she was determined to feel the same way. Ten minutes into the journey and Phoebe had called, but on seeing her number Annie had hesitated before flicking the phone on to silent mode. Having never ignored her daughter before, Annie had felt guilty, but she wanted to make the most of the time away from her normal life, and another telling off from Phoebe would put a downer on things before she had even got to Paris.

They had spoken several times since Annie had first mentioned the trip to Paris, and each time Phoebe had tried again to persuade her to retire and move two hundred miles away up to Yorkshire. Annie wondered why the insistence, and had made a note to herself to visit Phoebe to see if she could have a proper heart-to-heart and find out what was really going on. She had promised to call Phoebe when she got to Paris but, for now, she figured that her daughter would be OK for a few hours. Judging from the latest pictures on her daughter's Instagram page, Phoebe appeared to be having a wonderful time. She had been out last night with her boyfriend, Jack, enjoying a sumptuous tasting menu at a Michelin-starred restaurant, followed by cocktails at a new bar with special invites to the exclusive VIP area. The pictures all looked amazing and extremely glamorous, with Phoebe wearing a new figure-hugging dress with a side slit up to the top of her tanned and toned thigh, smiling and glowing into the camera. Annie would call her later as soon as she was settled into her room at the Airbnb.

Turning her attention to the *Eating Out in Paris* travel guide she had bought in one of the kiosk shops at the station, Annie flicked through the pages, admiring the pretty canopied cafés and cobbled plazas and noting down a few names of some that she'd like to visit. One in particular on the Right Bank or La Rive Droite, the far more romantic-sounding French name, had caught her eye with its corner location and red canopies at street level, fuchsias and white geraniums tumbling from pots on the three ornate balconies above. It was called Odette, and having also checked the maps app on her phone, Annie was delighted to see that the café appeared to be almost next door to the Airbnb. Visions of taking her book and strolling along to sit outside the café in the evening with a delicious glass of *vin rouge* and a basket of bread came to mind, making Annie smile to herself as she enjoyed the rest of the train journey.

Annie felt a fizz of anticipation as she wheeled her suitcase through the grand Gare du Nord station, crammed with crowds of people, with its soaring windows, steel and glass high arched ceiling and lampposts with chic twin white domes to light the way. Soon she emerged into the dazzling Parisian sunshine. The bustle and noise of people and cars and coffee shops, and music floating from open windows and bars was overwhelming. Sensory overload. But she had arrived. In crazy, cacophonous, perfect Paris. And it was exciting and exhilarating! And her phone was buzzing now to signify a WhatsApp message from Beth.

Just a quickie to say ooh la la! And make damn sure you enjoy Paris. Are you there yet? xxx

Grinning, Annie quickly typed a reply, snapped a pic of the Parisian street scene before her and pressed send. Moments later, a picture of her best friend appeared on the screen with her eyes and mouth wide open, as if screaming in delight for her. Ah, Annie momentarily pressed the phone to her chest, delighted to have heard from Beth but a little despondent that she wasn't here with her so they could experience this amazing city together.

Popping her sunglasses on, Annie spotted the taxi sign and made her way to join the lengthy queue. Twenty minutes later, it was eventually her turn. She told the driver the name of the street where the Airbnb was. He stared blankly, tilted his head to one side and did a nonchalant one-shouldered shrug, as if he didn't understand. Annie tried again, 'Rue du Moulin. *Merci*,' in her best French accent, and then ruined it by babbling, 'It takes about twenty minutes from here by car, I think. That's what it said on the maps app. Thanks,' in perfect southeast London, England style. Smiling hopefully, she fished inside her bag for the piece of paper she had printed off and went to hand it to the driver. He ignored it but did manage to move his head ever so slightly to the right as she lifted the paper to his eye level, wondering if all French men were as casually indifferent as this one.

'Ah, Rue du Moulin,' the driver bellowed, flicking the paper as if to punctuate his point, giving Annie another shrug, even though she reckoned he'd pronounced the name of the road in exactly the same way that she had. After casting a lazy eye over her luggage and muttering something about *la valise*, he sauntered out of the car, took her suitcase and stowed it in the boot before sauntering back to the car and getting himself comfortable in the driving seat, then beckoning for Annie to get in too, and instantly speeding off through the busy traffic. Barely giving her time to close the door and tug a seatbelt over her shoulder.

Annie sat back and let out a long breath as she

gazed out of the window, taking in the scenes as they raced through the Parisian streets. Dense traffic was punctuated with the sounds of a random cacophony of car horns; some people were milling around, some striding along with purpose. Two older men were standing on a street corner and appeared to be arguing, gesticulating wildly at each other before doing big belly laughs and then hugging it out before going their separate ways. Past restaurants, hair salons with glamorous interiors, an elegantly dressed woman emerging from one with perfectly coiffured platinum tresses, carrying a white Bichon Frise with a pink crystal collar under one arm, dangling a Chanel bag from the other. Annie was in her element watching it all go by. Even the square road name signs with their white lettering on a French navy background were incredibly chic. The wide tree-lined streets were populated with magnificent multistorey mansion houses. Statues. Fountains. It was like being in a film. *Funny Face.* She half expected Fred Astaire and Audrey Hepburn to come dancing along singing '*Bonjour, Paris*'. It was another world, exhilarating, and it was making her feel properly alive for the first time in a very long while.

The taxi turned into another street and Annie gasped, pleased that she had asked the taxi driver to go via the main sights. The Champs-Élysées! She swivelled in her seat to get a better look, not wanting to miss a thing as she saw cafés with crimson-and-gold-trimmed canopies, leafy green trees lining the iconic street on both sides, the glamorous Art Deco style Yves Saint Laurent building on one corner, the pretty pastel green frontage of the Ladurée patisserie on another. As the taxi slowed in traffic, Annie was able to catch a glimpse of the ornate black and golden lit interior, highlighting rows and rows of macarons – lemon, raspberry, chocolate, pistachio, next to beautifully crafted cakes and *gâteaux*. Maybe she could buy a box of macarons to take back for Phoebe, a little part of Paris to soften her annoyance over Annie's last-minute decision to come on the trip. On second thoughts, maybe not. Phoebe wasn't one for sweet treats, and the last thing Annie wanted was another lecture from her daughter about the dangers of sugar addiction.

Instead, Annie made a mental note to pop back here during her time in Paris and perhaps treat herself to the afternoon tea that was advertised on a board outside. And for a moment her heart saddened, for here she was in the most romantic and beautiful city in the world, but all alone. It felt like such a shame. She couldn't help wondering what it might be like to have a partner here with her to share and enjoy the experience together. Someone to wander around Paris with, take silly selfies, making heart shapes with their hands held up to the Eiffel Tower. Someone to love and get that fluttery butterfly feeling on seeing them walk towards you. She had felt that in the early days with Mark, and with a couple of men since then but, to be honest, there had been no butterflies for a very long time now.

As they passed by the impressive Arc de Triomphe at the end of the boulevard, Annie cast her mind back to the last time she'd had a boyfriend. Adam. He had been nice. Very nice – kind and well mannered – but had never set her heart alight. There had been no butterflies. And so the companionable relationship had fizzled out just over a year ago. Annie inhaled and smiled to herself, musing that perhaps she'd quite like to meet a new man. She felt ready for a rush of butterflies to explode within her. *What if I meet a man here in Paris?* Dipping her head, she allowed herself to ponder on this extremely unlikely possibility before gathering herself and focusing once more on the glorious scene outside the window.

The taxi turned into a side street and came to a halt outside a tall, grey, inconspicuous building that looked very much like an office block to Annie, and not the traditional Parisian place with romantic wrought-iron balconies at the floor-to-ceiling windows that she had seen when she booked online.

'*On doit marcher*,' the taxi driver said over his shoulder, lifting his left hand in the air and waggling his fingers, as if to indicate that she must now walk for the rest of the way.

'*Pardon?*' Annie attempted, wondering where she had to go from here. After taking the payment and removing her suitcase from the boot of the car, the driver pointed towards a cobbled alleyway to the side of the building.

'*Trois minutes*,' he said, lifting three fingers, then adding, '*pas de voitures*,' and shaking his head at the taxi.

'Ah, it's three minutes away, but no cars!' Annie nodded, getting it now, and after saying a cheery, '*Merci beaucoup*,' she headed off in the direction he had told her to go, dragging her wheelie suitcase over the cobbles until she came to a junction. There was another cobbled alleyway running parallel, but which way now? Just as she was pondering on whether it was likely to be left or right, and scanning the walls of the tall white-shuttered apartment buildings looking for a street name, a woman with wavy brown hair tied back in a chignon appeared, wiping her hands on a flowery apron and beaming from ear to ear as she bustled towards Annie.

'Annie Lovell?' the woman asked brightly in English, with a lovely, melodic French accent, her strikingly blue eyes searching Annie's inquisitively.

'Oh, um,' she smiled, before taking a moment to remember what she had practised, and then added, '*Oui, je m'appelle Annie.*'

'*Enchantée.*' The woman clapped her hands together. '*Parlez-vous français?*'

'Oh, um,' Annie hesitated, trying to remember what 'just a little' was in French but then figured it best to be honest and so shrugged, laughed and added, 'No, not really.'

'Ah, it's no problem as I love to practise my English.' The woman laughed too. 'Now let's go inside. I imagine you're thirsty and hungry after the long journey. Here, let me help you with your luggage.' And before Annie could say any more, the woman had taken the suitcase and was herding Annie along the alleyway, into another one, and on towards an apple-green shabby-chic wooden door with a small plaque next to it saying Odette, with some more words in French and an L-shaped arrow, as if indicating that the entrance was around the next corner.

'Ooh, I spotted this café in my travel guide,' Annie started, but was cut off when the woman spied a black cat and yelled something at it in French.

'*Pardon*! Sorry to shout. Is bad luck, they say. If a black cat crosses your path.'

'I thought it was good luck,' Annie suggested.

'Really?' The woman stopped in her tracks and stared at Annie before nodding and adding, 'I never knew this! I'm Marguerite by the way, but everyone calls me Maggie,' she said. 'And I can see that you and I are going to get on very well, I've always liked an optimist.' And she held out her hand. Annie reciprocated with a friendly handshake, noticing how lovely and warm it was.

Maggie motioned for Annie to follow her inside the building, which didn't look like a café at all. In front of them was an old store cupboard leading into a narrow corridor. 'Please be careful here,' she said, pushing a stack of wooden bread crates out of the way.

Moments later, and Annie was enveloped in a cocoon of sweet warmth. The comforting aroma of hot chocolate, mingled with the smell of freshly baked baguettes and garlic, filled the café, with its black-and-white chequered floor and rustic old wooden tables with red leatherette-topped stools and wicker chairs. At the windows were white lace curtains draped back and clasped behind big brass hooks, and it looked out on to a small cobbled courtyard filled with more tables, some with trees, their slim trunks growing up through the middle in place of umbrellas to provide leafy shade from the afternoon sunshine.

'Wow, this is gorgeous! And my favourite meal too,'

Annie smiled, looking at a big chalk board on the wall, with today's special of *steak frites avec salade de roquette* written on it in white chalk.

She loved the traditional feel of the place. It was sumptuously warm from the big brick bread oven mounted into the wall on one side, and full of elderly men, mostly yelling at each other as they played cards and drank beer from half-pint glasses or red wine from very small glass tumblers. Melodic accordion music floated through the open door from the courtyard, giving the whole place a nostalgic feel of traditional times gone by. Black-and-white photos in gilt-edged frames hung higgledy-piggledy on the walls with what looked like chic bohemian beautiful people of the 1920s. The men in suits with waistcoats were smoking pipes, the women wearing cloche hats over bobbed hair, long ropes of pearls over low-waisted knee-length dresses, fur wraps around their shoulders. *C'était magnifique* indeed.

Taking it all in, Annie glanced around again and could see that Odette was probably exactly the same now as it had been in the Café Life era of the 1920s, *Les Années Folles*, or Crazy Years, that she had read about, when poets, artists and writers would gather and the cultural and creative life of Paris was buzzing. She could picture Ernest Hemingway and James Joyce together, seated outside, drinking coffee from glass cups and ruminating, the smell of Gauloises cigarettes lingering in the air. Coco Chanel even – maybe she popped in for a croissant, in between creating her famous lipsticks and perfume. You never know, it could have happened! Maybe Joanie's benefactor, Beatrice Archambeau, had sipped *café au lait*, right here, back in the day. Annie made a mental note to look up the address of Joanie's inherited apartment to see how close it was to here; maybe she could walk the route that Beatrice may have taken.

Annie adored the sense of stepping back in time, not to mention the interior design in the café which was simply exquisite.

'Sit down, please,' Maggie said, pressing her palm onto the only free table and tucking Annie's suitcase in the corner next to her. 'We'll get you settled upstairs in your room as soon as you've had something to eat and drink. But I'm sorry we just served the last of the steak frites.'

'Oh, no problem, and that's very kind of you . . . thank you,' Annie said, then, 'Can I ask, do you work in here? Is the Airbnb room upstairs, above the café? Only, it wasn't clear in the online profile. Or maybe I missed it. And sorry if I'm being intrusive,' she quickly added, remembering they had only just met. But there was something about Maggie that made Annie feel as if they had known each other their whole lives.

'Well, yes and no. The Airbnb rooms are all upstairs, and this is my café, but,' Maggie said, gesturing towards the other tables, 'my late husband and I bought it ten years ago – he was English and we used to live in London – but it was always our passion to run a little café together here in Paris. He was a pastry chef at the famous Savoy Hotel in London you see, and . . .' She momentarily stopped talking, a flicker of emotion softening her features as she glanced downwards and fiddled with the edge of her apron.

'I'm so sorry,' Annie said quietly. 'What was his name?'

'Oh, err . . . Samuel. Sam to me and his friends,' she said, sounding surprised. 'And *merci*. Thank you.' She looked up with the jovial expression back in place. 'You are the first person who didn't know him to ask me what his name was . . . and that's very nice. It keeps him alive . . . it was a motorbike accident, just over a year ago now, but . . .'

Annie listened and nodded as a silence crept upon them both, unsure if she should ask more, but the decision was made for her, for now, when Maggie appeared to break from her moment of reverie with, 'And, well, as I was saying, the café was our dream and Sam was in his element back there in the kitchen.'

She glanced over her shoulder. 'We have a chef now to do the cooking. I like to look after people, so I mostly manage the B&B, but we are short staffed in here today so I'm helping to make coffee and clear the tables.' Maggie dipped down into the free stool opposite Annie. 'Don't worry, I shall not hang around and bother you, but I have been on my feet all day so I am due a short break, yes?' and she tilted her head to one side and grinned.

'Oh please do, you most definitely do deserve a break,' Annie said, knowing how tiring waitressing could be having worked in a café when she was a student. 'I'm happy to chat,' Annie smiled, grateful for the company and thinking how kindly and welcoming Maggie was. She was probably about the same age as Annie, but she had a motherly way about her, sort of comforting and calming, and it made her seem older somehow. She reminded Annie of her own mother too, who coincidentally had also been called Maggie. She had died a few years ago, in her eighties, having lived a happy and fulfilling life. Always with a smile, and a comforting word or two in times of trouble. Annie missed her, and still forgot sometimes that she couldn't pick up the phone and call her for a chat about mundane, silly things that wouldn't mean much to anyone else except them.

A waiter appeared and placed cutlery wrapped in a starched white cotton napkin, a basket of bread, a jug of water and a carafe of wine on the table.

'Do you like red?' Maggie asked, turning over a small glass tumbler and filling it to the brim with wine before going to place it in front of Annie.

'Yes, thank you,' Annie said, taking the glass and tasting the deliciously fruity liquid. Maggie poured herself a smaller measure, citing the need to keep a clear head as she would need to tally up the till later on and it confused her at the best of times.

'So, what brings you to Paris?' Maggie asked, offering Annie the bread basket.

'Thanks.' Annie helped herself to a warm mini-baguette, broke it in two and smoothed a slick of butter over it. After explaining about the apartment and Joanie's inheritance, Annie bit into the bread. Maggie sat back in her chair and nodded her head, impressed.

'This is very intriguing!' Maggie took a piece of bread too, buttered it and took a big, hearty bite, as if in celebration of such a revelation. 'I wish somebody would leave me an apartment in Paris.' She laughed, widening her eyes. 'When are you going to see it?'

'Tomorrow, hopefully. That's when I'm meeting the *avocat*, a Monsieur Aumont, to pick up the keys,' Annie explained further through another mouthful of gorgeously crispy yet doughy bread.

'Ooh, I'd love to come with you,' Maggie said, and then quickly held up a hand, '*Pardon*, sorry, that was very presumptuous of me. And nosey! But who doesn't love looking around other people's homes?' Annie laughed and tilted her glass towards Maggie in agreement.

'Nobody I know. That's for sure!' a tall, slender, dark-haired woman said in an American accent – New York, if Annie wasn't mistaken.

'Oh, hi Kristen, this is Annie. She's just arrived today.' Maggie jumped up and introduced the effortlessly chic woman wearing a gorgeous black silk jumpsuit cinched at the waist with a large Hermès gold-buckled belt. Several big shopping bags were looped over her arm.

'Nice to meet you,' Kristen smiled warmly, offering a hand to Annie.

'Nice to meet you too,' Annie replied, standing up to shake Kristen's hand, liking her right away.

'How long are you staying in Paris?'

'Two weeks! How about you?' Annie asked.

'As long as possible! This place is a charm,' she laughed throatily, before lowering her voice and leaning in towards Annie with a conspiratorial look, 'and it's a very long, long way from my crazy ex-husband!'

'Oh?' Annie lifted an inquisitive eyebrow, but didn't like to enquire further. Maggie, however, got straight to the point.

'Kristen is another of my guests. She arrived last week and is celebrating her divorce.'

'That's right!' Kristen nodded, as she adjusted the sunglasses holding back her mane of big hair. 'I've filed the papers and so now I'm free! I thought, why the heck not! I'm off to Europe. The Louvre – I'm a big art freak, you see, and it drove Chad nuts – he hates all kinds of culture.' She rolled her eyes. 'So I deserve a treat after putting up with his narrow-minded crap for all that time.' She stowed the bags on the floor before planting her hand on her hips. 'Why are you here?'

'Oh, um,' Annie started, a little taken aback at Kristen's boldness. 'Well, I—'

'Mind if I sit?' Kristen jumped in. 'My feet are killing me. I must have walked a million steps today in these heels.' And she tilted her right leg out slightly, revealing a red-soled Louboutin stiletto. 'New today! From that darling boutique on rue du Faubourg Saint-Honoré. Have you been there? It's a shopper's dream.' And she clapped her hands together in glee.

'Err, not yet!' Annie ventured, her mind boggling. Kristen was a whirlwind, her energy invigorating. Annie sat down too, as did Maggie, and the three women chatted for a few minutes as if they were old friends, until the conversation came back to Joanie's apartment.

'Wow! It's so intriguing,' Kristen declared, draining the glass of wine that Maggie had poured for her. 'And sorry for butting in like that earlier, I've got a habit of diving right in without thinking . . . Come to think of it, that's where I went wrong with Chad!' she sighed. 'Anyway, my ears pricked up when I walked in and overheard the tail end of what you were saying about other people's homes. I love all those real-estate programmes on TV. Mind if I tag along too?' she grinned, naughtily.

'Of course!' Annie laughed. 'The more the merrier. In fact, you'll be doing me a favour as I have no idea how to get there, so if one of you knows how to navigate the maze of cobbled alleyways to find the apartment, it's in a private courtyard apparently, then you'll save me getting lost. I'd be terrified to rent a car and attempt to drive in the busy Parisian traffic, and I certainly don't want to trouble another taxi driver. The one from earlier who drove me here seemed most put out!'

'It's the Parisian way,' Maggie shrugged nonchalantly, and they all laughed. 'Do you have a street name?'

'Oh yes, it's called Cour Felice. Just off the Place de la Bastille,' Annie told her, thinking how chic it sounded.

'Wow! Yes, I know the place,' Maggie's eyes widened. '*Très branché*. It's a smart area not far from here,' she explained, 'and trendy as well, with lots of art studios, galleries, artisan bakeries, hand-poured candle places, expensive dress boutiques and so on. Your friend may have inherited a lovely, large nest egg . . . especially if there is a shop with it too, as you say.'

'Really?' Annie's interest was piqued. Perhaps Joanie could have her dream home with Sandra after all.

'Yes. It's a very much sought-after area. Real estate is expensive in that part of Paris. Prestigious. Although . . .' Maggie paused and glanced around before leaning forward covertly. 'Infamous too, I've heard,' she lowered her voice. 'Not these days, but years ago . . . back in the war. The Second World War.'

'In what way?' Annie frowned.

'During the Occupation. The Nazi soldiers. They used to frequent the shops around Cour Felice; they paraded around like tourists, buying gifts and taking pictures . . . some of the older men in here have spoken about it. I've overheard them even saying that certain residents and shopkeepers around there were in cahoots with the Gestapo, the ones who rounded up the Jews. Friends with them even. Frequenting bars and restaurants for dinner and drinks together.'

'Oh dear,' Annie shook her head.

'Disgusting!' Kristen expelled, curling her top lip dramatically, then adding, 'My grandparents were Polish immigrants, Jews driven out of their homeland. Many of their friends and relatives weren't able to escape and were murdered in the camps. I hope your Beatrice wasn't friends with the evil ones!' And poured herself some more wine.

'It is shocking! But the passage of time can muddle things up,' Maggie said soothingly and then asked, 'Did Beatrice stay in Paris during the Second World War?'

'We don't know, but I'm hoping to find out,' Annie said.

'Many French people left as the Germans arrived, and many more weren't able to escape, but endured the most difficult of times, often doing all that they could to protect their neighbours and friends, putting themselves in extreme danger too. Maybe the *avocat* will know more – how your Beatrice Archambeau fitted in to that time in history.' Maggie handed Annie and Kristen a menu each. 'Do you know much about Beatrice?'

'Not really. Other than that she was a hundred and four when she died many years ago in 2002 and – aside from the last ten years of her life, when she lived in a retirement village – she had lived in the apartment since the Twenties. There's paperwork linked to the property that verifies this.'

'Hmm, in that case a neighbour or someone is bound to know of her if she lived there for all those years,' Kristen said, her eyes sparking.

'That's what my friend Joanie and I are hoping.'

'We'll find out more tomorrow, I guess.' Maggie tapped the menu to change the subject. 'I can recommend the cassoulet with tasty sausages from Toulouse. It comes with green beans and pommes frites in a garlic butter drizzle. *Très bon!* And my treat, ladies. To welcome you to Paris,' she added, curling the fingers of her left hand into a chef's kiss on her lips.

'That's very kind of you, but—' Annie started and Kristen continued with,

'Maggie, you must stop being so hospitable.' She turned to Annie, 'You know, this gorgeous woman has refused to let me pay for my own dinner far too many times now.'

'No buts, you're my guests,' Maggie beamed, 'and besides, I like you both.' She chuckled and stood up to go to the kitchen to place their order.

'In that case, thank you very much,' Annie smiled, tilting her head and lifting her glass again, thinking what a wonderful welcome this was. She really liked Maggie, her warmth and openness, and the café, and was sure her room would be just as welcoming. And Kristen made her laugh with her frankness and in-your-face attitude. She was also now utterly intrigued to find out more about Beatrice and her apartment. She hoped the *avocat* would be able to help, with the history behind it all . . . maybe he could even shed some light on who Beatrice was in relation to Joanie.

As they waited for Maggie to return, Annie and Kristen chatted some more, until the door opened and a tall, incredibly good-looking man with dark, curly hair wearing faded jeans and an open-neck shirt walked in and over to another man sitting at a table near the courtyard.

'Oh, hello!' Kristen nudged Annie and whispered, 'Did you see that dreamboat?'

'Um,' Annie managed, after swiftly swallowing the too-big piece of bread that she had torn off and pushed into her mouth just as he passed by their table, his evocative scent of lemon and spice teasing her nostrils. She felt her cheeks warm as she gulped down some water to prevent a choking fit, and allowed her gaze to drift in the direction he'd gone. The cut of his Levi jeans accentuating his slim hips, nicely shaped bottom and firm thighs; his tanned hands pushing the messy curls back from his face.

'I wonder who he is . . .' Kristen said, running her

index finger around the top of her glass. 'We should ask Maggie to find out. Or better still, we could send over a drink, like they do in the movies! What do you reckon?' she laughed, her eyes dancing mischievously.

'Well, I, err . . . you could, I guess,' Annie said vaguely, dabbing water from her lips with a linen napkin, distracted by the sudden quickening of her pulse – a feeling she hadn't experienced in a very long time. It was as if something had awakened within her, especially when the man sat down and, on catching her eyes with his own, smiled and held her gaze a little longer than was probably necessary. Surprised by her reaction, Annie quickly looked away. 'But what if he's married or—'

'I don't think that matters here in Paris. Don't all Frenchmen have mistresses? Mind you, if I was married to him then I wouldn't let him out of my sight. Would you?'

5

Western Front, France, 1917

Beatrice pulled the blanket tight around her shoulders in an attempt to utilize her own body heat to keep warm amidst the bitterly cold wind. It had been blowing relentlessly into the bell tent she shared with Cissy, one of the other VADs, with no sign of letting up any time soon. Rubbing her hands together to ease their numbness, she leant in closer to the candle lamp, the page of her diary barely visible as she tried to capture her feelings since first arriving at the camp hospital. It had been all go from the first day here after sailing from Southampton, working long shifts with very little time for confiding in her constant companionable diary, which she kept locked within her writing slope. Unable to bear being parted from it, having sought so much solace in her diary-writing since Mother had died, Beatrice had wrapped the wooden slope, containing all her diaries and private letters, inside her clothes within the one suitcase that she had brought with her from home. It hadn't left much space for anything else, but she had her uniform and essential hairbrush and toiletries and that was enough. She had freedom. A life of her own. And this meant the world to her.

My naivety is all consuming, such was the sight that first greeted me on arrival here. The images that Lady Dorothy shared back in the village hall were a mere fantasy of opportunity, efficiency and duty, or perhaps figments of my imagination, so keen was I to paint a pretty picture. The reality is not at all as I had anticipated. I have gone from having to be chaperoned by Iris on a tea date when men were present to having responsibility for many battered male bodies. But I am here now, and getting on with it as best I can. Everywhere there are tents full of men, wounded and broken. Some seeking solace through sleep, others groaning and writhing in their beds. The thundering sound of gunfire and piercing whistle of shells can be heard. The mud, dense like clay and the colour of soft charcoal, the rain torrential and relentless. The stench of death and infection – mingled with carbolic and chemicals

– lingers in the sad, dark air. The other girls are pleasant, though, and there is a cheery sense of camaraderie, especially when Sister isn't around. She runs a very tight ship, but I suppose we need that. I've been here for a month now and it's been an educational experience. My first day being a disaster when it became perfectly clear that I didn't have an inkling when it came to simple things such as lighting a cigarette or shaving the chin of an injured man incapable of doing such things for himself. It's all well and good knowing how to clean the sluice room, fold a sling, take a pulse or clean a wound, as I was taught during my training, but sometimes it's the home comforts that mean the most to the soldiers we serve.

Cissy swiftly showed me the ropes and, after talking late into the night, I confided in her about my love for Bobby, showing her the small photograph I have of him in his uniform, standing next to Queenie's brother, Stan, and my brother, Edward, taken on the day they all left Tindledale, and feeling proud when she remarked on Bobby's handsome face. Cissy and I are now firm friends, which is just as well given that our living quarters are so cramped. Two camp beds, two wash bowls on a stand, two canvas chairs that topple over every time one of us brushes past them with any kind of haste, and our tent is full. The central tent pole serves as our wardrobe, with a strap hanging from it on which we loop over our top coats and uniforms. A small metal mirror dangling on string is all that we have to see ourselves in but it is sufficient for us to keep smart. It is the least we can do to boost the morale of our men. A cheerful face and groomed hair beneath our caps is often remarked upon as a welcome sight to help ease the awful images of the trenches that the men have trapped inside their weary heads.

Cissy and I were fortunate enough to be given a few hours' leave yesterday afternoon and so we cycled to the seaside, where on checking that the coast was clear we unbuttoned our boots, lifted our skirts and paddled in the gloriously crisp clear waves. The salty sea air an elixir floating in our hair and on our faces. The sun was shining, and for a brief moment our minds were released from the troubles of war and caring for the wounded as we basked in its warm rays.

As we cycled back, we came upon a babbling brook at the foot of a sloping wood, the grass a carpet of colourful flowers. Periwinkles, oxlips, anemones. Vibrant bursts of yellow, white, violet and crimson. Rosemary, wild garlic and lavender bushes too. The scent an irresistible perfume that graced me with an idea to alleviate the acrid smell in the camp. With Cissy's help I managed to gather a fair bundle of flowers and sprigs of sweet rosemary and lavender, just as Mother and I had done in the fields of my childhood. With a little oil purloined from the storeroom I have concocted a rather joyful scent that when rubbed onto the inside of my wrist helps to ease the task of removing a soldier's pungent, soiled bandages. A young private named Monty Franklin, when I had embalmed the top half of his head in fresh bandages, held my wrist to draw in the comforting fragrance before asking me to sit with him a while as he reminisced about his fondness for the garden he tended back home in the Kent countryside. Another young soldier, Karl Müller, a German, murmured gently about the süßer Duft von Blumen, or sweet scent of flowers, to which I whispered a short prayer in German, for fear of catching Sister's eye, as I cleaned the wounds on his shattered legs. Karl, certain to be vilified back home in Tindledale, yet his hand as I held it the following day, during his final moments, felt much the same as my darling Bobby's had, the last time we embraced before he left to travel to this awful place.

Not a moment goes by when I don't think of Bobby, with his aquiline nose and high forehead, thick dark hair, silky soft when entwined in my fingertips. His sparkling, curious blue eyes fixed on mine. His zest for life and how he seemed to truly understand me. Keen to hear my opinion on a whole raft of subjects from politics to planets as we lay together in the grassy meadow in the dark of night, whenever Father and Iris were socializing in London and the servants were sleeping, to gaze at the stars and dream of a time and place where our love will no longer need to be clandestine. Oh, how I yearn to see him again. To rest my face on his shoulder and draw in the sweet scent of his cologne. If I close my eyes, I can almost transport myself back to the meadow once again.

The power of perfume is quite remarkable, the way it evokes memories of more pleasurable times. It's a small thing that I can do to bring a moment of release for these courageous, but broken soldiers. I overheard one of the surgeons saying that our sense of smell is one of the last of our faculties to leave us when the end is near. So I shall endeavour to bring sweet, comforting fragrance to all in my care, together with soothing words of comfort in English, French and German if needs be, as I have seen first-hand the fear in all of the souls in my care. Death doesn't distinguish, or indeed vilify, when the final moments are calling.

On a cheerier note, I have been thinking of Queenie and hoping that my letter reaches her, for she was most devastated on learning that her young age prevented her from joining me in France. Without wanting to scare her with the reality of what it is really like here, I would want her to know that her work in the post office now is sure to be far more satisfactory than the ammunitions factory or indeed these muddy fields, and so she really must not feel aggrieved on missing out. I was comforted to receive her letter some weeks ago with news of her new position covering her brother Stan's postal delivery route around the village while he is stationed somewhere here in France. I have assured her that I shall keep a lookout for him. My own dear brother, Edward, too. And Bobby, of course, for I yearn to know where he is and that he is safe. The last I'd heard from him was two months ago, a letter to thank me for the parcel I'd sent to him a month previously. A few comforts to help ease his time in the trenches – two pairs of socks that I'd knitted using wool unravelled from a cardigan I'd had the foresight to bring with me,

*a book of poems I'd found in a shop when Cissy
and I went to the village on an afternoon off, and
a small bar of chocolate that Queenie had sent to
me, for I was sure that Bobby would be in more
need of the sweet comfort than I. Although every
day that passes when I don't see Bobby, Edward or
Stan – wounded, or worse – is a blessing, and they
are all in my thoughts during our prayers at the
start and end of every shift.*

*Less can be said for Father and Iris, who,
although having eventually given their blessing to
my departing for France, have since written to
inform me that I must not forget my quest to find
a suitable husband, and urge me to not ruin my
chances by being overfamiliar with men of unsuit-
able rank. It is an utter disappointment to them
that I have reached such an age and to still not
have entered into matrimony. They fear that I am
now marked as a lost cause! If only they could
know of my love for Bobby and his love for me,
surely true love conquers all. That's about it for
now. My eyelids are drooping and I must try to
sleep since I have the opportunity to do so before
Cissy returns from her shift and wakes me with
her chatter. Cheerio for now.*

6

Beatrice Archambeau's Parisian apartment in Cour Felice was accessed through a majestic, if shabby, wrought-iron black gate, leading into an ornate arched stone passageway. Vivid red geraniums tumbled from window boxes on the Juliet balconies of the tall, six-storey white buildings set in a square around a cobbled courtyard. Wisteria the colour of Parma Violet sweets trailed up and around all the doorways; together with the bright afternoon sunshine bathing it all in in a golden glow, it gave the whole place a gloriously halcyon atmosphere. Even the streetlights looked romantic, with ornate glass lanterns hanging from swirly black brackets on the walls of the buildings. Annie wondered if Beatrice had enjoyed living here in such a pretty, timelessly chic place. Surely she must have done. But to leave her home in this marvellous location to a complete stranger, as far as Joanie believed, well . . . there must be a truly significant reason for her doing so. Having seen what a special place this was in the heart of Paris, Annie was even more curious now to find out why.

'Oh my, this is too adorable!' Kristen gasped, on taking in the view. 'What a lucky woman your friend Joanie is.'

'Wow! She sure is,' Annie agreed, turning a slow 360 degrees as she admired the whole area before pulling her phone from her pocket and taking lots of pictures to share with Joanie later on. They had agreed that Annie would email a nice selection of pictures over, and even a video of the inside of the apartment to Joanie's friend, Sandra, and then her daughter was going to show them to Joanie on her iPad.

'Here it is!' Maggie said to Annie, pointing to a smaller, three-storey, buttery yellow painted building tucked away in the far corner. There was a faded sign above the boarded-up bay windows with a padlocked door in the middle. 'This looks like it might have been a chemist once upon a time.'

The women glanced up to the top of the windows to see the smudgy outline of a picture depicting an old-fashioned glass bottle with a stopper in the top. The paint was cracked and peeling off, exposing the bare wood underneath which was faded and weather-worn. They spotted a small gap in the wooden board at one of the windows and so took it in turns to press their noses up to the glass. With their hands either side of their heads they tried to get a glimpse of the shop's interior, a chink of sunlight revealing a maze of cobwebs hanging from an old, tarnished chandelier and looping outwards like eerie bunting to the rows of shelves set against the walls. A circular wooden block stood in the middle, the mirrored counter top cracked and mottled with black age spots.

Annie stepped away and turned around to take in the rest of the square, trying to imagine Beatrice being here, wondering when did she first move to Cour Felice? Or was she born here? Or perhaps she came here when she married. If she married. But if she had married then wouldn't she have had other relatives, people in her husband's family to leave the apartment to? There were so many questions and Annie was keen to get inside to see if there was any trace left of the woman who had lived within the apartment, and, Annie presumed, worked in the shop as well. When Monsieur Aumont had handed over the keys and paperwork earlier, he had been very vague. It could have been his age, for Annie was surprised to see that he was in his seventies at least, possibly older, but he was just doing his job – he had made that quite clear – processing a will that had been filed with his office several decades earlier. In fact, if the retirement home hadn't contacted him then he would have been none the wiser regarding his client's passing in 2002, with the search for Joanie being triggered by the caveat in the will when another tenant decided to move, is how he had presented the situation. And the Englishwoman, Joan Smith, she was not mentioned in any of his client's other files, only in the will document itself, with a last known address in London, so tracing her had 'taken almost a year and had been complicated and time-consuming, as is often the case with these obscure foreign beneficiaries' is what he had said in heavily accented English, before exhaling a large sigh of impatience, or maybe it was the exertion of rummaging with trembling hands through his battered old leather document case to find the keys, Annie had wondered, giving him the benefit of the doubt. He had also been equally vague, with a curt, 'My client was a very private person with exemplary discretion. Her personal history is confidential. Those were her exact wishes,' when Annie had ventured a few questions about Beatrice Archambeau's life and circumstances in an attempt to find out more about her and why she might have left her home to Joanie. Monsieur Aumont had also declined to accompany Annie inside the building, looking panicked and then almost fearful at the prospect of doing so. In fact, it was as if he couldn't wait to get away from Cour Felice.

'Shan't be a second,' Annie said to Maggie and Kristen, who were now looking at a quant old-fashioned black wrought-iron water pump they had spotted a little further along in the square. 'I'd like to have a little look around the area before we go inside.'

'Sure, we'll join you in a moment,' Kristen smiled, lifting her phone to take a picture of Maggie standing next to the pump, her hands on the lever as if she were about to start filling a bucket with water, as they would have done many years ago.

At the far end of Cour Felice, near the opening into another street, there was a more imposing building, the only one that wasn't white and didn't have balconies with pretty flowers. Its door was large, solid dark wood, with a rusty old brass knocker in the centre. Wandering closer to get a better look, Annie thought it might be an official building of some sort, a government office, an institution even, as it had a coldness about it which was in stark contrast to the rest of the places in the pretty square. As Annie moved closer, a sudden sense of foreboding descended, causing her to shiver as if somebody had stepped on her grave. She stopped moving, and listened for the sound of birdsong, which seemed to have dulled suddenly, or was that just her imagination getting carried away? She drew in a big gulp of refreshing air to clear her thoughts away.

Turning, she saw Maggie and Kristen walking towards her and felt happy to have her new friends here with her today. After the delicious dinner they'd enjoyed together last night, they had sat up late, and long after the last customers had left Odette, drinking red wine and putting the world to rights, and so now Annie felt as if she had known Maggie and Kristen for ever. And Kristen hadn't gone through with her plan to send a flirtatious drink over to the gorgeous Frenchman. Not because of a change of heart, but because he and his friend had left the café before she'd had a chance to. That hadn't stopped Annie from wondering what would have happened. How she might have felt if he and his friend had joined them, like they did in rom-com movies, where they end up chatting and flirting and ultimately living happily ever after. How would she have felt? And more to the point, how would she have behaved? It had been a long time since she had last been in the company of an extremely attractive man, not to mention one that she had felt an instant attraction to.

'Are you OK?' Maggie asked. 'You look as if you've seen a ghost.'

'Yes, I think so,' Annie frowned, and glanced back over her shoulder to indicate where she had just come from. 'It's the strangest thing. See that building at the end over there?'

'I see it,' Maggie replied, following Annie's gaze.

'Well, it gave me the creeps.' Annie shuddered, before folding her arms and rubbing her hands over the tops of her arms as if to comfort herself.

'Hmm, it is a bit creepy looking,' Kristen said. 'But then old boarded-up buildings always give me the creeps. I've watched too many horror films with vampires running around derelict buildings.' And the three women laughed.

'Maybe the building is haunted,' Maggie said, lifting her eyebrows. 'There are rumours about places built on sites where a guillotine used to stand.'

'No way! Actual sightings of ghosts dressed in eighteenth-century peasants' outfits or whenever it was all that brutal stuff went on,' Kristen added, shaking her head and sliding a dramatic index finger across her throat. Then, pulling a spooky face, she looped her left hand through Annie's arm and her right hand through Maggie's arm and steered both women away. 'Come on, let's get away from this mood-sapping building. I'm excited to see inside your friend Joanie's new apartment.'

7

After Annie had found the right key to the main door of Beatrice's home, the three women entered the hallway and exhaled a collective impressive sigh on seeing an elaborate chandelier twinkling in the sunshine above a beautiful brown and ivory check tiled floor. The walls were white, the bottom half decorated in a perfect Parisian blue paint, the exact shade that Annie had been coveting for her own hallway at home. She looked around, loving the interior so far, even if it was a little faded and neglected, she knew that with some time spent cleaning and repainting it could be restored to a gloriously chic space. To the left was a door marked with a gold number one, and at the far end of the hallway were carpeted stairs in a black and gold pattern that appeared to lead to another apartment.

'I wonder if someone else lives in this building?' Annie said, spotting two grey metal mailboxes on the wall.

'Looks that way,' Kristen nodded, dipping her head to take a look at the names on the mailboxes. One had a small metal plaque with *Archambeau* on; it was difficult to see the initial or indeed salutation as the letters were so faded. On the other mailbox the letters were far clearer, *M. M Ramond*. 'Ooh, a Monsieur Ramond lives in the building too, that could be useful. He'll probably be able to tell us about Beatrice. I wonder what the M stands for?' Maggie asked, a curious look on her face.

'Hmm, well let's hope he's charming and accommodating, unlike that cranky lawyer from earlier.' Kristen pushed her shades back and pursed her lips. The others nodded in agreement.

'Yes, he was an odd one, wasn't he? Couldn't wait to get away from here . . . we're not that scary, are we?' Maggie added.

'Of course we aren't. Forget him! And let's concentrate on why we are here. It's exciting and we don't need a Debbie Downer of an old man spoiling it,' Kristen stated, making it clear that all talk of Monsieur Aumont was over.

'OK, so here goes!' Annie turned the key in the door of Beatrice's apartment. 'Are we all ready?' Maggie and Kristen grinned, their eyes sparking in anticipation, as Annie pushed open the door and stood aside to let them in.

'No, after you!' Maggie gave Annie a gentle steer. 'You've come all this way to help out your friend so it's only right that you get the first look. We're just here being nosey,' she chuckled.

'Absolutely! Go right ahead,' Kristen said, her phone poised. 'I'm going to capture it all for you and Joanie, so you just put your phone away and drink it all in. You have your very own one-woman film crew at your service!' she insisted, standing to attention and doing an exaggerated salute.

And so Annie led the way through a narrow, plain white-walled corridor and up a small flight of stairs that took the building over the boarded up boutique below. At the top of the stairs was a square landing with four closed doors. She chose the door that she assumed must lead into the main living room, given that it would be at the front of the apartment, over-looking the pretty square outside. With Maggie and Kristen on either side of her, the three women moved into the room and just stood, staring open-mouthed at each other for a while, holding their breath and not daring to make a sound in case it broke the spell of what was set out in front of them.

It was magical.

Like a movie set.

A period drama.

A Postcard from Paris

Downton Abbey, perhaps, circa 1920s.

A gold silk Jacquard patterned chaise longue. A circular rosewood table in the centre of the room with a crystal square vase in the middle. Two sets of floor-to-ceiling windows – flanked in heavy gold brocade curtains, sumptuously swept back with matching ties held on crystal-tipped hooks – allowed glorious sunlight to bathe the room, the dust motes dancing in its rays. There was a well-worn, comfortable-looking couch beside a grand marble fireplace, the mantelpiece housing an oval Art Deco-style dark wooden clock, giving the room a comforting tick-tock sound as if time really had stood still. There was even a magazine lying open on a lamp table next to a Louis XV chair with intricate cabriole legs and upholstery that matched the curtains.

Framed black-and-white photos filled a marble-topped console table. One showed a beautiful woman from the Victorian era, looking very resplendent in a Bertha low neckline dress, with a full taffeta and tulle skirt, her hair pinned up in an elaborate bun, a parasol at her shoulder. Another of a strikingly handsome and distinguished young man in a khaki soldier's uniform, an officer in World War I, perhaps, given the peaked hat and high buttoned jacket collar. A large, sumptuous cream-coloured rug lay on the polished wood floor.

Framed paintings hung on the walls. There was even a library area of shelves stacked with old-fashioned encyclopaedia-style books. A padded window seat looking out over double glass balcony doors completed the picture-perfect scene.

Annie wandered towards the window seat and imagined Beatrice relaxing on it with a book in one hand and a glass of champagne in the other as she gazed out at the scene, Paris in Springtime. Sighing in contentment, she could see that Beatrice would have had a perfect view of the gorgeous square and beyond. Over the rooftops and pastel-pink cherry blossom trees towards the Eiffel Tower. Yes! Annie leant forward. Like everyone else she had seen pictures of the tower so many times in magazines and films that it took a moment for it to sink in . . . that she really was looking at the Eiffel Tower. Incredible. The domed top of the sweeping, iconic metal structure was right there in the distance.

'*Ooh là là! C'est magnifique!*' It was Kristen who broke the awed silence.

'I can't believe it,' Annie gasped, trying to take it all in. Her heart was racing as she turned back around and away from the window, admiring the amazing interior again. She clapped her hands together in glee. Beatrice must have had a very keen eye for design, or had someone in, a design expert, surely, to make her home this beautiful. It really was like stepping inside one of the home interiors magazines that Annie loved to flick through to gain inspiration, often with a wistful sigh. There was also an air of opulence and heritage, quality furniture passed down through generations, as some of the furniture appeared to be antique. Annie wasn't an expert but the cherrywood armoire with delicate carved floral detailing on the doors, which stood in an alcove, looked very much like one she had spotted at an antiques market in Edinburgh many years ago when she was a student. Price tag £3,000! She remembered doing a superficial laugh in a desperate attempt to cover up her embarrassment over thinking she might have been able to afford to buy it as a restoration project to rub down and paint in a trendy shabby-chic colour, as was the fashion back then.

'Wow! Look up there,' Kristen yelled, waving a pointed index finger in the air towards another chandelier as she tilted her phone to capture its beauty. Even with a thick coat of dust and a few cobwebs tangled amidst the crystal cut glass drops, the chandelier was majestic.

'It's incredible, like time has stood still,' Annie said. 'I never imagined there would be furniture. I just assumed the apartment would be empty.' She rang a finger over a dust-coated console table that housed an old-fashioned cream-coloured telephone with a dial in the middle, just like the one in her childhood home of the 1970s. 'Monsieur Aumont never mentioned contents, and Joanie didn't mention it either. Not that I'm complaining, of course,' she laughed, imagining Joanie's reaction on seeing all of this.

'And the artwork is incredible,' Kristen gushed in awe, moving towards the wall now, darting from one painting to the next, her phone still recording it all.

'Come on, let's take a look at the other rooms,' Annie said, quickly heading to another door and feeling like a child at Christmas, keen to open the presents under the tree. The kitchen this time. Galley style with traditional blue and white fleur-de-lis-patterned tiles and dark wood cabinets. Next door was the bedroom. 'Oh no!' Annie said on entering. It was another magnificent room, with a lovely large window seat too, but two of the gold and yellow vertical-striped papered walls were covered in a greenish-black substance, possibly from a water leak as there was a large stain, the shape of it like a map of France, on the ceiling above. The paper had peeled off from the top of the wall, so it was now drooping downward and making the room look sad and derelict. On the upside, there was the now obligatory crystal chandelier hanging over a king-sized bed covered in a yellow floral Marie Antoinette-style fabric that matched the curtains.

'Oh, what a shame,' Maggie said, lifting one of the curtains away from the wall. 'It's covered in mould!'

'Ah, I'll have to take them down,' Annie said, placing her hands on her hips as she surveyed the room, her mind boggling while planning what she could do to restore things. 'Or, I could make new curtains, it wouldn't take me long, and I do have two weeks here. But . . .' She stopped talking.

'What is it?' Kristen asked, inspecting the curtain that Maggie still had in her hands.

'A sewing machine!' Annie sighed, despondently. 'I never envisaged the apartment would need upholstery work doing so didn't think to bring mine with me. Not that it would have been practical to have carried it all that way on the train.'

'Well, that's no problem. You can use mine,' Maggie grinned, letting go of the mouldy curtain before spritzing her hands with sanitizer gel and offering a squirt to Kristen.

'Oh, yes please,' Annie said, her mood lifting. 'That would be wonderful. I'm sure I could redecorate the walls too.'

'You'll need to get the water damage looked at first,

and the mould treated, but we'll find someone to help with that – I'll translate for you, of course,' Maggie beamed, seemingly keen to get involved too. Annie felt a bubble of excitement at the prospect of getting her hands on a project such as this and made a mental note to discuss it with Joanie later – her inheritance might be dusty and faded, but still, it was truly delightful, elegant and chic, and Annie couldn't wait to share the news with her. That en-suite room in the luxury living place could well be Joanie's very soon. Annie had no idea about the value of property in France, but surely an exquisitely furnished apartment such as this, in a gorgeous courtyard in a lovely part of Paris, with a distant view of the Eiffel Tower would be worth a very nice nest egg, just as Maggie had predicted last night over dinner.

After taking lots of pictures and promising to return the next day to have a proper look inside the cupboards and cabinets to see if there was any personal information about Beatrice that had been left behind, the three women went back down the stairs and realized there was one last door in the hallway at ground level to explore.

'Oh, we must have missed this on the way in,' Annie said, trying the door handle.

'Hardly surprising, we were all so eager to get inside

the apartment and take a look around,' Maggie said, making them all laugh.

Annie opened the door which led into another small corridor and then on into the back of the boutique.

'Eew, it sure is musty in here!' Kristen coughed, using the end of her silk scarf to cover her nose and mouth. 'And what is that smell?'

'Damp?' Maggie surmised.

'No, I don't think so, it's warmer, sweeter. Floral perhaps,' Kristen pressed the torch button on her phone so they could see inside the boarded-up shop.

'Almonds. Or vanilla maybe,' Annie sniffed the dark air as she flicked her phone's torch on too.

'Yes, that's it. I just got a faint whiff of vanilla, sugary almost, like birthday cake,' Kristen agreed, ducking as her head made contact with a large cobweb. 'Ugh, I hope there wasn't a giant, hairy spider working away in there.' She batted a hand over the top of her head to be sure.

'Look at this,' Maggie said, shining the torch on her phone towards the old mirror-topped counter in the centre of the room. 'There's a cupboard underneath here.' She crouched down to show Annie and Kristen.

'Ooh, is there anything inside?' Annie moved in closer and crouched down too. After carefully opening the creaky, precarious cupboard door that was hanging by one hinge, Maggie turned her torch to the inside of the cupboard so that Annie could get a good look. 'Oh, it's just a big old black ledger by the looks of it,' she said, lifting the battered book out of the cupboard.

'Beatrice Archambeau,' Kristen read from the front cover, after finding a tissue in her bag and using it to clear some of the dust away. Annie opened the book, which at first glance appeared to contain recipes of some sort. But not ordinary cooking recipes; these had ingredients like bergamot, orange, lemon, neroli, sandalwood and myrrh. One of the recipes was titled *Simple Perfume No. 7* and listed ¼ part clove and ¼ part lavender and possibly 1 part lemon – it was difficult to tell for sure what the other ingredients were, as the ink had smudged with age, or perhaps it was a liquid stain, water or oil. Annie hoped it wasn't tear stains.

'Wow, it's fascinating!' Kristen said over Annie's shoulder as they all took a look at the old ledger.

'It sure is. It's like an Aladdin's cave in here,' Maggie said, 'and I'm so pleased I invited myself along to see all this with you.'

'Me too!' Kristen agreed, and the three women laughed.

'I'm going to have a look at the shelves over there, see if there are any more hidden gems lying around.'

Maggie directed her torch towards the other side of the shop.

Annie carefully turned a few more pages, all of them revealing recipes listing essential oils, flowers, herbs; there were even some with titles such as *Nausea* that listed ginger beside it, another *Insomnia* and lavender given as a remedy, there was also one for *Tension* with a camphor, menthol and clove oil paste prescribed to be applied to pulse points and temples for 'soothing relief'.

'Do you think Beatrice was a pharmacist?' Kristen asked, leaning in closer to Annie.

'Maybe, or a perfumier perhaps? The faint scent of vanilla, the glass-topped counter right in the centre of the shop, which would have been very chic back in the day, and . . . see up there,' she paused and they both glanced up towards the ceiling where there were the remnants of another old beautiful crystal-glass chandelier. Some of the droplets were missing, but with some restoration it could be magnificent again, thought Annie. 'I can imagine this boutique being enchanting once upon a time, and to have Beatrice's perfume and remedies book is amazing,' she mused, tilting the ledger to get a better look in the torchlight.

'But, hang on a moment!' Kristen took another look at the ledger before folding her arms across her chest and tilting her head to one side as if deep in thought.

'What is it?' Annie wondered.

'Well, why haven't we noticed?'

'Noticed what?' Annie looked up at her friend.

'The words, here . . .' Kristen tapped the opened page. 'They are all written in English!'

They both fell quiet for a moment. Annie looked again at the page.

'You know, you're right! I didn't even consider the significance of this.' She was baffled. Why would a Frenchwoman fill a ledger with recipes for perfume and prescriptions in English?

'Of course you didn't! The brain sees what it expects to see, and I guess we're used to seeing English words . . . or something like that. I read a piece about it once in one of those psychology magazines,' Kristen explained, grinning and shaking her head. 'But seriously though, don't you think it's odd?'

'Yes . . .' Annie nodded slowly, mulling it all over, '. . . it is unusual. And makes me even more determined to find out exactly who Beatrice Archambeau really was.'

Just as Annie was wondering whether to put the ledger back inside the cupboard or take it with her to look at properly back in her room at Maggie's place, there was an almighty walloping sound behind her, followed by smashing glass. Dropping the ledger on the counter, Annie pivoted around to see Maggie toppling sideways through a section of shelving that was now bouncing against a wall in what appeared to be another space.

'Whoa! Maggie,' Kristen bellowed, darting from across the other side of the shop. But it was Annie who got there first, managing to grab her friend's arm and save her from toppling down a narrow and very steep set of concrete steps.

'Are you OK?' Annie asked, as Maggie stumbled back into the shop.

'I think so!' Maggie replied, panicked and visibly shaken.

'What happened?' Kristen yelled.

'I'm not sure! One minute I was looking at the shelves, went to pick up an old glass bottle in the far corner, and then the next thing I know is that the bottle has been flung across the floor and I'm being catapulted forward after losing my balance. It was as if I just stepped through the shelves, like going through the back of the wardrobe into Narnia! Only this isn't Narnia, it looks more like a dank old dungeon down there.' Maggie shook her head, waving a hand into the darkness.

'How strange. But see here . . . it's not an ordinary shelving unit, it's more like a door that has had shelves attached to it.' Annie gestured to the section of shelving that had hit the wall.

'There's even a hinge,' Kristen said, carefully stepping over the pieces of the glass bottle and then down onto the first concrete step, shining her torch around the edge of the moving shelf unit to get a better look. 'It's a secret trap door!' she added, dramatically. 'Must be. And my guess is that it was triggered when you reached towards the back of the shelf to lift the bottle up.'

'Ingenious! But why would you have a secret trap door in your perfume boutique?' Maggie muttered, smoothing her hair and gathering herself.

'Who knows, who cares! But, much more to the point . . . let's see what's down there.' Kristen directed her torch towards the eerie steps, her words quickening in anticipation.

'I'll wait up here if you don't mind. I've had enough surprises for one day.' Maggie laughed nervously as she moved away.

'Are you up for it?' Kristen turned to Annie, an eager look on her face. 'I was only joking with the guillotine gag earlier, there won't be any ghosts. I bet it's just a storeroom and not a dungeon at all!'

'Oh, um,' Annie swallowed. It was a long way down, and pitch black, but she had come here for Joanie, promising to take a look at her inheritance, and so she couldn't let her down now. She found herself saying, 'OK.' There were ten very narrow steps in total. Annie had counted them as she trod carefully, her foot still a little sore and unsteady; she didn't want to trip over and bump into Kristen who was leading the way.

Now they were standing in what appeared to be a cellar with a small, oblong-shaped grilled window high on the wall at street level outside, giving a shaft of light.

'What a dark place this is.' Kristen shone her torch around the bare brick-walled basement room. 'Imagine getting locked in here . . .' And her voice trailed off.

There was nothing to see, apart from a few old pieces of furniture – a metal bed frame stacked up on one end in a corner, a small table, a couple of folding chairs and some empty cardboard boxes. A crumbling mantelpiece over a brick fireplace housed a few old books.

'Yes, it is a bit claustrophobic,' Annie said, not wanting to imagine being locked in such a small space as this.

'The perfect hiding place though,' Kristen said, directing her torch towards the heavy door at the entrance to the room. 'We never would have known this tiny room was down here if Maggie hadn't inadvertently opened the secret door.'

'Ah, yes, good point. And I've heard about people

hiding in the war – I remember helping my son, Johnny, years ago with his history project about France when it was occupied by the Germans during World War Two.'

'Ooh, how intriguing,' Kristen's eyes widened.

'But it's just a storage room now by the looks of it,' Annie said, picking up one of the books that was written in French. Flicking through it, she realized that it was a child's book, with pretty pencil-line drawings of teddy bears having a picnic.

'Did Beatrice have children?' Kristen commented, taking one of the other books.

'I don't think so. We assumed not, Joanie and I, given that Beatrice left all this to her. Why would she do that if she had children to leave everything to? And probably grown up by now, and with their own children too. So Beatrice would have had grandchildren if that were the case. And if there were living relatives then wouldn't they have contested the will? Isn't that what people do when a family member leaves everything to a complete stranger? I don't know for sure, but it happens in films.' Annie put the book back on the mantelpiece and shrugged. Both women pondered for a moment.

'Maybe they were estranged! Or maybe they all just hated each other. Families can be fickle things. I learnt that the hard way,' Kristen's voice drifted off as she positioned her phone on the mantelpiece next to Annie's so as to get a better look at the books. 'Chad's parents won't talk to me these days. They even turned around and walked in a different direction one time when they saw me coming out of Macy's on Fifth Avenue. Like it was my fault the marriage fell apart. It was their cheating, dirty rat of a son who ruined it all.'

'Were you married for a long time?' Annie asked, gently.

'Five years. Things took a downturn when the last round of IVF didn't work,' Kristen said, blankly, a slight wobble in her voice. 'Then it all got snippy and Chad started playing around. You know, his girlfriend is now pregnant! Through IVF. And after everything we went through to try to have a family . . .' She paused momentarily. 'Good luck to him, I guess, he gets the happy family, but that's why I had to get away. Out of sight, out of mind and all that.'

'I'm so sorry.' Annie gently touched Kristen's arm, surprised and touched that her new friend was talking so openly about such a deeply personal matter. There had been no mention of this last night when they had bonded over the bread basket and red wine. Maybe it was the semi-darkness, the confined space they were standing together in, giving the moment an intimacy, like a confessional of sorts, and so Kristen felt comfortable in showing a vulnerable side to her usual bold, indomitable spirit.

'Yeah, it was a real shame. But for his parents to blank me . . . well, it hurt,' Kristen drew in a big breath before letting out an even bigger sigh of resignation.

'I know how that feels. Mark's family – my ex-husband – they did the same. I never really heard much from his parents after the divorce. That hurt a lot, it was probably one of the most difficult aspects of the whole thing, to be honest,' Annie confided, 'for my children's grandparents to fade away from their lives too was hard for them . . .' Falling silent, Annie momentarily remembered Phoebe crying on her birthday because Grandma hadn't come to see her with a new little knitted outfit for her doll, as was the tradition. It had broken Annie's heart and so, to make up for it, she had saved up for weeks and then taken Phoebe and Johnny on a day trip to the famous Hamleys toy store in London to let them choose a present each, followed by a tour of the sights on an open-topped red bus. Johnny had been thrilled with his Lego police station, whereas Phoebe had been angry, refusing to pick a toy, culminating in her screaming at Annie on the train on the way home, telling her she hated her and it was all her fault that

Grandma and Daddy didn't love them any more. Annie had felt inadequate and hopeless for days after that.

'That's really shitty!' Kristen tutted, interrupting Annie's thoughts.

'It felt so at the time. But then, later, I used to wonder if it was because they just felt awkward over how Mark behaved, how he left and then drifted away and then moved on with a new family unit. His new wife came between Mark and my Phoebe and Johnny, and so maybe she did the same with his parents to pull them away from us too,' Annie said, softly, picking up another book.

'You reckon?' Kristen tilted her head to one side. 'I didn't see it that way.' A short silence followed as the two women flicked through more of the books, taking them over to the stream of sunlight flooding in now through the small window. 'But I like this perspective. Yes! Thanks Annie, you've a kind heart as I never considered that could be the reason, but I will from now on. Sure beats feeling lousy about it, like it's all my fault. Maybe Chad's parents feel awkward too. And maybe I'll reach out to them one day and let them know it's OK, I get it.' And she flicked through the book in her hands. 'I can't make sense of any of these words. Is it even French?'

Annie leant over and took a look. 'I think the words

are German!' she said, taking the book from Kristen and looking at the front cover.

'Really?'

'Yes. See there! And, oh no . . .' Annie stopped talking.

'What is it?' Kristen stared at her.

'See this indented shape.' And they turned the book over again.

'Is that a swastika?' Kristen breathed.

'Yes.'

'Give it here! Maybe Maggie was right and Beatrice was one of the shopkeepers in cahoots with the German soldiers!' Kristen puffed, clearly aghast.

'We don't know that. The book could belong to anyone,' Annie said, playing devil's advocate. She still knew nothing about Beatrice but, having seen her gloriously decorated home, she wanted to like her because she felt a modicum of affinity with the mysterious woman who clearly had a keen eye for design.

As Kristen snapped the book shut, and went to return it to the mantelpiece with the other books, something fell from the pages and fluttered onto the ground.

'Oh, what's this?' Kristen crouched to pick up a piece of folded, faded paper. Annie moved closer so she was standing alongside Kristen as she opened what appeared to be a short, one-paragraph letter. It was handwritten in French, in black fountain pen, swirly old-fashioned cursive writing, and addressed to *Ma chère Beatrice* and signed *Ton amie, Paulette x*.

'Amazing. But my French isn't good enough to understand what this says,' Annie said, picking her phone up from the mantelpiece.

'Maggie will know. Come on, let's take it.' And Kristen folded the letter and handed it to Annie.

'Do you think we should? I'm not sure if Joanie will want anything removed,' Annie pondered.

'Sure it'll be fine. We can always bring it back later,' Kristen decided, and after picking up her phone too, she turned to leave.

Back outside, and the three women gawped open-mouthed at each other before shaking their heads and laughing.

'Thanks so much for letting me tag along today, Annie. That was incredible. It's like a museum in there, with us lucky enough to enjoy a private viewing,' Maggie said. 'Even if I did get the shock of my life.' She shook her head, looking much more relaxed now.

'Can we come back another time? I want to take a closer look at those paintings in Beatrice's sitting room. They were quite something!' Kristen whistled, impressed. 'And I promise not to touch, or steal one,' she laughed.

'Sure. But I'll have to talk to Joanie and see what she wants to do – she might say to just close it all up and find an estate agent to sell the boutique and apartment, in its current state, contents included, as – apart from the bedroom – it's perfectly lovely and suitable to be seen for viewings as it is,' Annie sighed.

'*Mais, oui*,' Maggie shrugged. 'But wouldn't it be lovely to spruce it up and return it to its former glory?'

Annie nodded, excited at the prospect.

'And she'll need someone to itemize and value the contents. They could be worth a fortune!' Kristen said. 'We'll have to find someone to help you. Plus, I want to know why Beatrice would have a German book with a swastika on the cover inside her property!'

'*Pardon?*' Maggie stopped walking.

'That's right. It's still in the basement. Could it be a Nazi handbook, you know, a manifesto or something?' Annie asked, concerned, sincerely hoping not and wondering what Joanie would make of it. She remembered Joanie telling her about her parents being killed during the Second World War. Her mother when their house was bombed and her soldier father in France.

'Surely not,' Maggie added. 'And I'm sorry . . .' She shook her head on seeing Annie's face. 'I shouldn't have said anything last night about the shopkeepers around Cour Felice. It's not right to speculate when we don't know anything about Beatrice and the type of women she was.'

'True,' Annie nodded. 'Maybe the letter will give us a little insight.'

'Let's hope so,' Maggie agreed.

'Come on, let's go! Ladies, it's been an eventful afternoon and we need a flagon, at least, of red wine,' Kristen declared. 'Each! Maggie might even need two. Are you sure you're OK after your trip through the bookcase?' she said, laughing kindly and putting her arm around Maggie's shoulders, giving her a squeeze. Maggie nodded and laughed too, seemingly relieved to be chatting about something else now.

'And we need a debrief! My mind is boggling after seeing all of that, plus I can't wait to have another look through this,' Annie laughed, lifting her arm where she had Beatrice's ledger tucked safely away. 'I've always fancied mixing up some potions so I might take some photos of Beatrice's recipes to try when I get back home.'

'And the letter,' Maggie added. 'I wish I had brought my reading glasses. To be honest, I'm not keen on wearing them. They make me look old.' And she pulled a face.

'Old? You're not old! A hundred and four is old, like Beatrice. She was old,' Kristen said, nodding impressively. 'Anyway, how old are you actually?' she stopped walking and turned to Maggie with a forthright look on her face.

'Oh, um, I'm fifty-four,' Maggie replied, hesitantly.

'And you?' Kristen looked at Annie.

'Forty-nine.'

'And I'm thirty-eight. So, there you go! We are in the prime of our lives. Now, come on, let's go,' Kristen instructed, doing a shooing motion with her hands, her confident stoicism firmly back in place, with no trace of the softer, more vulnerable side she had revealed to Annie earlier in the basement.

Annie smiled inwardly as the three of them headed off with a definite spring in their steps. She had come to Paris hoping for adventure, to step out of her comfort zone and put the spark back into her life . . . and that's exactly what seemed to be happening.

8

'Hello, darling. Or should that be *bonjour*,' Annie answered brightly, on seeing Phoebe's name appear on the screen as she picked her phone up from the table. She took another sip of the delicious drink that Maggie had prepared for them all. Her treat, she had insisted, once again, refusing all protests and insistence of payment from Annie and Kristen. The three women were sitting outside the Odette café, in the still warm early evening Parisian sun, enjoying very potent French 75 cocktails and bowls of garlicky black olives, chunks of warm crusty baguette and various wheels of ripe, gooey cheese and plump purple grapes. Sultry accordion music was floating in the warm breeze, mingled with the sweet fragrance of the early blooming honeysuckle from the delicate white flowering plants climbing the trellis on the stone brick walls of the café. And all around there were people, families, couples, the old men playing cards and doing their usual animated remonstrating with intermittent jovial laughter, giving the atmosphere a wonderful, carefree, holiday vibe.

Annie felt relaxed and happy with her new companions and couldn't think of anywhere she'd rather be right now. She had even managed to see Beth in Australia when she had FaceTimed earlier, and they had chatted for well over five minutes, before the screen went grainy and disconnected. Annie had also spoken to Joanie, and emailed the pictures and the film that Kristen had made over to Joanie's friend, Sandra's daughter, who was delighted to hear how marvellous the apartment was. Joanie was also very keen to find out more about Beatrice, fascinated by news of the ledger with her fragrances and potion recipes inside, saying that she would love to know who she was, what type of woman, the kind of life she had led . . . anything that Annie could find out would be of interest as she was ever so grateful to her for giving her such a lovely sounding inheritance. Joanie also wanted to explore the option of doing some home improvements, if they weren't going to cost very much, and if Annie was absolutely sure she didn't mind getting a quote for the damage on the bedroom ceiling and walls. Joanie didn't want to encroach any more on Annie's precious time in *'gay Pareee'* as she had said in a very jolly French accent before adding, '*au revoir*' as Sandra's daughter was at the front door with her iPad. And Joanie couldn't wait to see the pictures and video of the inside of the apartment and shop.

'Where are you, Mum, are you OK? I've been so worried about you,' Phoebe jumped in, her voice full of anxiety. Annie's smile dipped in concern as she lowered her glass.

'I'm fine, love, thanks, really I am. No need to worry,' Annie replied. 'I'm with Maggie and Kristen—'

'Who?'

'New friends, darling.'

'Oh, Mum, what do you mean, new friends? You've only been in Paris for one day, barely even that. Who are they? Where did you meet them?' she let out one of her long sighs of exasperation.

'Here, in Paris. I met them yesterday, soon after I arrived,' Annie said, smiling around the table at Kristen and Maggie who were chatting and sipping their drinks in the sunshine.

'Mum, please just be careful, are they anything to do with the apartment you've gone there to look at, by any chance? Because remember what I told you about fraudsters and con artists—'

'They are not fraudsters!' Annie said too quickly, regretting the words as soon as they popped out of her mouth. She lifted her glass to take a fortifying gulp and glanced sheepishly at Maggie and Kristen, hoping they hadn't heard her, but they had both stopped chatting and were giving her sympathetic looks. Maggie leant towards Annie, her forehead creased in concern as she mouthed, 'Everything OK?'

Annie grinned and nodded, managing a weak smile, but immediately felt self-conscious as her cheeks were flushing. Phoebe sounded genuinely worried, but cross too, in her usual perpetually exasperated way, but Annie felt that she couldn't really have this conversation with her daughter right now. Certainly not in front of Maggie and Kristen. And it might spoil the carefree, holiday vibe they had all been enjoying until a few minutes ago. She figured, instead, that a calm, diplomatic response was the way to go; she could always ring Phoebe later on and talk to her properly then, and so she settled for,

'They are both lovely women. You'd like them, darling.'

'How do you know that?' Phoebe kept on, having none of it. 'How did you even meet Maggie and . . .' She paused momentarily. '. . . whatever you said the other one is called? You only got there yesterday. Did they befriend you right away? At the station or wherever? The taxi queue! You know, you need to watch out for that kind of thing, it's the oldest trick in the book – they lull you into a false sense of security, flattery, friendship, especially lone travellers who might be nervous and feeling vulnerable. And you have been feeling lonely lately, since Beth left you, haven't you?' Annie went to answer but Phoebe ploughed right on. 'Have you given them any money? Have they got you to pay for stuff? Really, Mum, you should have let me come with you—'

'Phoebe! Stop it,' Annie leapt in, desperately trying not to raise her voice but failing catastrophically when it jumped up several octaves making her sound shrill and frustrated. 'Like I just said, they are not fraudsters or con . . .' She closed her mouth and swallowed down her embarrassment, cross with herself for reacting and forgetting to keep calm, and inwardly praying that Kristen and Maggie, who were chatting politely now, but were still sitting close to her around the small circular table, couldn't hear what Phoebe was saying. Because both women were kind, wise, funny and down to earth. Annie was convinced they were the type of people that she wanted to be around. To be friends with. But Phoebe had shot a dart of doubt into her head now. It was true, Maggie had been waiting for her when she arrived. And she had to admit that it was a bit unusual the way Kristen had joined in their conversation right away as she walked past the table in the café yesterday. And both women had been very keen to come with her to the apartment today . . .

No.

Stop it!

Why on earth would you doubt your own judgement all of a sudden?

Maggie was waiting because she was expecting you, obviously, and wanted to make you feel welcome, as any kind, decent host would do. And Kristen is American! A New Yorker, no less. Outwardly confident. What you see is what you get. Effervescent and bold. Nothing wrong with that. And she shared a vulnerability today which she didn't have to, and that takes courage.

Annie closed her eyes momentarily and shook her head, as if to recalibrate her thoughts. But it was hard. Why must Phoebe have such a suspicious mind all the time? It was unkind, bordering on mean even. And Annie hated that she felt this way about her own daughter. But more worryingly, why was Phoebe behaving like this? It was creating a knot of alarm inside Annie, making her fearful but she wasn't entirely sure why . . . it was as if there was a screen, a barrier of some kind between her and her daughter and she couldn't quite get a glimpse round or through it to see what was really going on.

'OK, what's the matter, Phoebe? You sound cross with me,' Annie trod tentatively, inwardly wishing she hadn't taken the call at all now as she stood up and went to move away from the table in an attempt to find a more private space. She felt rude and awkward too, having this type of conversation in such a public place, and she presumed it must be making Maggie and Kristen feel uncomfortable as well.

'I'm not cross, Mum, really I'm not.' There was a pause, then she added, 'But I can't help it if you don't like a few home truths.'

'Come on now, Phoebe. Home truths? Really? I am a grown-up, sweetheart, and I know how to look after myself. What is it that you are really bothered about?'

Silence followed. Annie waited patiently, wanting to give Phoebe space to think about her answer, but none was forthcoming. 'Are you still there?' Annie checked the screen of her phone to make sure the call was still connected. It was. 'Phoebe?' she tried again, softening her voice. 'What is it, love? What's wrong? I can't help you if you don't talk to me. Is it something to do with Jack?' Annie remembered a while back when Phoebe and Jack had argued – they had very nearly split up – Phoebe had been just like this, tetchy, anxious and even more exasperated than she usually was, but Annie had never really got to the bottom of it all and, come to think of it, she had never found out what had caused the argument in the first place. She had asked, several times, and had offered a shoulder to cry on, but Phoebe had just shut her down every time.

'It's nothing,' Phoebe eventually said in a quiet, almost resigned-sounding voice, followed by more silence.

'OK. Then why don't you tell me about your evening out?' Annie changed tack. 'At the Michelin restaurant with Jack. I'd love to hear all about it. The pictures were amazing. And you looked gorgeous, darling. Was the food nice? It looked delicio—'

'Stop it! Why would I want to talk about food?' Phoebe cut her off. 'And why are you going through my Insta grid?'

'Oh, I, err . . .' Annie managed, taken aback and unsure of what else to say. It had never been an issue before. 'Um, sorry . . . what do you want to talk about then?' she tried again.

'Why did you ignore me?' Phoebe blurted.

'What do you mean?' Annie said, mentally searching for a clue, and then on remembering that she had ignored Phoebe's call on the train yesterday, she felt relieved that it was nothing more, and added, 'Oh, darling! Is that all you are worried about?'

'That all?' Phoebe's voice cracked slightly. 'I called

you. But you didn't answer. And then you just disappeared. I had no idea where you even were.'

'You knew I was coming to Paris, love. And that I would be on the train,' Annie attempted, trying again to keep her voice even and calm but a sinking feeling had replaced the one of relief because she had promised to call Phoebe when she got to Paris. And had totally forgotten to do so. She had enjoyed herself so much last night. Laughing and chatting to Kristen and Maggie. She hadn't given her own daughter a second thought. And suddenly she felt bad. Inadequate. And what kind of mother did it make her when she knew Phoebe was concerned about her coming to Paris on her own? Surely, she should have made time for her. Annie bit down hard on her bottom lip.

'And then when I call you,' Phoebe said, her voice wobbling as if she were on the verge of tears now, 'I find out that you're drinking, *again*, and with complete strangers this time!'

'I'm so sorry, darling. I genuinely forgot, I guess the travelling and then the excitement of being here in Paris, meeting new friends . . .' Annie lowered her gaze as her voice trailed off, conscious that Kristen and Maggie were both busying themselves by being engrossed in their own phones now. But then Maggie stood up.

'I'll refill the olive bowl,' she said, placing a kind hand on Annie's arm as she walked past her into the café.

'I'll help,' Kristen said, quickly draining her cocktail before standing up too. Both women made a tactful, swift departure leaving Annie feeling mortified for having driven them away.

Later, in her room, soon after Phoebe had hung up on her, Annie heard a soft knock on the door.

'Just me,' Maggie said cheerfully, and then when Annie opened the door, added, 'I thought you might like some tea while I translate Beatrice's letter for you.' And she wheeled a little gold and glass three-tiered trolley into view. On the top shelf next to the letter that had fallen from the book there was a big pastel pink teapot covered with a striped knitted cosy and two matching pink china cups on saucers with plates and dainty gold forks. The second shelf was laden with traditional French sweet treats – croissants, crème brûlée in pots, macarons and a beautiful selection of little tarts – lemon, raspberry and pistachio, plus profiteroles too. 'Did I mention that we have a room service afternoon tea trolley?'

'Oh, Maggie!' Annie smiled, clasping her hands together in joy before giving her wonderfully welcoming host a hug.

'I hope you like the tea, I perfected the art of making it the English way when I was living in London,' Maggie said, proudly.

'You're so thoughtful. And I'm so sorry,' Annie said. 'What for?'

'Well, you know . . .' She stepped back, raised her eyes upwards and pulled a face before shaking her head. 'The phone call earlier. I never should have answer—'

'From what I could hear, not that I was eavesdropping, but it was hard not to,' she swiftly explained, 'you did the right thing to answer the call. Whoever you were talking to was obviously upset, and you certainly were too . . . that's the impression I got, and it's never nice to hear someone upset. It's much better to get it out than bottle it up. Want to talk about it?' Maggie asked. Annie nodded, her smile widening as she opened the door fully and helped Maggie in with the trolley.

Seated in armchairs by the open windows looking out onto a small Juliet balcony, vibrant with colourful potted plants, the two women sipped tea and savoured the taste of the pastries. Annie had just devoured a lemon tart, or *tartelette au citron*, as Maggie had said on offering it to her, and was now sure it was the most delicious, crumbliest and butteriest and lemoniest cake that she had ever tasted.

Maggie sighed and shook her head.

'If you don't mind me saying so, I think you're being very harsh on yourself. I know "mum guilt" can be tough, but still . . . you're only human and we all make mistakes.'

'Do you really think I am?'

'Yes, very harsh!' Maggie nodded.

'But I feel terrible for forgetting to call her.' Annie had explained how Phoebe was so cross and concerned when she had called.

'But you didn't do it on purpose . . . these things happen. I wonder why she reacted in the way she did? It seems a little disproportionate from what you've told me,' Maggie suggested, popping a final sliver of pastry into her mouth before quickly adding, '*Pardon!* I probably shouldn't have said that. It's not really any of my business.'

'It's OK. I probably shouldn't have gone into as much detail as I have, and then going on about my family problems when you hardly know me. But thank you for listening.'

'It's no trouble. I like having you here and, to be honest, I feel as if we've been friends for ever.'

'Yes, I agree, it does feel that way,' Annie smiled, taking a sip of her tea.

'Do you think something more is going on for

Phoebe? I don't know her, of course, so my apologies if I'm making assumptions; maybe she is just cross because you forgot to call, but . . .' Maggie's voice trailed off as she wiped her fingers on a napkin.

'I honestly don't know. She's always been intense and hyper-focused, and usually this works well for her when she channels it into her career – she's very hard-working and ambitious, but when the intensity becomes anxiety and exasperation . . . well, maybe there is something more,' Annie pondered, having had the same thoughts herself. What was wrong with Phoebe? She had always been controlling, but it seemed there was more to it somehow; she had been very panicked and cross earlier, even telling Annie she was selfish as she had ended the call. 'I wonder if I should go home,' Annie said quietly, still deep in thought. She had seen the apartment now, and Phoebe was her daughter, her child, albeit a grown-up one, but that didn't really make much difference somehow. Annie still felt protective and that would never change. But was it right to stay in Paris having a fun time with new friends when Phoebe might need her?

'You could always ask your daughter to come here,' Maggie suggested. 'Maybe a change of scenery – a holiday in marvellous Paris – would cheer her up?'

'Ooh, maybe . . . but would you really mind?' Annie

cast a glance around her room. There was certainly enough space in the lovely large bedroom. They would have to share the bed, but that would be fine – they had done it before on holiday when Phoebe was younger. And it would give them time together, bring them closer, hopefully, which Phoebe had seemed very keen for them to do in that FaceTime call, with her suggesting that Annie should retire and move to Yorkshire.

'Of course not. It would be a pleasure to have her here. If you think so too . . . if it would help?' Maggie lifted her eyebrows, as if to check it was what Annie wanted.

'I can certainly suggest it to her,' Annie nodded. 'And she did say that she should have come with me. But to be honest, that was more for my own good than hers. She seems to have got it into her head that I'm old and can't look after myself properly – I had a silly fall not so long ago and managed to fracture my foot. It's much better now though,' she quickly explained.

'Oh dear, but could that be it? Maybe she's worried you'll have another accident or that you're not safe here in Paris? And who can blame her with all that goes on in the world these days.' Maggie broke off to glance upward and laugh, 'I know this makes me sound old . . . but it really isn't like it was when I was in my twenties. The worst thing we had to worry about then was having something nice to wear out on a Saturday night. We didn't have phones and social media, and instant access to minute-by-minute accounts of all the awful things happening in the world. There's no switching off from it these days. And there's just so much pressure on teens and twenty-somethings too, with everything having to be rated. Like this. Love that. Swipe left. Right. Up and down. It's exhausting!'

'True.' Annie was thinking about what Maggie had said, and it would be nice to spend some time with Phoebe, but what if she did agree to come to Paris and then continued being anxious and critical . . . perpetually exasperated? What if it put a dampener on the trip? Annie's chance to put the spark back into her life would vanish in an instance. But then again, maybe Phoebe would arrive and be happy to spend time with her and they'd go to the Ladurée tea room for cake and macarons and . . . on second thoughts, no, perhaps a trip there wasn't the best idea as Annie didn't want a lecture about healthy eating. They could visit Notre-Dame, walk along the Seine. The Louvre. Sephora! Yes, Phoebe would love a trip to Sephora. Annie could treat her to some new make-up and they would make it a proper mother-and-daughter day . . . She couldn't remember the last time they had done anything like that together.

Maybe this was the real problem, they just hadn't spent any proper time together in a while, Annie thought, feeling bad. Then again, that could easily be fixed, she reckoned, which in turn quickly lifted her spirits again.

'Why don't you call her?' Maggie suggested. 'And then come downstairs and join us for dinner? I'll clear this away and see you soon.' She placed the teapot back on the trolley. Annie stood up to help her friend but Maggie was having none of it and motioned for her to sit back down. 'Oh, I almost forgot,' she added, fishing in her pocket before producing Beatrice's letter. 'Shall I leave this here?' Maggie went to put the letter on the table, her face suddenly sombre.

'Sure. I'm keen to know what it says. Does it say anything important? You know, to give us any clues about Beatrice?' Annie unfolded the piece of paper and took another look.

'Not really. But it's a little odd in the way that it is written.'

'Oh, really? In what way?' Annie asked, keen to hear more.

'It's very formal and detailed . . . It's dated 1944, so was sent during the Second World War.' Maggie cleared her throat and began reading.

A Postcard from Paris

My dearest Beatrice

I write to thank you for the perfume. The phial containing the scent made up of Patchouli, Indole, Echinacea, Rose, Rose de Mai and Eucalyptus has arrived safely and is quite the sweetest fragrance yet. Sadly, the herbal remedy accompanying it made up of Juniper, Elderflower, Rosehip, Evening Primrose, Myrrh and Ylang-Ylang was less fortunate, the body of the glass bottle damaged beyond repair. I trust that you will send a suitable replacement in due course.

Until we meet again.

Your friend,

Paulette

'And it's finished off with a couple of kisses,' Maggie said, folding the letter in half and handing it to Annie.

'Thank you. I shall put this back where Kristen found it when I next go to the apartment.' And Annie walked across the room to where her handbag was on the bed and put the letter inside for safe-keeping. She had no idea who Paulette was but felt it right to return the letter, wondering if it might make sense after she had sorted through the rest of Beatrice's things in the apartment. A photo perhaps. There were a few in the sitting room, perhaps one of them would have a name on the back to let her know who Paulette was.

'Intriguing, *oui?*' Maggie said.

'It is. And with two lots of rose.'

'*Oui*,' Maggie nodded. 'The rose de Mai – rose of May – is harvested in the month of May and comes from the Grasse region of France.'

'Ooh, that's interesting.'

'I read all about it after first reading Paulette's letter. Apparently, this ingredient must have the unique blend of the rich soil in the French Riviera and the aquatic breath of the Mediterranean Sea to become rose de Mai.'

'Wow! So Paulette must have been important for Beatrice to send her phials of perfume with high-grade ingredients during wartime. Quite extravagant! Or maybe the ingredients were all that Beatrice had. I assume there was rationing or short supplies of other goods here in Paris during the war, the same as there was in Blighty,' Annie said.

'Blighty?' Maggie's eyebrows raised.

'Oh, Britain, the UK. It was called Blighty during the war.'

'Ah, I see.' Maggie nodded, her eyes lifting, as if filing this new English word into her vocabulary.

'I'd love to know who Paulette is, if she's even still alive? I wonder if she could tell us about Beatrice . . .

She might even know how her friend is connected to Joanie. Wouldn't that be amazing?' Annie said, pondering all the possibilities. 'I might also try Monsieur Aumont again. I'm not convinced he knows nothing at all about Beatrice. Surely he must have met her at least . . . if she was his client. Just to know what Beatrice looked like, a glimpse into the kind of person she was would be something to share with Joanie.'

'Maybe he could put you in touch with Paulette, if she's still alive? We have no idea how old she was when she wrote the letter during the war, of course, but I imagine he knows how to trace people,' Maggie suggested.

'Oh yes, good idea,' Annie agreed enthusiastically, making a mental note to ask him if it might be possible, but then realized that she should really focus on Phoebe and not be getting carried away trying to track down people from the past who may or may not remember a friend they wrote a short letter of thanks to, about some perfume, over seventy years ago. She inhaled and let out a long breath, as if to clear her head, but couldn't resist probing just a little bit. 'And what did you mean by intriguing? The letter seems very concise . . . although a little sanitary and devoid of emotion. But that could just be the era it was written in, more formal, a time when emotions were kept in check.'

'Ah, *mais oui*,' Maggie shrugged. 'It is interesting that Paulette doesn't ask how Beatrice is. I assume she was in Paris during the German Occupation when the letter arrived, so wouldn't you enquire as to how your friend is coping during wartime? Paulette addresses Beatrice as "my dearest", so it would seem that she cared for her as a friend rather than an acquaintance that she has simply bought perfume from. And she signs it, "*Ton amie*", which is the familiar form.'

'Maybe she didn't dare,' Annie surmised. 'We don't know where Paulette is when she writes the letter. Perhaps she was scared . . . "loose lips sink ships", and all that. Wasn't that one of the slogans during the Second World War?'

'True.' Maggie nodded. 'But it is odd, yes? That Paulette lists out the ingredients of each perfume, when she could simply say thank you for sending the perfumes . . . Perhaps it is a code for something.'

'Ooh, yes, how exciting! And it was wartime!' Annie said, and both women laughed. Annie, suddenly remembering Phoebe's Miss Marple quip, pushed her hair back from her face and scooped it into a ponytail, as if to draw a line under the conversation. Besides, she was only here in Paris for a couple of weeks, so there really wasn't enough time to get carried away with engaging solicitors to trace people from the past and concocting elaborate notions of having discovered a coded wartime letter. She would be busy enough with making new curtains and getting a plasterer in to repair the damp in the apartment. And hopefully, Phoebe would be here soon and they would then be busy seeing all the sights and shopping together.

'I have to go now and check on the café,' Maggie said, patting Annie's arm. 'I will see you later when you are ready?'

'Yes, you will. And thanks again, Maggie.'

After Maggie had wheeled the trolley away, Annie made the call to Phoebe. There was no answer. She tried again, but the call went through to voicemail so she left a message saying that she'd love Phoebe to join her in Paris if she still wanted to, and to call her back so they could sort out the arrangements.

After hanging up she made a little wish, inwardly hoping she had made the right decision and didn't end up regretting it. Her time here in Paris was precious, and so the last thing she wanted was for Phoebe to arrive in a mood and make the magic and sense of adventure evaporate. But she had to try, offer an olive branch at least. She loved Phoebe, and you never knew with her, she could also be such fantastic company, fun and enthusiastic if she was excited about something. Annie had seen how she was when teaching her cheerleading classes, raring to go and full of energy as she danced and jumped around, cheering everyone on to 'reach new heights' and 'show your body some love'. It was infectious, and very exciting, and if she brought that enthusiasm with her to Paris then the rest of the trip would be even more of a wonderful whirlwind for sure.

9

Back downstairs in the café and Annie spotted Maggie and Kristen deep in conversation with a group of the old men who usually sat around playing cards and drinking wine. A white-haired elderly woman wearing a black crocheted shawl over a black serge dress was there too, drinking coffee, and appeared to be arguing with one of the men seated beside her. Wagging her finger in his face, she was yelling,

'Non, elle était allemande.'

It was Kristen who spotted Annie first when she entered the café, and after pulling a small round stool out from underneath the table, she beckoned for Annie to join them. Slotting one leg sideways around the stool to squeeze into the small gap at the table, Annie managed to slide into a seated position, swivelling her head from side to side in an attempt to take in all the animated yelling and hand waving. The old men appeared to be arguing with the elderly woman in black.

'What's going on?' Annie whispered to Kristen.

'I don't know exactly, but Maggie asked one of the men – that one over there in the beret,' she pointed discreetly, keeping her hand at table level, but Annie couldn't be sure as there were at least three men wearing black berets, 'if any of them remembered Beatrice in Cour Felice, and, well . . . all hell broke loose. They all started babbling and arguing and talking over each other.' She laughed and, shaking her head, she tore the corner off a packet of brown sugar and tipped it into a large mug of coffee. Stirring vigorously, she added, 'It's like watching a foreign-language film without the subtitles. The action is fascinating, but it's really frustrating when you have absolutely no idea what they are arguing about. I want to know. Only then can I pitch in and holler away with the best of them.' And she shook her hair back and gave a big throaty laugh.

'Oh, they are not arguing . . . not really.' Maggie appeared. 'The animated conversation is the French way, but there does seem to be some disagreement,' she acknowledged.

Crouching down in between Annie and Kristen, Maggie steadied herself with one hand on each of their stools and quickly brought them up to speed. 'OK, so this man here,' she indicated with her head over to the other side of the table towards the man who was doing most of the remonstrating with the elderly woman sitting next to him. 'He says he knew Beatrice, and that yes, it was a perfume shop that she had in Cour Felice – she sold remedies and medicines too, apparently, in the old days. He says she was a pleasant old lady who kept herself to herself and that she was a renowned perfumier. But Madame Bardin next to him – she's his mother – disagrees. She has just said, "No, she was German," and now she is telling them that Beatrice was a traitor, nobody wanted her perfume, and that she spoke German and had a German lover. Oh, *un moment*,' Maggie paused to listen to Madame Bardin who had now lowered her voice and was shaking her bowed head.

'Is she OK?' Annie whispered, 'she looks as if she is about to cry.'

'Ah, yes, she's sad . . . she's recounting an incident in the Second World War when Paris was occupied by the Germans. *Le bâtiment!* It means building. Oh, I think they're talking about the building opposite Beatrice's place at the far end of Cour Felice, the one that gave you the creeps today.' Maggie stopped talking to Annie and Kristen in English and said something in French to the group around the table. There was a brief moment of silence as they listened to her followed by many nods and answers of, '*Oui, oui, l'orphelinat.*'

'*L'orphelinat?*' Annie attempted.

'What is it?' Kristen asked keenly, hanging on their every word as if she were indeed watching a movie.

'It means orphanage.' Maggie briefly looked down at the table before adding, 'Now they are saying the building was an orphanage for Jewish children and that during the Occupation the Nazis came in the middle of the night and loaded all the children into a truck and took them away . . . They were never seen again.' The three women fell silent. 'And then the following day, Madame Bardin says she saw Beatrice laughing and talking in German to the soldier who ordered the round-up and even gave him a phial of perfume as a gift for his wife! There was also a picture on the front page of a German propaganda newspaper of Beatrice shaking hands with Kurt Lischka, who was head of the Gestapo during the Occupation and responsible for the deportation – and ultimately the death – of more than 30,000 French Jews.'

Annie inhaled sharply.

Kristen pushed her coffee away before placing a hand over her mouth and shaking her head.

Maggie didn't say another word.

10

The next day, and Annie was in her bedroom, spritzing her wrists with a new Chanel perfume she had treated herself to for the trip, when her mobile beeped to signify a text message. She popped the bottle back on the dressing table and picked up her phone. It was from Phoebe. At last. Annie had been worried when she hadn't heard back from her daughter yesterday, and had sent a short text message before she went to bed last night just to say that she hoped Phoebe was OK and that she loved her. Annie had never been one for ending the day on a bad note.

Sorry Mum, I can't to come to Paris now, I'm busy teaching classes. Fully booked for the next two weeks and I can't let my clients down at short notice ☹

Ah, Annie felt a wave of disappointment. After sleeping on her decision yesterday to invite Phoebe to join her in Paris, she had actually been looking forward to having her here, quite sure now they could have a fun time together away from the stresses of normal life. Even though Annie knew how important the gym was to Phoebe, she couldn't work out if this was a snub or not? Was Phoebe still cross with her? She had seemed so keen to come on the trip. Annie went to type a reply, but, oh, hang on, three dots appeared on the screen showing that Phoebe was sending another message.

And you're not selfish. I didn't mean to say that. Sorry xxx

Annie typed a reply.

I know. I hope you're OK darling and call me any time. I love you and will see you soon. Love to Jack too xxx

She waited a moment to see if Phoebe was going to reply, but there were no dots this time so she put her phone in her bag and pulled it onto her shoulder. After picking up her sunglasses she put them on and used them to push her hair back before going downstairs to meet Kristen for a breakfast of home-baked croissants and coffee in the courtyard outside the café. She felt excited as she and Kristen were going on a sightseeing bus tour of the city that took in all the iconic landmarks, finishing up not far from Cour Felice, so they were going to hop off there and call in to meet Étienne, the builder that Maggie had found to take a look at the damage in Beatrice's bedroom. Maggie had assured Annie that Étienne spoke perfect English and so there was no need for her to come along and translate. She would have loved to have seen the apartment again, of course, but they were two waiters down in the café today so she really needed to stay and help out.

Annie was halfway along the landing when her phone buzzed in her bag. Another text message. It was from Phoebe again.

Love you too xxx

Ah, Annie smiled to herself as she returned her phone back to her bag. Maybe Phoebe had just been having a bad day yesterday. Stress, most likely, from being so busy with the gym – back-to-back classes were exhausting, and with all the administration and management side of the gym to deal with too, it was a lot of work. Phoebe had never been shy of hard work, though . . . she took after Annie in that way. Annie made a mental note to make sure she called Phoebe later; instinct told her that she needed to keep the communication going, as the last thing she wanted was for Phoebe to work herself too hard and end up exhausted or, worse still, so tired and tetchy that she fell out with Jack and then shut Annie out like she did the last time it had happened. Jack was good for

Phoebe. He was a calm, steady influence, nothing seemed to faze him, but Annie imagined even his inordinate amount of patience would be tested with the way Phoebe behaved at times.

It was a beautifully warm afternoon with a soft, powdery blue sky smudged with wisps of cloud, reminiscent of a Monet painting, when Annie and Kristen eventually found the right bus stop and managed to get on the right tour bus. Annie was excited at the prospect of seeing the sights, doing the whole tourist trip of Paris first before exploring the hidden gems that she had read about. Having never been to Paris before, she didn't want to miss a thing.

Seated together side by side on the top deck, they had a perfect view as the bus meandered along the pretty pink-cherry-blossom-lined boulevards of Paris until the famous river Seine came into view. Annie turned to look at the breathtaking scene, the water glistening in the now golden afternoon sun, an ornate grey-stone bridge arching gracefully from one side to the other. People were wandering along the banks of the river, browsing the bookstalls selling books and paintings, stopping to admire the sketches on the street artists' easels.

'Hey, look down there. Boat trips! See the sign by the steps,' Kristen said, waving her hand over the side of the bus towards a wooden board beside a small jetty. 'What do you reckon?'

'I reckon it's a great idea,' Annie grinned, enthusiastically, thrilled at the prospect of a river cruise. Not that she was a seasoned sailor; the last time she had been on a boat was a ferry trip to the Isle of Wight as a child. It had been a choppy crossing and she had felt bilious for hours after arriving. But this was different. This was Paris! And she couldn't wait to glide elegantly along the famous river and see all the magnificent sights up close along the way. 'Do we have enough time though? We're meeting Étienne at the apartment . . .'

'Sure. Come on. We can hop back on the bus further along the river when we disembark and will have plenty of time to get there.' And Kristen was out of her seat and making her way towards the stairs to exit the bus. Annie dashed along after her, excited about the spur-of-the-moment change of plans.

Moments later, and they were sitting in the glass-roofed, open boat with a much better view of the heart of Paris, or so it seemed. Annie took a quick look at the map of the city that the boat cruise operator had given them, showing how the river Seine meandered right through the middle of Paris. She had her phone poised to take pictures. But then paused, wondering if she'd be better off just sitting back and enjoying the whole experience first-hand, instead of second-hand through the lens and then later looking for filters and frame sizes to make her pictures look perfect, like Phoebe always managed to do on her Instagram. Annie decided to put her phone away and instantly felt lifted. Such a treat. To relax and take it all in with no pressure to capture every moment on her phone, taking photographs that she most likely wouldn't even look at again.

A man with a microphone welcomed them onboard, his English accent stylishly chic and Parisian, and then when he switched to French, Annie smiled contentedly, pondering on how romantic the words sounded, transporting her to a world so far away from her normal life back home in London. And then they were off, the water rippling as the boat glided gently through the silvery green water.

'Oh, wow!' Kristen breathed, swivelling her head as the glorious gold-trimmed dome of the Institut de France came into view. 'Built by Louis Le Vau in the seventeenth century,' the tour guide told them.

'It's fantastic. And so old! And look at the French flag up there above the clock.' Kristen was in awe. Annie smiled, pleased to see her friend having a good time. A group of people sitting on benches and enjoying the spring sunshine on the towpath waved as the boat drifted on. Annie waved back, resisting the urge to say a breezy, '*Bonjour*' for fear of coming across as an embarrassing tourist. Kristen, however, had no such qualms, and leant right across Annie, and almost over the side of the boat too, in her enthusiasm to wave and yell, '*Bonjour*' and '*C'est magnifique*', before blowing kisses and collapsing into a fit of laughter followed by exuberant chatter about the awesomeness of it all. Annie was delighted to see her friend enjoying herself, fully immersed in the sightseeing experience – Kristen had explained over breakfast this morning that she had never travelled outside of America, apart from Canada to visit her cousin, and so this was her first time in Europe!

They sat back to enjoy the trip, relaxed in each other's company for a while, and soaking up the atmosphere.

'Wait till you see over there,' Annie nudged Kristen, smiling and holding her breath to see how she would react on realizing that the world-famous Louvre Museum was coming into view now, sited at the eastern end of the Tuileries Gardens. Annie gazed from left to right through the glass windows of the boat, keen to not miss any of the magnificent historical buildings.

'Oh my goodness, is that the actual Louvre?'

'Yes, here we see the world's greatest art museum,

the wonderful Louvre,' the tour guide confirmed with a flourish, right on cue, making Kristen instantly lift her phone, turn her body around and snap several hundred selfies, or so it seemed, of her smiling and pointing an index finger at the majestic stone building.

'And now the Orsay Museum, which used to be a railway station. Here you can see many works by the French Impressionists,' the guide continued, pointing to what Annie was learning to call the Left Bank.

'Oh yes, you can see that, can't you?' Kristen nodded, studying the building, engrossed in hearing the history as the guide told them it was built between 1898 and 1900, 'with all those beautiful, big arches turned into windows. And the architecture, it's incredible. So detailed.'

'And look at the flowers there,' Annie said, spotting a huge array of scarlet roses in a wooden cart which, from their low angle where they were sitting on the boat looking up at the brick wall to the side of the river, appeared to be backlit with the prettiest powder blue sky. Annie momentarily closed her eyes, as if to save the beautiful scene inside in her head for ever more. It was truly idyllic.

Motoring on, and under another bridge, Annie marvelled on seeing a row of gorgeous houseboats moored to the side of the Seine. A colourful yellow and white painted wooden barge with half-barrel tubs crammed full of pretty flowers, a fluffy cute caramel-coloured cockerpoo jauntily sauntering along the deck as his owner, sitting in the sunshine enjoying a leisurely drink, raised his glass and tilted his head. Annie waved and smiled back, feeling a little self-conscious when the man lifted a leisurely hand in response and gave her a quizzical smile, one eyebrow arched.

'Ooh, did you see him? I'm sure that was the hot guy who was in the café the other night,' Kristen breathed, her eyes widening.

'Really?' Annie said, turning to take another look.

'Yes. You must remember, the young George Clooney lookalike.' Kristen craned her neck to get another look as their boat moved on and the man faded from view. 'Very suave, with his messy black curls and that whole wealthy shipping magnate look he had going on.'

'Shipping magnate?' Annie laughed. 'What do you mean?'

'Oh, you know, the crisp white made-to-measure shirt with sleeves casually rolled up, blue jeans and loafers. The leather bracelet and platinum bangle on his wrist. Designer shades. The easy confidence. A sophisticated glass of cognac in his hand. The cute dog!' She paused to nod and place a hand on Annie's arm, as if to underline her theory. 'Trust me. And we know he smells divine. Of expensive aftershave. And money!' she laughed, her eyes widening as she shook her hair back. Then, leaning forward into Annie, she lowered her shades and peered over the top of them to give her a cheeky look.

'And you got all of this from a momentary glimpse of a total stranger?' Annie mused, intrigued by another side of Kristen that she hadn't seen before. But it was true, he had smelled divine, although Annie had no idea if the tantalizing scent that she had caught a delicious whiff of as he had walked by the table in the café was expensive or not, but she did remember the quickening of her pulse in response.

'Sure. But not a complete stranger. I mean, we've met before . . .' Kristen shrugged nonchalantly.

'Well, that's stretching it a bit. He made a fleeting appearance at Maggie's café,' Annie said, suddenly feeling the same way again . . . that fluttery awakening sensation fizzing within her.

'Honey, you have to be quick these days! Dating in New York is all about the instant impression. You have to know how to spot the good 'uns worth spending your precious time on . . . even if it's only for a few minutes,' Kristen stated, clicking her fingers as if to demonstrate just how quick the decision-making process must be.

'OK,' Annie said slowly, not entirely convinced. 'But tell me . . . if he's a shipping magnate, then what is he doing living on a barge on the side of the river Seine in Paris? Wouldn't he own a superyacht and be sitting on the deck, moored up somewhere like . . . oh, I don't know, a Greek island?' Annie joked, relaxing back into her seat and lifting her hair up before securing it with a bobble to make a messy bun.

'Hmm, I guess so,' Kristen shrugged and laughed some more. They sat in silence for a little while longer, contentedly taking in the view and the atmosphere together until Kristen spoke again. 'But he did look like George Clooney!' she swooned. And Annie had to agree. He did look like a young George Clooney. Curly black hair, tanned, and that smile! He had been very easy on the eye with his athletic physique and laidback manner. But then the whole scene with the pretty barge and cute dog and . . . well, she couldn't believe that she was doing it now . . . giving a complete stranger far too much of her headspace when she should be enjoying seeing all the other sights of Paris. He most likely also had an equally gorgeous wife.

Drifting on and towards another bridge, and in Annie's opinion, the best one of all they had seen in Paris.

'We are now passing under the Alexander the Third Bridge,' the tour guide told them, and Kristen took more selfies as the ornate construction passed overhead.

Built in the Beaux-Arts style, it had four huge pillars topped with gold-embossed winged horses. Ornate triple-plumed Art Nouveau streetlights dotted the whole length of the bridge, with more gold-embossed statues, the detailing and craftsmanship incredibly intricate. It was spectacular, and the epitome of timeless Parisian chic and architecture. And then the moment Annie had been waiting for.

The Eiffel Tower.

It was truly magnificent up close. Surprisingly emotional too. Annie caught her breath as its true splendour came in to view. And she couldn't resist quickly finding her phone and taking a few pictures as the afternoon sun gave the brown metalwork a beautiful rose-gold sheen. It was now or never to capture the moment.

'Would you like me to take a picture of you both together?' an older guy sitting behind them offered, as the boat slowed to a standstill.

'Sure, that would be great,' Kristen said, moving alongside Annie, and then with their backs to the tower they both smiled.

'Thanks,' Annie said, taking her phone back from the man.

She gazed at the towpath, where more people were sitting around chatting and eating lunch and just taking time to be outside and enjoy the sunshine. Smiling, she tried to remember the last time she had sat outside back home in London, and was stunned on realizing that it never happened. Most of her time outside was spent travelling to work, crammed onto an overcrowded train and then in the office on the twentieth floor of a tower block with only the obligatory chain cafés and restaurants nearby. Annie made a mental note to get outside more. Find a park near her office. A small patch of green space would do, or maybe she could walk along the river Thames, her office wasn't that far from it. Or she could do more travelling. There were so many places that she had never visited. Being here in Paris was giving her the opportunity to see her life from the outside, as an onlooker, and making her start to realize just how confined and boxed in it all felt. Especially with Beth so far away.

She hadn't been gone long but Annie was already dreading going back home and being on her own without her best friend to socialize with. Maybe Phoebe had a point about moving. It wasn't as if she had to work, not like the old days, and she was incredibly grateful to have been able to pay off her mortgage, even though she'd much sooner her dad was still around. But maybe it was time to do something different, instead of commuting to work every day and then spending her weekends indoors, making yet more cushions or moving her furniture around to try out different interior design ideas. It was pointless really, seeing as she always ended up putting everything back where it was in the first place. The best place. Because she already knew this from having tried every conceivable option over the years. And the truth of it was that she kept everything in the same place because it felt safe and comfortable . . .

11

Later, having finished the boat trip, Annie and Kristen found a quintessentially Parisian little café called La Bastille near Cour Felice, and enjoyed deliciously gooey and cheesy croque monsieur sandwiches with a glass of fruity red wine before heading to the apartment to meet Étienne. They waited outside for a while but, when he was near to being ten minutes late, they went inside and Annie went into the bedroom to make a start on measuring the windows for the new curtains, while Kristen took a proper look at Beatrice's, now Joanie's, paintings in the drawing room, having declared that the enormous queue outside the Louvre was not for her. Not when there was Beatrice's very own private art gallery right here to view.

Carefully lifting the old, damaged curtains out of the way and tucking them back as far as she could, Annie slipped off her ballet pumps and tentatively stepped up on the window seat in order to reach the pelmet. She made sure her feet were properly planted on the sturdy wooden frame of the seat so there was no risk of her falling off, as she had from the loft ladder back home. Phoebe would never forgive her if it happened again. Having got her measurement of the pelmet, she took a step sideways and leant against the wall as she inspected the lining of the curtains, impressed to see that it was embossed, the sign of an excellent quality fabric, but such a shame that it was now ruined with stains. On second thoughts, though, much of the fabric was still in pretty good condition, so perhaps she should try to get the curtains professionally cleaned. It might be a cheaper option for Joanie and would mean that these curtains, so beautifully in keeping with the rest of the apartment's design, could stay in place and gain a new lease of life. Yes, and maybe Maggie might know where she could find an upholstery cleaning place in Paris.

Just as Annie was pondering on whether to try this option first, she pressed a hand onto the corner of the wall so that she could step down safely onto the floor, and felt something move beneath her fingertips. It was as if the plaster or brickwork underneath the wallpaper was loose. She took a closer look, curious to see a section of wallpaper that was carefully cut out like a flap; the crease was hidden underneath where the curtains would fall when hanging down properly, so it wouldn't have been noticeable normally. Intrigued, she gently peeled back the section of wallpaper, revealing four loose bricks, the dried-out white plaster around them disintegrated and crumbling away. Annie touched the corner of one of the bricks and was surprised to see that she could tilt it outwards and away from the wall, creating a kind of cavity within. So, after tentatively checking that the surrounding bricks seemed to be securely in place, she carefully removed the loosened brick and looked inside. There was fabric of some sort, a silk scarf perhaps, but it was tricky to tell for sure as it was covered in brick dust and nestled in cobwebs so had clearly been inside the wall for a very long time.

Annie hesitated, unsure if it was acceptable to remove the bundle from its hiding place within the wall, even though she was excited to take a look right away. Would Joanie want her to? Would Beatrice have wanted her to, come to think of it? Whatever was inside the bundle had obviously been stored away inside the wall for a reason. Hidden like treasure. She took a deep breath and went to call Kristen into the bedroom, wondering what she would say, but then heard her mobile ring and Kristen saying, 'Hi' to answer a call, and so she didn't want to disturb her.

Figuring that Kristen would most likely say go right ahead, and Joanie had been fascinated on hearing about Beatrice's perfume recipe ledger, even asking Annie to bring it back with her if she had space in her suitcase so she could have a proper look at it, Annie made her decision.

After removing all of the loose bricks, she was able to lift the silk bundle out too and carefully place it on the window seat for safekeeping as she stepped down onto the carpet. She sat in an armchair nearby to take a proper look. Gently unravelling the fabric, she discovered a collection of papers and an envelope containing some dried pressed flowers bound together with string and a bundle of small leather-bound books. Diaries or journals of some kind, she did a quick count-up and was fascinated to see there were ten of them at least. Some of the books were damaged with age and damp, most likely, as the pages were all pulped together and impossible to separate, let alone read, but Annie managed to find a tissue in her bag with which to carefully wipe enough of the cover on one of the books to see that it was a diary dated 1926 with a gold embossed *B.C.* monogram at the corner. *Beatrice? But why a C?* Annie opened the diary and there on the inside was the answer, *Beatrice Crawford*, which she thought sounded very English indeed and would explain why the perfume ledger was written in English. So maybe Beatrice wasn't French at all. And as if to confirm Annie's thinking, she turned to the first page and saw that the words were indeed all written in English.

Intriguing then that the men and the elderly woman in Maggie's café were convinced that Beatrice was German and was in cahoots with the German Nazi soldiers during their Occupation of France. Why would they think so? There must have been good reason. Had they heard Beatrice talking to the soldiers in German? Seen her socializing with them, they had even accused her of having a German soldier lover . . . but she was *Madame Archambeau*. Annie knew this for sure as it was on the paperwork for the apartment. The only explanation that Annie could think of was that Beatrice had married a Frenchman or simply changed her surname for some other reason.

Annie's pulse quickened as she read the first paragraph, keen to see what Beatrice's life was like way back in 1926. Would there be any clues as to who she really was? And why she wrote her diary in English, and her perfume recipe ledger too. And, more excitingly, would there be any clues as to how she was connected to Joanie? Annie couldn't wait to find out, and so she turned the page . . .

New Year's Eve, and what a marvellously exhilarating evening it was, celebrating with all of the gang. My feet are still tingling from dancing the Charleston at the smart new Zelli's club, on rue Fontaine, and my head is still throbbing from sipping far too much champagne followed by a lethal concoction of Pernod and iced water with an absinthe chaser. Monty insisted on having magnum after magnum of bubbles brought to us at the table, or 'royal box', as Joe Zelli himself called our private booth when he escorted us there. Equipped with our own telephone on which we could call and chat to the rest of the gang in their respective booths – it was such fun. There was the most splendid view from the balcony as we watched the cabaret stage and bandstand on the floor below, the lights glittering as they sparked off mirrored archways and the marble pillars at the corners of the dance floor. The delicious scent of cigarette smoke, mingled with pomade and perfume, made for an evocative atmosphere, still clinging to the exquisite silk tasselled dress that I wore last night. Barely skimming my knee, the dress was marvellously risqué but nothing compared to the cabaret of dancing girls with their feather boas and long beaded necklaces nestled between glistening bare breasts that jiggled around as they performed exhilarating high kicks, much to the delight of the audience. We clapped and cheered them on with fevered enthusiasm and utter awe. Oh to have the skill, not to mention the courage, to dance and perform on a stage. With shimmering sequin scarves to barely cover their bottoms, my thoughts drifted to Iris and how very much she would disapprove. Of course, this in turn made the evening all the more exquisite, for she continues to be tiresome and disapproving, commenting at every opportune moment, to the point that I am convinced she is quite obsessed with me. But I really do not care for it any more. I have come back to France to escape her and Father's relentless disapproval of me and so far it has done the trick. Paris really is the very best place to be. I can be happy and frivolous here. I can be Trixie and not boring Beatrice who must be on her best behaviour at all times!

Paris is the City of Light, that's what they say; more rather fun and frolics in the dark of night, is what I say. I feel alive and gay when I'm here and extremely grateful that Father agreed to Iris's insistence that I live in the little apartment that she keeps on Cour Felice, citing no need for it now as she would no longer frequent Paris if I was going to be there 'flaunting yourself around like a common floozy' she informed me when Father had left the room. The place is pretty and utterly perfect for me, with its floor-to-ceiling shuttered windows that look out onto wrought-iron balustrade balconies providing a perfect view of the city. I enjoy it immensely, gazing from an open window on a warm evening to see the twinkling Eiffel Tower in the distance set against an indigo night sky, a red Metro sign beneath a glowing golden ball nearby. There is always something new to discover across the rooftops and in the cobbled streets below, where the sound of life and honks of motor-car horns drift upwards in the breeze to invigorate and make me feel part of the world at last. I have everything I need here with Monty and the gang to frequent the fashionable cafés that are only a stone's throw away, and there's even an empty, disused old stable below the apartment that I have plans for – I have every intention of turning it into a shop, or boutique as they say here in Paris, so I can finance myself and be free of the beholden constraint that a monthly allowance brings.

Iris had insisted I have the allowance if I was going to Paris, and was furious when I refused at first, stating that I would not embarrass Father by being a poor shop girl (my original plan was to keep myself by working in a dress shop) and making people presume that he was not in a position to provide for me. Although I rather think Iris's and Father's motives for housing me here in Paris were more to do with keeping me from embarrassing them within the society circles they frequent. Especially as Clement, on returning from the war and realizing that he was never going to get his own way and lure me to be his wife, has since washed his hands of me. As he wishes! For I am having a ball and meeting the most fascinating people – Americans and poets, playwrights, artists and authors. Everyone is here to be free and have the most splendid time. Last night at Zelli's I was introduced to a young, tremendously handsome and talented trombone player called Maurice, his ebony skin, sumptuous lips and sparkling dark eyes so attractive as to bring a blush to my cheeks when he kissed them both, as is the French way, before lifting my hand and planting a lingering kiss there too as he murmured, 'Enchanté, Trixie,' then lifted his trombone, tilted it towards the ceiling and performed a triumphant blast. Maurice certainly dazzled me with his youthful zest for life! And then there was Jacques! The moment our eyes met is *one I shall never forget as my pulse galloped like a racehorse headed for the finishing line. Tall, dark and devilishly handsome, with conker-brown eyes and beautifully chiselled cheekbones, I fear he stole my heart in that very first moment. He talked to me in perfect English with an exquisitely romantic French accent, although I have no recollection of the words he spoke, such was the giddy state of my head and heart! I must learn to compose myself when we next meet, which I truly hope will be very soon.*

And what a stroke of luck, meeting my sweet Monty before I had even arrived in Paris. There he was with a battered brown suitcase, wearing a flat cap and his best suit on the deck of the ship bound for France, a kindred spirit, also keen to escape the confines of his life back in England, where being queer is quite out of the question. It is quite extraordinary that he recognized me from Étaples where I had tended to his head wound. The fear in his young eyes had faded on hearing a comforting poem whispered to him in the dark of the night, for he had suffered so greatly in the war, cooped up in the trenches with the other soldiers mercilessly bullying him for his effeminate ways. But he continues to be the most wonderful friend. Queenie, when I brought her to Paris for her birthday treat, adored him too, for he really is the gentlest of men, with a kind word for everyone lucky enough to meet him, although he has a wicked tongue when he's in one of his exasperated moods.

Annie smiled to herself, thinking how Monty of 1926 sounded very much like her daughter, Phoebe, today. Charismatic but quite exasperating at times too. And Annie felt an affinity with Beatrice, or Trixie as she preferred, as well, understanding about her wish to escape the confines of her life back in England. Keen to discover more about Trixie's life, Annie read on.

It is such a pity that Monty isn't one for the women, with his dashing looks and love of life, or joie de vivre, as the French say, being so very appealing. Queenie was taken with his charm and felt like a perfect chump when I explained that her flirting with him was quite futile. Although I do fear for him dreadfully with his predilection for men being wholly indiscreet at times. Nobody cares in the cafés and clubs we frequent, but the stolen glances he shared with a man at one of the other dining tables in Maxim's last week, was noted, I'm quite sure, by Lord Asbury who made no attempt to hide his disgust with an enormous huff and puff

Alex Brown

*harrumph as he promptly steered his dowager
mother away to the perceived safety of their motor
car waiting outside . . .*

'Annie. *Annie.*' Kristen appeared in the bedroom,
waving her hands in the air with an excited look on
her face. Annie quickly closed Trixie's diary and took
a second or two to bring herself back to the present
moment. Kristen stopped short and looked concerned
now. 'Gosh, Annie, are you OK? Sorry, I didn't mean
to startle you . . . You look stunned!'

'Oh, um . . . yes, I . . . sorry, I was reading this . . .
Beatrice in the Roaring Twenties, well, 1926 to be
precise. And I think she's English. She sailed from
Southampton, that's a port town in England, and there's
even mention of friends . . . Monty and Queenie, who
came from England too. I wonder if there is a way to
find out more about them – obviously they won't still
be alive now if they were adults in the 1920s but we
could try to find younger relatives or friends who
might have heard of Beatrice. Wouldn't it be wonderful
if they could unravel the mystery of the link from
Beatrice back to Joanie? The clues could all be right
here,' Annie marvelled, tapping her fingertips on the
page. 'Can you believe it?' And she closed and then
lifted Trixie's diary up to show Kristen.

'And I'm intrigued to read more and find out why she felt compelled to stash them away inside the wall. You know, her friend Monty was gay and that would have been out of the question back in 1926; homosexuality was illegal in England, but people were more relaxed about it here in Paris. I wonder, though, if Beatrice wanted to protect him and so stowed his secret safely away? How sad if that was the case.' Annie shook her head.

'Whoa! Slow down, honey. I can see that you're excited, but what is it you have there?' Annie went to explain but Kristen cut in with, 'Fascinating! And I can't even imagine how terrible it must have been to have to keep a secret like that. You are who you are! Why would anyone have a problem with that?' she puffed, placing her hands on her hips as she momentarily considered the injustice and swiftly dismissed it as an inconceivable nonsense, before adding, 'But wasn't Paris pretty progressive and hedonistic back in the Roaring Twenties? They had nude cabaret bars and same-sex clubs and nobody minded at all! It was very carefree, and so I bet there's more to this than meets the eye.'

'Do you reckon?' Annie said, turning the diary over and wondering what other secrets might be held within its pages.

'For sure! I sat next to a guy on the flight over from New York and he was telling me all about the book he's writing – something to do with the history of jazz. Anyway, he said there were loads of gay clubs in Paris in the Twenties,' and she paused as if recalling a detail. 'Clair de Lune! That was the name of a famous one. I remember it because my dad loves classical piano music and Debussy's "Clair de Lune" is one of his favourites. But enough of all this.' And she flapped her hand excitedly. 'You need to come with me right away. We can talk more about this hidden stash later,' and took the diary out of Beatrice's hands and placed it on top of a burr-walnut writing slope on the lamp table next to the armchair. Then, lowering her voice and leaning in with a covert gleam in her eye, she pressed her palms together and whispered dramatically, 'Trust me, this is way, *way* more exciting than finding an old diary!' She practically pulled Annie from the armchair and propelled her out of the room.

Before Annie had a chance to ask more, Kristen had gripped her arm and babbled something about Maggie's café, the boat trip, and it being a small world, and then pulled open the front door to the apartment. A man was standing in the hallway with his back towards them. 'Étienne is here!' And Kristen gave

Annie a quick nudge as the man turned around and put his hand out towards her.

Annie opened her mouth.

Closed it.

And then opened it again.

It was the man who had made her pulse quicken in the café. The man from the houseboat. A young George Clooney was standing right in front of her with possibly the sexiest grin that she had ever seen in real life! With a natural tan that accentuated his sparkling brown eyes, he was wearing those jeans, the ones that clung nicely to his hips and accentuated his firm thighs, and a navy polo shirt, his unruly curls flopping onto his forehead. And there was the divine scent again . . . vanilla and warm spice. Although he was younger close up, early forties perhaps, taller too, than he had looked when seated on the deck of his boat.

'*Bonjour*,' Étienne's smile widened, making his eyes crinkle at the edges. 'I am very sorry to be here late,' he added in English, with a very appealing French accent. 'The Parisian traffic is, how you say . . . rushing along!' he shrugged.

'Oh, um, no problem. It's . . .' Annie shook his hand and then gestured for him to come on inside. 'Well . . . this is a surprise, a lovely surprise and you're . . . well, you're not what I, um, expected a

Frenchman, err . . . a French builder to look like . . .'
She stopped talking, inwardly cringing at how ridiculous she sounded, especially when the truth of it
was that she hadn't given a moment's thought before
now as to what a French builder would look like. Or
a Frenchman should look like. What had she had in
mind? A stereotypical beret, stripy T-shirt and rope
of onions around his neck! Gathering herself, she
promptly continued with a more appropriate, 'It's very
nice to meet you, again!' And then when he stared
at her blankly, Kristen jumped in with:

'The boat. We waved to you on the Seine. You have
a very cute dog. And a cute smile too.' And she laughed,
coquettishly, ruffling her hair around before giving it
a big flick over her shoulder. Étienne's forehead creased
as a flicker of a smile danced on his lips before he
nodded casually, as if it were an everyday occurrence
for women to wave at him and tell him he had a cute
smile. Annie grinned awkwardly, wondering what
Kristen might say, or even do, next. She was coming
to realize that her new friend was not only bold, but
quite unpredictable too and, given her dating pep talk
earlier, there was a high chance she might whip out
her phone and waste no time in taking Étienne's
number and setting herself up on a date with him.
Pronto! It was about the instant impression and

moving in fast, after all. Although he was here to look at the water damage, not have Kristen flirting with him, or indeed to deal with her own inane babbling, blithering like an idiot about French builders.

Annie inhaled through her nose and wondered why she felt so bamboozled all of a sudden. It was unlike her. She was usually fairly relaxed around men, so why had she reverted to her 13-year-old self-conscious self? Where she would have had Beth by her side as they giggled and gawped at the boys in the school disco, neither of them with any confidence, or knowing what they would do if a boy actually came over and spoke to them. But that was a lifetime ago. And now Annie was a grown woman with a failed marriage plus a multitude of lacklustre relationships under her belt so she really ought to know better. Kristen was puckering her lips at Étienne's back now as he walked past her, so Annie gave her a glance as if telepathically telling her to stop it at once for she was being far too full on and what would Étienne think if he turned around and caught her carrying on like a lusty lunatic?

Leading the way into the bedroom, Annie showed Étienne the water damage, desperately trying not to catch Kristen's eye as she was leaning seductively against the doorframe, now sneaking up-and-down looks at Étienne's impressive physique as he bent over to inspect the skirting board that they hadn't noticed was coming away from the wall.

'Come, see this here,' Étienne said, gesturing towards the bottom of the wall, and Annie wondered if she should crouch down beside him. Casting a quick glance over her shoulder, she saw Kristen flapping her hand in the air as if motioning for her to get down there immediately. 'Look, Annie. You see this?' When she nodded, but didn't actually engage her mouth to say something useful, he instructed her to sit, seemingly oblivious to the effect that he was having on her. And so she did. Kneeling down next to him, the close proximity of his body beside hers and the quick burst of warm vanilla making her feel ridiculously self-conscious, and why was it so hot in the bedroom all of a sudden?

Annie surreptitiously tweaked at the neck of her T-shirt and tried to focus on Étienne's fingers as they gently lifted the skirting board away from the crumbling plaster. 'This wall must be fixed. Scraped off and fresh plaster put on. And then there must be new wallpaper. The ceiling too,' he said, lifting his face to look upwards and then directly towards her so his face was practically right next to hers now. His stare so intense that she had to look away and pretend to be inspecting the patch of wall where he had been pointing. Just as she went to stand up, he added, 'And this must be a new one on here,' slapping a hand on the skirting board, startling her so that she almost toppled over, only managing to rescue herself by grabbing the side of the bed and doing a kind of lame, crouching kind of pirouette before hauling herself upright into a standing position. She didn't dare look in Kristen's direction for fear of laughing, as she could already see in her peripheral vision that her friend's shoulders were bobbing up and down in a silent guffaw.

Managing to compose herself as Étienne stood up and strode over to inspect the rest of the room, Annie attempted to ask about costing and explain that her friend Joanie had only a modest budget to spend on repairs.

'Is no problem,' he said, shrugging and lifting his palms up. 'I like to help you. My grandmother used to live in this neighbourhood and so I have happy memories of running through Cour Felice on my way to visit her. There was a small garden that I helped her with and her apartment was like this one with the old furniture and decorations. And there are not many like this one left now; everyone prefer the new modern style instead, so I help you make this one good again, *oui?*' He folded his arms and scanned the room appreciatively. 'Did you see the . . . how do you say? . . .

pompe, for the water, in the street?' Both women nodded. 'My brother and I loved to jump on it and my grandmother would get so mad with us.' He smiled and shook his head as if recalling a fond memory.

'Oh, thank you,' Annie beamed, knowing Joanie would be delighted too.

'*Excellent!* So you help with scraping the walls and it cost less money, but I will consult with you throughout and this way you not outspend the budget. I work out the price and you can call me tomorrow. Give me your mobile and I will put my number inside it.'

'Um. Yes, of course. Well, that sounds pretty decent. Are you sure?' Annie managed, and then cringed all over again at how prim and stereotypically British she suddenly sounded.

'Is more fun with a friend to help, *oui?*' he said, pushing his hair away from his forehead, his mouth hovering on the brink of a smile as he pulled out a little black notebook and a pencil from the back pocket of his jeans in which to make a few notes, presumably, about the work that was required.

'Err,' Annie lifted one shoulder and attempted a nonchalant, '*oui*,' in agreement, as if it was an everyday occurrence for a very attractive French builder to recruit her as his workmate.

'Awesome!' Kristen chimed, wandering over towards Étienne, who was busy inspecting the area around the windows, trying to establish where the mould on the curtains was coming from. 'So, how many helpers would you like?' she drawled, her New Yorker accent sounding stronger, 'because I have my phone right here if you want to put your number inside mine too.'

Annie silently shook her head and went to find her handbag so she could check her phone and take Étienne's number. Heading back to the room, Annie almost bumped into Étienne's chest as he came towards her through the doorway.

'Oh, I'm so sorry,' she started, as he sidestepped and said,

'*Pardon*,' before taking her phone from her hand and tapping his number into her contacts lists. Annie could see Kristen hovering in the hallway now with a very mischievous glint in her eye. '*Merci*, Annie. I look forward to your call,' and before Annie could respond, Étienne put his hands on her shoulders and gave her a quick kiss on each of her cheeks, making her blush just as Trixie had all those years ago when Maurice, the jazz musician, had done the same to her.

Utterly oblivious to Annie's mixture of emotions, Étienne made his way towards the front door. Kristen dashed after him, clearly keen not to let him out of her sight. But there was something Annie wanted to check before she left the apartment. So after quickly explaining to Kristen, who waved a quick, 'Sure, we'll see you downstairs,' over her shoulder, Annie darted into the sitting room and over to the console table where the photos were displayed. She picked up the picture of the handsome soldier and nodded to herself; it hadn't registered on that day when she had first come here and admired him. The soldier was wearing a British army uniform – there had been one just like it of Annie's great-grandfather on the sideboard in the home she had grown up in. Annie pulled out her phone and quickly searched for a picture of World War I British army soldier to check. Bingo! She found a picture and it was exactly the same as the uniform of the man in the framed photo. She took a picture of the photo and then carefully opened the frame to see if there was a clue as to the name of the soldier, knowing that sometimes people wrote on the back of photos. And sure enough, there was . . . *My darling Bobby 1918*. So the photo was taken during the First World War. A husband perhaps, given the affectionate inscription. But he looked so young. A lover or sweetheart, as they said in those days.

Annie paused her thinking to do a rough calculation in her head. Given that Trixie was 104 when she died many years ago in 2002, Annie tried to work out how old that would have made her in 1926. Late twenties. So she would have been sixteen, perhaps, when the First World War broke out in 1914. It was fascinating, and Annie was even more determined to find out more. Especially after reading Trixie's diary. Annie felt as though she knew her, the glamorous, champagne-drinking Charleston dancer, who bravely broke free from the constraints of her stifled life in the 1920s, which Annie knew would have been no mean feat for a young lady of those times.

Annie went back into the bedroom and picked up the diary. She was just about to walk over to the window seat to wrap it inside the scarf with the bundle of letters when the walnut wood writing slope caught her eye. She hadn't noticed it the first time she had come here, but looking at it now she could see that it was exquisite, with gold inlay and polished wood, and clearly well used, for the varnish had faded around the edge of the lid. Annie carefully tried opening it, excited to see inside. Would there be more diaries and letters to reveal more of an insight into Trixie's fascinating life? But it was locked. There must be a key somewhere. She looked around on the lamp table. Inside the wardrobe. Even opened the drawers of the cabinets beside the bed, but nothing, other than a faded old Christmas card tangled in a few balls of wool. She opened the card and saw that it was dated December, 1952.

Ma chérie Trixie

Mon amour toujours

Maurice xxx

Annie looked again at the card and, remembering her rudimentary French from school, felt sure it said, 'My darling Trixie, my love always, Maurice', which sounded very romantic indeed, the message compounded by the picture on the front of the card showing red roses nestling on a bed of glistening snow beside a Christmas tree with heart-shaped baubles dangling from its branches, making her wonder how the relationship developed after that night back in 1926 when Trixie first met the handsome jazz trombonist, Maurice . . .

After replacing the Christmas card, she wandered back into the sitting room and over to the mantelpiece where there were a couple of little trinket pots, but they were both empty. The drawers of the console table too. Annie was sure that Joanie wouldn't mind her searching through everything, or indeed Trixie, for Annie felt as though she were being guided somehow, spurred on to unravel the truth. It was a strange feeling, and Annie didn't believe in ghosts as such, or forces from beyond the grave, but in the moment she was certain that she could feel a presence with her within the sitting room. It wasn't scary. More calm and comforting.

Going into the kitchen, Annie opened all the drawers and cupboards and was just about to give up her search for the key when she spotted a little red leather coin purse hidden behind a pile of plates. Pulling the purse out, she opened it and rummaged through the collection of old French francs, but still no luck. She closed the purse and went to return it to its strange home inside the kitchen cupboard, when she felt something sharp on the side of the purse, so she opened it up again and felt around the lining inside. There was something hidden in there. Annie carefully separated the fabric from the metal frame. Bingo! A small brass key. She raced back into the bedroom and slotted the key into the lock of the writing slope. After jiggling it around a few times, she heard a soft click and was able to open the lid. She gasped. Inside, it was crammed with pieces of paper and several more of the small leather diaries. A small scrapbook too, filled with pretty pressed flowers, their Latin names written in old-fashioned cursive writing underneath.

Annie glanced at her watch, realizing that Étienne and Kristen would have been waiting for her for over fifteen minutes by now. So she took out the diary on the top of the pile, fascinated to read more about Trixie's life, but inwardly promising to bring the diary back, and closed the writing slope before carefully stowing the key back in the purse and returning it to its place in the kitchen. She then gathered up the silk-scarf bundle from back in the bedroom and tucked it under her arm, pulled her handbag over her shoulder and left the room . . .

12

Western Front, France 1918

Beatrice heard the now familiar clanging of the bells signifying the imminent arrival of the field ambulances, lorries and horse-drawn trucks bringing yet more wounded men from the trenches. She flew off from her bed where she had been catching a quick few minutes' nap and hurriedly made her way to the arrival point, securing her apron and headscarf on the way. With her feet desperately trying to navigate the slippery, thick, ankle-deep mud to keep her body upright, she went to take her place in the chain to help lift and pass the stretchers along to the trestle tables in the triage tents. Where she would then cut away uniforms and clean and dress as ordered to by the fully trained nurses, and on occasion a doctor too could shout for her assistance to help stem the flow of blood or clean soiled swabs away after he'd patched up a poor soldier and sent him back to the trenches.

'Crawford. The sack?' Sister barked on seeing Beatrice's empty hands. 'Fetch it at once!' Beatrice immediately gathered up the hem of her ankle-length skirt and sped off back through the mud as fast as she could, not daring to hesitate for fear of further incurring Sister's wrath. She had forgotten to bring the sack containing the brandy, cocoa and biscuits to comfort those wounded who were not in immediate need of treatment. Also knowing that a warming tin cup of cocoa with a dash of brandy in was all that could be done for some of the other men too, the ones beyond repair, for whom morphine was their only release, often accompanied by murmured, desperate last messages to loved ones.

Reaching the canteen tent, Beatrice grabbed the sack from the hook where it was kept and hurtled back across the muddy field towards Sister, skidding along for much of the way, deftly swerving to avoid tripping on a stretcher or the outstretched leg of a soldier sitting with a cigarette dangling from his motionless lips. On arrival, it was Cissy's ghostly white face that Beatrice saw first.

'Oh, Trixie, please, wait, you can't—' She stopped talking to clasp both hands to her face, turning away from the commotion going on behind her.

'What is it, Cissy?' Trixie scanned the scene, quickly trying to fathom what had happened. Everywhere she looked there were soldiers. Some on stretchers lined up side by side on the ground. Many men, the walking wounded, just wandering around as if in a daze. Like rabbits caught in headlights, Beatrice thought, on seeing the look of bewilderment and confusion in their eyes. The relentless sound of gunshots, screaming and sheer terror could be heard in the distance, the moans and cries of the men closer by. Beatrice moved nearer to Cissy, conscious of Sister whipping the sack from her hands without saying a word, which registered as odd, for usually Sister would have scolded her for forgetting it in the first place, but then it all became clear.

And it was as if time had stood still.

Silence descended as Beatrice felt a falling sensation.

And if Cissy and one of the medical soldiers hadn't caught her by the elbows, then her knees would have buckled completely and she would surely have slid downwards into the mud in a faint.

13

'So what have you managed to find out about Beatrice so far?' Kristen asked, wiping her hands on a napkin before carefully picking up one of the little leather books from the silk-scarfed bundle that Annie had brought down from her bedroom and placed on a table in the Odette café. The three women were in the courtyard enjoying the evening sunshine with the familiar sound of the accordion as they tucked into the *plat du jour* of bouillabaisse with succulent salmon, cod, prawns and black olives in a tangy, tomato herb sauce, mopped up with warm wedges of crusty sourdough slathered in salty butter. A rainbow salad on the side with a carafe of crisp white wine too. Maggie had insisted again on treating Annie and Kristen, refusing to let them pay or even consider letting them split the bill. Annie had made a mental note to chat to Kristen about this later, to see if she was also wondering if there might be more to this than Maggie just being wonderfully kind. Plus it didn't feel right to Annie, to accept such generosity, and she was starting to feel reluctant to dine here for fear of potentially being seen as taking advantage. But at the same time she didn't want Maggie to feel snubbed or disappointed if she went somewhere else for her meals.

'Ooh, I've found out quite a lot!' Annie started. 'Firstly that Beatrice preferred being called Trixie.' She lifted her sunglasses and pushed them up on her head. 'And obviously she was English.'

'Ah, interesting . . . so not German then?' Kristen asked, putting the book back on the table and picking up her glass to take a big mouthful of wine. 'I wonder why she was in cahoots with the Nazis then? Maybe she was politically that way inclined.'

'We don't know for sure that she was in the cahoots, as you say,' Maggie jumped in, diplomatically. 'It could all be hearsay and speculation, embellished over the years. You know how these things get distorted through the mist of time. There were many French people, and British people too, who were Nazi supporters. What we really need to do is to find someone who actually knew her. A friend, or a neighbour. What about the man who lives in the same building? I can't remember the name on the mailbox, but we must try, no? Better to get at the truth?'

'Yes, it's a good idea,' Annie said. 'I thought I'd knock on his door when I'm next there.'

'Well, it's a crying shame that prickly solicitor, Monsieur Aumont, refused to help out,' Kristen puffed. 'And then to not even agree to try to trace the woman who wrote that letter about the perfumes – Paulette . . . If she was young when the letter was written then she might still be alive and able to satisfy your curiosity about Trixie, just like that.' And she clicked her fingers.

'I agree. It was very odd indeed . . . the conversation you had with him, Maggie,' Annie nodded, taking a sip of wine and turning towards her friend. Maggie had called Monsieur Aumont earlier, to see if he might be more accommodating if a fellow French person asked for his help in finding out a bit more about Beatrice and tracing Paulette. At first he had been quite charming, saying how he did indeed provide a tracing service, as do many solicitors, although he would need more than a first name from a letter that was seventy years old. But as soon as Maggie had mentioned the name Paulette and an odd letter to Beatrice thanking her for sending perfume and listing out the ingredients, he had turned very terse indeed, claiming to have another client waiting to see him and saying that he had to end the call at once, leaving Maggie having to say, '*Monsieur, êtes-vous là?*' several times into a void, as if he had hung up on her, which it turned out was exactly what he had done. 'But anyway, if Monsieur Aumont doesn't want to help out then I guess I'll have to glean as much as I can from Trixie herself in her diaries and letters that we have here.'

'Exactly! Who needs a man when you can do it yourself?' Kristen picked up her glass and swallowed the last of her wine in one big gulp before prompting Annie to tell them more.

'So, I found out that Trixie left England some time in the 1920s and travelled here to Paris, and had an absolute ball by the sounds of it, making the most of the Roaring Twenties,' she started.

'Ah, *Les Années Folles*, as we call that decade in French,' Maggie told them, 'the crazy years full of partying and extravagance. Flapper girls and ragtime music on gramophones. Liberation and promiscuity. Coffee and Pernod in cafés just like this one,' she gestured around the courtyard. '*C'est incroyable* that you have found a first-hand account of what life was like then, just like the pictures on the walls there inside.' She gestured over her shoulder to the café's interior and the marvellously evocative images that Annie had admired on her first evening here in Paris, which suddenly struck her as seeming like a lifetime ago, when the reality was that she had been here only a few days. It was true that old adage, of time flying when you're having fun, but she really hoped the rest of the trip didn't whizz by as quickly, because she wasn't ready to go home any time soon. The thought of returning to her normal life at home and rarely going out made her heart sink. Being here was making her see that maybe Phoebe had a point about her having a 'basic life'. She had got herself in a bit of a rut, with only the familiarity of her home interior projects, sewing and crafting to keep her company. Annie was enjoying herself being here in Paris, seeing new things and making new friends. And she found that she wasn't missing Beth as much either. Yes, she still thought about her, but it was becoming more of a '*I wonder what she's up to*' thought instead of a '*I wish she was here as there's a massive gap in my life.*' Talking of whom, a WhatsApp message popped up on the screen of Annie's mobile.

'Mind if I see to this?' Annie said politely to Kristen and Maggie as she picked up her phone. 'It's from Beth.'

'Ooh, of course not,' Kristen grinned.

'*Merveilleux!*' Maggie said. 'It's exciting to talk to a friend on the other side of the world.' Annie read the message.

Morning! It's 1 a.m. here and just heading off to bed. Knackered after two encores. Not that I'm complaining as it's always nice when the audience want more ☺ Hope you're still having a ball in Pareeee. Maybe catch you tomorrow morning your time for a catch-up? Buzz me when you're awake and free to chat xxx

'Ah, that's nice,' Annie said, and then told Kristen and Maggie the gist of the message.

'She must be so talented,' Maggie said.

'I wish I could sing,' Kristen sighed, followed by, 'ask her what the Aussie men are like.' Laughing, Annie quickly tapped out a reply to say that she'd love a chat, but left off Kristen's question, figuring she could always ask it in the morning when Beth wasn't tired and about to go to bed. Putting her phone face down on the table, Annie asked,

'So, where were we?'

'Talking about the café,' Kristen said, 'the pictures inside . . . I thought they might just be for show. I didn't realize this place was really like that in the olden days.'

'Yes, it really was, and the pictures are all genuine,' Maggie replied. 'When Sam and I bought the café, the previous owner gave us a trunk full of pictures and old menus that he had collected over the years, so we thought it only right to have them on the walls for everyone to look at and enjoy and reminisce over . . . some of the elderly regulars remember coming here as children, I think one or two of them are even in the pictures with their parents.'

'Ah, how lovely. I wonder if Trixie came here; she could have sat and sipped her coffee in this very spot,' Annie smiled, contemplating the possibility.

'Amazing! When did she come to Paris?' Kristen asked.

'Remember, I mentioned it in the apartment . . . the section of Trixie's diary that I read to you was from 1926, where she writes about leaving England and being in Paris.' Annie turned to Kristen.

'Ah yes, sorry about that,' Kristen wafted a hand in the air. 'I wasn't really listening. How could I when the sexiest man in Paris was waiting at the door.' And they all laughed.

'Étienne?' Maggie confirmed.

'Yes, that's right,' Kristen said in a dreamy voice. 'Did you forget to tell us how incredibly hot he is?'

'Oh, I . . .' Maggie shrugged, smiling.

'Lucky Annie getting to be his workmate, is all I can say. Alone together in the bedroom all day long . . . I'm so jealous,' Kristen sighed, letting out a long whistle and doing a fanning motion with her right hand.

'Ah, I don't think it's like that,' Annie started, feeling her cheeks flush as she took a sip of wine.

'Of course it is! He couldn't take his eyes off you, honey,' Kristen laughed.

'I didn't notice,' Annie continued, wishing as soon as the words were out of her mouth that she didn't sound quite so prim. But the truth was that she did fancy Étienne; just thinking about him now was making her pulse quicken again, which was ridiculous really as she knew nothing about him and, besides, she had never been one to go purely on looks. Apart from Mark, but she had been young and naïve then, and look where that had got her! She had fancied Mark at first glance and then let lust control her common sense when it was perfectly clear that he wasn't right for her, yet she got swept along in the romance of it all. Or had it been that she couldn't disappoint everyone around her who wanted the fairy-tale wedding and happy-ever-after dream for her to be real? Her parents especially had been over the moon when Mark had proposed.

Annie thought a lot about her failed marriage over the years and had vowed never to rush into a romance ever again, and she hadn't, but she also hadn't really had another passionate and lasting relationship since. Maybe this was the reason why. She had grown too cautious, guarded, and so had inadvertently prevented herself from finding out . . . as the old adage goes, *love like you've never been loved before*. That was all well and good, but Annie had been determined to never get hurt again. It had always just felt easier that way . . .

Annie took another mouthful of wine, swallowed hard and pulled her thoughts back to the present moment, before turning to Kristen.

'Anyway, I thought you and Étienne were—'

'Oh no, that was just flirty fun,' Kristen waved a hand in the air, 'it was definitely you that he was interested in. He asked me about you when we were waiting outside for you.'

'Asked you what?' Annie felt her forehead crease in curiosity.

'The usual . . . you know, how long were you staying in Paris? Were you here with a husband, a boyfriend? Were we having a good time? Did we like the food? . . . Stuff like that,' Kristen said vaguely.

'So, general conversation then,' Maggie clarified, glancing at Annie, who smiled as a cover for feeling a little disappointed that he hadn't said more. But then who was she kidding, Étienne was way out of her league. Yes, she fancied him, but she wasn't deluded.

'Well, I guess so,' Kristen nodded, 'but he wasn't interested in me, that's for sure. Even though I flirted outrageously, he didn't so much as give me a second glance.' She laughed as if it were an everyday occurrence for her to flirt so confidently with incredibly good-looking men. Annie felt secretly in awe of her, but baffled that Étienne wasn't attracted to Kristen, with her being as beautiful as he was. 'But I guess men like Étienne are used to women flirting . . . he must know how gorgeous he is.'

Maggie shook her head, '*Oh non*, this is not the case . . .'

'*Really?*' Annie and Kristen chimed in unison, both twisting in their chairs to stare at Maggie.

'*Mais oui!* Sam often talked about Étienne and his laidback ways and lack of interest in the many women who flirted with him – that's how I know Étienne, he was one of Sam's friends. I don't know very much about Étienne myself, other than that he's always been very polite and courteous whenever I've met him. Sam had a lot of time for him and used to love sitting here in the courtyard with him, playing cards and catching up over a beer or two,' she finished, her eyes filling up with tears and her voice wobbling ever so slightly. Annie momentarily placed an instinctive hand on her new friend's forearm while Kristen topped up Maggie's wine glass before lifting it and handing it to her. Maggie had talked about Sam on that evening when the three of them had sat up and had a heart to heart as they got to know each other, but not once had she been distressed in this way and it was sad to see.

191

'Here. For fortitude!' Kristen said.

'Thanks, I'm being very silly,' Maggie said, taking the glass and glancing downwards as she swiftly brushed a sleeve across her eyes.

'No you're not! Don't you dare you say that,' Kristen quipped in her typically formidable way. On seeing Maggie take a quick gasp, Annie took over with a gentler,

'I think what Kristen might mean is . . .' she started slowly, not wanting to talk for Kristen, but she was busying herself by tidying the bowls and cutlery into a neat pile and hadn't noticed Maggie's reaction, '. . . that you're still grieving. It's perfectly normal to have moments when . . .' Annie's voice faded as Maggie nodded and responded.

'True. And most of the time I feel fine, especially when I am busy. I think that's why I like helping out in the café, it stops my mind from wandering, but some days the smallest thing can catch me off guard. Just last week, a tall, well-built courier guy arrived at the café with a delivery and, as he hopped off his motorbike, backlit in the glorious early morning sunshine in black leathers and a helmet . . . well, for a moment it took my breath away. It was as if Sam was right here, standing in front of me.' Maggie fell quiet.

'Oh, Maggie, I can't imagine how that made you feel,' Annie said.

'You know, it was actually very nice. In that moment. Because I was able to go back in time, to have another glimmer of Sam and to smile and wave again, just as I had every day for a lifetime, or so it seemed, before he went. It was only later, when the daydream had faded and the reality returned that it hurt . . . It was similar to that exquisite moment when I wake up and think he's still here, before the synapses of my brain kicks in and I'm reminded all over again.'

Silence followed as Kristen stopped tidying and the three women sipped their wine, sitting together with their collective thoughts, until Kristen piped up again.

'I used to wonder how I would feel if Chad had died instead of wanting to divorce me.' Annie shook her head, ready to step in for a second time, but it was Maggie who spoke next with wise words. 'Sometimes a divorce can hurt as much as a bereavement. The grief can be just as real. The loss of the life you hoped you would have together, gone in an instant.'

Again they sat quietly contemplating. Annie was the first to speak this time.

'I never really saw Mark again after the divorce.' Maggie and Kristen stopped sipping wine and waited for her to elaborate. 'Apart from a couple of times in the solicitor's office and the odd occasion when he was allowed to turn up to collect the children.'

'*Allowed?*' Kristen sat bolt upright, looking alarmed. 'What do you mean "allowed"?'

'Oh, his new wife never welcomed Johnny and Phoebe and so made it very difficult for them to see their dad . . . not that it excuses Mark for drifting away. It was very upsetting and stressful for them. And me too.' Annie glanced away.

'I'm sure it was,' Maggie said.

'Wicked stepmother!' Kristen huffed and shook her head.

'Yes,' Annie said. 'But Mark could have stood up to her and prioritized his children. You know, I remember one time in a restaurant in town when I was having lunch with Beth. Johnny and Phoebe were at school, and he was there with his new family. His toddler twins were throwing food all over the place and the wicked stepmother was practically yelling at him . . . giving him a telling off for not telling them off. '

'Shit, Annie,' Kristen exhaled, 'what did you do?'

'Nothing. Well, I had to talk Beth down from wanting to tip her Thai green curry over his head!' Annie nodded, remembering how furious Beth had been with Mark. 'But then I finished my meal and said a breezy, "It suits you" to him as we left. The look on his face was worth every second of the grief that I'd had to deal with when he realized there was bolognaise sauce smeared all down the side of his silly, overgrown new hipster beard with a gigantic brown splodge on his too-tight T-shirt.' They all laughed and the mood felt instantly lighter.

'Ah, I'm so pleased you are both here,' Maggie beamed. 'Great guests, such as you two, really help me as well,' and with a fond smile she nudged her shoulder sideways into Annie, and then Kristen.

'Is that why you won't let us pay for anything in the café?' Kristen blurted out, picking up the cutlery now and tidying that away on top of the stack of bowls and plates, making Annie inhale sharply and wonder if Kristen could really be any more insensitive, but had to admit she was curious on hearing that Kristen had been thinking about this too.

A few seconds of silence followed until Annie could bear it no longer and gave Kristen's thigh a swift shove under the table with her knee. Taking the hint, Kristen immediately stopped tidying and turned to Maggie, 'I'm so sorry. I didn't mean it to come out like that. I wasn't thinking properly.' She paused to let out a long breath and rake a hand through her hair, clearly embarrassed by her blunder, 'Well, that's a lie, I was thinking, inside my head. The words just tumbled out of my mouth. I'm sorry. I was tidying up and before I knew it my thoughts were actually being verbalized. It was rude of me, and well, you're the loveliest, kindest woman I know, and trust me, I know a lot of women, and not one of them has ever been as kind to me as you have,' she nodded. 'Except Annie, she was pretty kind the other day in the basement at the apartment . . . she sure gave me a different perspective too.' Kristen did a lopsided smile and lifted one shoulder.

'Ah, Kristen, it was a marvellous chat, just what friends do, and I appreciate you sharing something so personal with me,' Annie smiled kindly.

'Sure. But with you two women it's different,' Kristen said in a softer voice. 'I know we've only known each other a short while and . . . well, you are both just so genuine. Down to earth and not fake and phoney like some of my other friends back home, who dropped me like a hot coal as soon as they heard about the split with Chad. I'm so happy I came to Paris, it feels like starting over . . .'

'Kristen, I'm sorry to hear this,' Maggie started, 'not the happy you came to Paris part, of course – I'm thrilled that you have. But why would your friends drop you?'

'I guess they didn't want me around their husbands!' Kristen said flatly.

'Why on earth not?' Annie asked, but as soon as the words came out of her mouth she remembered how flirty Kristen had been with Étienne, so maybe that was why not. But then Annie immediately felt bad for jumping to conclusions, and rightly so as Kristen quickly clarified with,

'Which is ridiculous, as I'd never move in on a friend's man. Never. I know I can be flirty, but I also know what it feels like when a friend betrays you and it's horrendous. No, I'd never do that.' She shook her head adamantly, as if to underline her stance.

'Is that what Chad did to you?' Maggie asked carefully. There was a beat of silence before Kristen responded.

'Yes, that's right.'

'Oh, Kristen,' Annie caught her breath and then squeezed her friend's hand.

'Yep, my ex-best friend is now his pregnant girlfriend!'

'I'm so sorry,' Maggie said, 'that must have been very tough to deal with.'

'It was. I guess the only miserable and mean consolation was that the other women in our friendship circle dumped her too . . . as they sure as hell didn't want her around their husbands either.'

'Hmm, I'm not surprised,' Maggie rolled her eyes. 'But we mustn't forget the man in all this . . . I'm sure your ex-best friend didn't force him to do the dirty on you.'

'Of course not. Chad is the one to blame. She wasn't the married one, after all, and she tried to apologize, but . . . well, you know . . . it's OK now,' Kristen smiled wryly before staring into her wine glass.

'No it's not!' Annie said, and then gently added, 'don't you dare say that.' And gave Kristen a tentative look, wondering if she had overstepped the mark. Fortunately, she got the irony and laughed, and so Maggie and Annie did too.

When they had all stopped laughing, Kristen turned to Annie,

'Thank you.'

'What for?'

'Oh, I don't know,' her smile widened as she glanced upwards, 'for making me feel validated, I guess! For saying it out loud. I tried for so long to be "OK about it",' she paused to do quote signs in the air. 'I even went to therapy and learnt about "letting go" and not giving over my thoughts to it and all that crap, when I really wanted to scream and carve the pair of them up . . . and that was on a good day!' She inhaled through her nostrils. 'But it's not OK, not really, is it? The pair of them behaved like shits. Sneaky fucking shits. There, I've said it out loud and feel far better for doing so.' She nodded. 'I wish I had said it out loud sooner instead of spending hundreds of dollars on woo-woo therapy in a bid to be "OK" and all Zen-like about it. Or does that make me sound like a crazy bitch?'

'Who cares if you sound like a crazy bitch?' Maggie grinned, lifting her glass up in the air. 'I don't know what this woo-woo means,' and she shrugged. 'But I know a sneaky fucking shit when I see one.'

'Maggie!' Kristen and Annie roared in unison.

'Pardon?' she looked blankly.

'Um, you surprised us. We didn't have you down as a swearer,' Kristen said, still cracking up as she turned to Annie for confirmation. She nodded in agreement.

'Pah! If something needs saying then I say it. Why not?' and she tutted and lifted just one nonchalant shoulder this time. 'Plus, I'm very protective of those I care about.' Kristen put her arm around Maggie and gave her a quick kiss on the cheek. 'So, please tell me about the woo-woo. What does this mean?'

'It means a bit out there . . . kind of like psycho-babble, hippyish,' Kristen started explaining, but then gave up. 'Anyway, this isn't about me, this is about me being mean to you with my ungrateful comment. And again, I'm sorry, I'd never want to hurt you. Or get on the wrong side of you after that sweary outburst.' Kristen laughed, tilting her head to one side so it was resting on Maggie's shoulder.

'Really, there's no need to apologize any more,' Maggie said firmly. 'It's true! I do treat you to meals because I like your company. And I had been feeling a bit lonely . . .' Her voice faded on seeing Annie and Kristen both giving her 'that's enough of that' looks.

'And we like your company,' Annie said, quickly, not giving Kristen a chance to drop another of her clangers.

'Yes we do!' Kristen agreed, sitting upright. 'We love you, Maggie, and you don't need to treat us to dinner any more. We want to spend time with you because we like you. We're friends, the three of us, and you can't buy friendship . . . when it's good, it's good . . . so it's gonna happen anyway. So you're stuck with us and all our emotional complexities. Well, mine at least. We haven't heard about yours yet,' she finished, turning to Annie with an inquisitive eyebrow arched in anticipation.

'Oh, you don't want to hear about my . . .' Annie started, thinking about Phoebe and where to start on explaining to Kristen, when Maggie helped her out with,

'How is your daughter? Is she coming to join us here in Paris?'

'No, unfortunately, she's not able to,' Annie said, and then found the words to bring Kristen up to speed.

After listening carefully, Kristen took a deep breath and let out a long puff of air, flicking her eyes sideways, as if deep in thought on deciding what Annie should do for the best. A few seconds later, she instructed.

'Call the boyfriend. Jack will know!'

'Oh, I can't do that,' Annie said, 'Phoebe would never forgive me.'

'Of course you can. You tell him you're worried about your daughter. You can always ask him not to tell her you called.'

'I'm not sure that would go down well . . .' Annie felt uncomfortable; she'd never done anything like that and wondered how Jack would feel about being put in that position. She had always got on well with him and so the last thing she wanted to do was to alienate herself from her daughter's boyfriend by asking him to potentially betray his girlfriend's trust. If there really was something going on with Phoebe, then surely it was sensible to keep all the channels of communication open with her, and her boyfriend.

'OK. Then trawl her social media. Honey, the grid never lies . . .well, it does of course. It's all a big lie! That's the whole point of it. But it can also reveal so much truth too, if you know how to really *see* what you're looking at.' Kristen lifted her phone and tapped the screen.

'What is a grid?' Maggie frowned.

'Instagram, the pictures,' Kristen quickly explained, then asked Annie, 'what's her name?'

'Um, it's . . .' Annie wasn't sure if this was a good idea. Kristen could be impulsive. What if she messaged Phoebe or something? But then, as if reading her mind, Kristen reassured her.

'Just looking, I promise.'

'OK.' And Annie found her own phone and showed Kristen, and then Maggie, and they both commented on how beautiful Phoebe was.

'And impressive too,' Kristen added. 'Having her own successful business and only twenty-two. She must have worked hard. Annie, she's awesome,' she enthused, scrolling through Instagram and seeing all the wonderful pictures that Phoebe had posted there. Annie smiled on seeing her daughter's happy, glowing face on the screen and suddenly felt a bit foolish for worrying about her and thinking something wasn't quite right. Maybe she had got it all wrong and was just being an overprotective mother. 'And look at her gorgeous boyfriend.' Kristen tapped the screen and Annie saw a new picture that Phoebe had posted a few hours ago with the caption, 'Love this man so much, especially when he takes me out for cake!' and there she was outside a shop with a pretty pastel-pink frontage. Her arm around Jack, and a glittery pink-frosted cupcake in her hand, held up next to her face, poised as if she was about to take a big bite.

'Yes, Jack is great,' Annie smiled.

'So why does Phoebe look unhappy?' Kristen asked.

'What do you mean?' Annie scrutinized the picture more closely, convinced that Phoebe looked overjoyed; her smile couldn't have been bigger and Jack was leaning his head on the top of hers in a lovely, happy-ever-after-looking cuddle. They both appeared to be wonderful together.

'See her eyes . . .' Kristen enlarged the picture so Maggie and Annie could get a closer look. 'I know a bit about body language from years back when I did a course. Don't laugh – it was all about attraction and how to be better at dating – though clearly it didn't work of course as I totally misread Chad's body language when he was snaking around my best friend, but see how Phoebe is glancing sideways and slightly downward,' she paused, so they could check. 'Well, that means she's feeling sad inside!'

'Really?'

'Yes. I remember the dating coach telling us all about it.'

'Ah, I wouldn't read too much into this, Annie. Maybe she is looking at something that has caught her eye on the other side of the street,' Maggie said, soothingly.

'Sure. Maggie could be right,' Kristen agreed, 'but do you see my point? We all interpret stuff in different ways, sometimes seeing what we want to see, so you need to delve deeper, take a closer look. They could have had an argument a few minutes earlier, or there could be something about the picture that doesn't sit right with Phoebe.'

'Ah, well, now you have a point,' Annie quickly jumped in. 'Because, you know, Phoebe doesn't even like cake. She's not a fan of sweet, unhealthy foods. I wouldn't dare buy her a cupcake for fear of her giving me a lecture about sugar addiction,' Annie said, her thoughts going back to the taxi passing by the Ladurée shop on the Champs-Élysées.

'I bet that's it then,' Kristen said, 'a fake picture for the grid.' And although Annie nodded her agreement, she made a decision to ask Phoebe about it later.

'So now we have sorted this out and become even closer friends, we should celebrate . . .' Maggie paused and lifted her glass, to which Annie and

Kristen reciprocated, and the three women had a little moment of celebration, 'To us!' they chorused, finishing their drinks.

'Shall we get back to Trixie now?' Kristen asked. 'I can't wait to find out more about her,' and she motioned to Annie to open the scarf and bring out another diary.

'*Un moment*. I will get us another bottle of wine before we begin reading . . .' Maggie went to stand up, but Kristen put her hand out to stop her as Annie grabbed her handbag and pulled out her purse.

'My treat!' Annie insisted.

'In that case, I'm getting a bottle too,' Kristen stood up with Annie.

'OK. OK, if you insist,' Maggie said, holding up her palms to show her surrender.

'We do!' Annie and Kristen chimed.

And more laughter from the three new friends floated up into the warm Parisian evening air.

14

Back in the courtyard, an ice bucket tucked into her elbow, Annie placed it on the table, sat down, and picked up the diary that she had found on top of the pile inside the writing slope.

'OK, are we all ready to read more about Trixie?'

'*Oui, bien sûr,*' Maggie said, expertly opening the fresh bottle of wine and pouring them each a measure.

'So this one starts in 1918.' Annie stopped talking to cast her mind back to the other diary that she had read in Trixie's bedroom. 'Ah, that's it, Trixie mentioned first meeting a man called Monty in Étaples, on the Western Front. Do you remember me telling you about that bit, Kristen?'

'Oh yes, the poor guy who was gay in the 1920s and so left England in search of acceptance in Paris,' she said, looking pleased with herself for remembering something at least of what Annie had said.

'That's right,' Annie said and then, looking at

Maggie, she quickly told her what Trixie had written about in the New Year's Eve entry in 1926. 'So it sounds as if Trixie was a nurse in World War One,' she added. 'I'm not great at history but, from what I can remember, I think Étaples was where they treated the soldiers fighting on the Western Front in France.'

'Oh my God. Is this for real?' Kristen bellowed, clutching Annie's sleeve in excitement. 'This is amazing. It's proper history. Oh, Annie, you must take all these diaries and stuff to a museum. Or a newspaper. A publisher even; you have enough material here for a fascinating memoir.'

'Well, let's not get carried away, I want to find out more about Trixie first and why those people last night thought that she was German. And, most importantly, the link between her and Joanie.' Annie laughed, 'It is why I'm here in Paris, after all.'

'And to meet us, of course,' Maggie grinned. 'I have a feeling the three of us were destined to meet, because it's what we each needed.'

'OK, let's not have another emotion-fest.' Kristen shook back her hair and lifted her eyes skywards, making them all laugh. 'Let's get on with it,' and she tapped the diary that Annie had picked up. And the three women huddled together, engrossed, as they read about what another woman's life was like back in 1918, in the fields of France during the First World War.

My heart is shattered into a million pieces and I want to run far away from this godforsaken place. First to arrive from the trenches was Queenie's older brother, Stan, his face battered and broken as he lay motionless on the stretcher, the certain pain he had endured having mercifully lifted from his body mere moments earlier. Yet I still felt it important to soothe him by holding his hand in mine and speaking of his family, his wife, Mabel, and their baby, little Harold, and Queenie too, and how very proud they all are of him, and giving him my word that I would write to them to offer comfort in knowing that I sat with him as he died. For they do not need to know the truth, that he most likely departed this earth long before he was hauled onto the lorry that he was being taken off as I arrived back with the wretched sack. Next to arrive was my own dear brother, Edward, in marginally better shape, inasmuch as he was still with us, but in a dreadful way, with the lower parts of his legs mangled and maimed. I ran along-side his stretcher as the men rushed him to the operating tent, clasping his hand and all the while willing Sister not to make a fuss and insist on my returning to distribute the biscuits and cups of cocoa. On arriving in the tent, and mere moments before Edward succumbed to the ether for the operation to saw off his legs, he managed to utter a name, the name of my darling 'Bobby', to me. 'Bobby has gone, my dear sister. His last words were of his love for you and his sorrow for distracting you from making a suitable marriage. I assured him there was no need for sadness when he gave you great happiness.' As I gasped and clasped Edward's hand tighter, he stared into my soul and told me, 'Bea, your love for one another was honourable and true. Never let them take the memory of it away from you . . .'

'Oh dear, it's so sad,' Annie said softly, giving Maggie a tentative glance as she was biting her bottom lip and dabbing a napkin at the corners of her eyes. 'Are you OK? Would you like me to stop?'

'No, please carry on, Annie. Let's see how Edward got on in the operation.'

'Yes, poor guy . . .' Kristen exhaled.

Annie read on.

Edward never awoke from the operation. And I will always cherish his final words. My dear, kind, selfless brother, who – even in his last moments – chose to confide in me, to let me know that he had kept my secret safe, without judgement, for he must have known all along of the clandestine love that Bobby, the stable hand, and I shared . . . But I never knew, Edward never asked me, or indeed betrayed my secret to Father and Iris. Although, I do recall on one occasion, when I was walking with Bobby in the flower meadow and Father and Iris returned early from one of their trips to London, and Edward yelled across the field in an unusually loud voice for me to come back to the house at once, thereby alerting Bobby and me to their imminent arrival. In hindsight, there were other clues that Edward knew, and this is a measure of the decent man that he was, for he chose not to confront me with his knowledge either. I presume to preserve my dignity . . .

The three women sat in silence, united in their contemplation and compassion for Trixie and the heartbreak she endured on losing her brother, and her lover – a love that she was never allowed to fully embrace and celebrate openly.

'Oh, Trixie, I feel like I want to reach right inside that diary and give her a huge hug. How absolutely crushing and devastating it must have been for her,' Kristen said. 'And I wonder what does she mean about "secret love"; why wasn't she allowed to be with Bobby?'

'I guess because he was the stable hand – a servant. Things were very different back in those days,' Annie said, 'which is interesting because that would mean she was from the upper classes, aristocracy even.' She took out her phone from her bag to make a note, figuring that this could be very helpful in tracing Beatrice and Edward Crawford, especially if they were from a prominent, well-known family. There might even be something on the internet about the Crawford family, something to take Annie a step closer to discovering the connection between Trixie and Joanie . . . Although when Annie had last called Joanie, she claimed she had no knowledge of the name Crawford; but then, having been orphaned as a baby, she knew almost nothing about her parents, their lives before she was born or indeed who their friends were.

'Interesting, yes. But horribly sad and unfair for poor Trixie and Bobby who couldn't be together,' Kristen sighed. 'I don't get this class thing you have going on.'

'It was a very long time ago,' Annie clarified, 'not that it makes it right, of course, and it wouldn't have been just about marrying within your own class. Women had very few freedoms or choices in those days, and often their lives were mapped out from a young age. If she was born into an aristocratic family then there would have been an expectation of her marrying well, to someone of her parents' choosing perhaps, and to have children – marriage and motherhood; that was the path for women in those days. And marriage to Bobby, the stable hand, would have been out of the question.'

'Well, love is love in my book,' Kristen declared. 'And I'm so grateful that I wasn't a young woman in those days, for I would have been in serious trouble from the get-go! Oh yes. I would have loved whoever I damn well wanted to, and I would have run away to Paris too in a heartbeat. And as for all the men in the war, such a sad loss of life. War is a terrible thing. In fact, I think we need another toast,' and she lifted her glass.

'To Stan and Bobby and Edward,' the three women said, before silently bringing their drinks together in acknowledgment of the ultimate sacrifice made by the three brave men.

15

A few days later and Annie was in Cour Felice looking at the boarded-up shop from the outside and imagining Trixie standing here in the exact same spot and doing the same thing, admiring her beautiful boutique. Annie closed her eyes momentarily and tried to imagine how glamorous and chic the boutique would have been in the Twenties when it was likely that Trixie had first opened her perfume emporium.

She had discovered from reading more of Trixie's diaries written during World War One that Trixie had developed a number of potions and fragrances while she was volunteering as a Voluntary Aid Detachment in France, and had then continued building up her knowledge and collection of concoctions in the years that followed, so it would seem a natural progression and a marvellous idea for her to open a perfume shop when she came back to France in the 1920s. But what Annie couldn't work out was why Madame Bardin had said that Trixie gave a phial of perfume to a German soldier in World War Two . . . If it was true, then why would she do that? Especially as she was British. Yes, she had considered Maggie's point about there being French and British Nazi supporters too, but it just didn't seem feasible, not when her brother and her lover, plus Stan, the older brother of her child-hood friend, Queenie, had been killed by Germans in the Great War. All of them had been in the PALS regiment from the same village. Tindledale. Annie had read about that too in one of the earlier diaries, when Trixie had written that a German soldier would be vilified back home in Tindledale. And then something struck her. The picture-postcard village with the water mill. The place Annie had travelled through on her scenic route before taking the Eurostar to Paris. Yes. What a coincidence.

She remembered it now, Tindledale, and so pulled out her phone from the pocket of her dress and did a quick search to be sure. There it was. The train route went through the Kent countryside, and so now she knew that Trixie, aka Beatrice Crawford, came from Tindledale in England. It looked so quaint, with a traditional little village pub – she saw on the Google search that it was called the Duck & Puddle and there was a haberdashery shop too. Hettie's House of

Haberdashery. Maybe someone in the village might remember the Crawford family, Beatrice, or her brother Edward. Annie made a note in her phone to mention all these details when she next called Joanie to update her. And she would tell her about Tindledale too and ask her if she could remember any kind of connection to the village.

Bringing her thoughts back to the here and now in the cobbled courtyard of the Parisian Cour Felice, Annie looked again at the boarded-up boutique in front of her, focusing her mind, as if telepathically trying to connect with the woman who had lived here for near on eighty years. *Please tell me, Trixie. How did you know Joanie? What's the missing link between you both? And what happened all those years ago? Why did you give perfume to a German soldier? Why do the people here think you were in cahoots with the enemy? Did you really have a German lover? Is that what happened – did you fall in love again? Maybe another German soldier, a prisoner of war who you tended to in the Great War. As Kristen said, love is love, after all. And I'm sure there were young German men who were there in the trenches for no other reason than that they had to be, to do their duty to their country. I've read about the historical World War I Christmas Day truce, where the ordinary British and German soldiers played football together with the Live and Let Live sentiment, high-lighting the futility and sadness of it for all the ordinary young men. But then the atmosphere in WW2 would have been vastly different . . .*

As Annie was pondering on all the possibilities, a loud bang made her jump as the double doors of the shop were flung wide open from the inside. Étienne appeared wearing a white T-shirt and jeans, with a tool belt skimming his hips, his dark hair speckled in plaster dust. Annie caught her breath for, even though he was covered in debris, he looked incredibly hot with the sun sparking off the tools in his belt, the dust from the shop rising like smoke from behind him and his gorgeous cockapoo – a caramel-coloured cutie called Bijou, the French word for jewel, Étienne had told Annie – springing along behind him, her little tail wagging excitedly.

'*Pardon*, Annie. Sorry to scare you,' Étienne said, coming towards her with his arms outstretched, a quick burst of his intoxicating scent making her stomach do another little flip, which seemed to be a frequent occurrence now whenever Étienne was nearby. She smiled, thinking how thoughtful he was, but wishing her cheeks wouldn't flush too every time he appeared close to her. 'I managed to break it.' His grin widened as he looked over his shoulder towards the door of the boutique. After talking to Joanie about the state of the apartment and getting her permission to repair the bedroom wall and replace the curtains, she had also asked Annie to look inside the shop to assess the possibility of getting it opened up and perhaps tidying it up to make it more presentable for when potential purchasers came to view. The wooden double doors were practically welded together with age and neglect, so Annie had come outside to see if she could pull them open while Étienne pushed from inside, before asking her to stand back, presumably so he could give them a good shove with the side of his right shoulder, which he was now brushing to remove flakes of cracked paint and wood that had landed on him during the breakout.

'You sure did.' She glanced at him sideways, trying hard to resist the urge to dust the flakes still clinging to the dark hairs of his tanned bare forearms too.

They had been together in the apartment for two days now. The bedroom walls and ceiling had been stripped back and Annie had set up Maggie's sewing machine at the table in Trixie's drawing room and was making good progress on creating a pair of new curtains with a matching pelmet and tie backs. Maggie had taken Annie to a specialist upholstery cleaner but, as soon as he had inspected the original curtain fabric, he had shrugged and declared them '*impossible de nettoyer*' – impossible to clean – on account of the fabric being too delicate and him not wanting to take the risk of it disintegrating and then being held responsible. He wouldn't be swayed, even when Maggie had translated Annie's instructions saying they'd sign a waiver, so keen was she to restore the curtains to their former glory. Instead, the man had directed Maggie and Annie to a gorgeously chic fabric shop in a side street off the magnificent Avenue de l'Opéra where Annie, after checking with Joanie and agreeing a modest budget, and with Maggie's bold bartering skills, had managed to buy a reasonably priced bolt of fabric in a very similar style to the original curtain material.

They had then wandered in and out of all the lovely little boutiques, marvelling at the glorious architecture of the famous Galeries Lafayette department store before moving on to Printemps to pick up some bargains – shoes for Annie and stylish silk scarves for Phoebe and Joanie, and a new handbag for Maggie. Then the gloriously, warm, sweet scent wafting from the open doors of the Pierre Hermé patisserie had tempted them inside, where they had gasped at the gorgeous array of exquisitely hand-decorated delicate cakes and macarons before moving along to the cold counter crammed with giant swirls of ice cream in every flavour they could have wished for. Annie had settled for the creamy, summery peach melba. Maggie the pistachio with tutti-frutti sprinkles on top. The next stop had been in La Cure Gourmande, an equally sumptuous cake and biscuit shop, where Annie had bought tins of traditional French butter biscuits with a creamy chocolate centre as another gift for Joanie, and a tin for Johnny too, for when, hopefully, he made another impromptu visit – at Christmas time, perhaps.

'Come on inside and see the shop,' Étienne said, clicking his fingers for Bijou to follow them, his French accent getting stronger in anticipation, and Annie noticed again how lovely his coffee-coloured eyes were, sparkly and warm. 'It's, how you say . . . amazing!' And laughing, he lifted his eyebrows and playfully batted her arm – it had become a joke between them after Étienne had picked up on how frequently Annie commented on everything in Trixie's apartment being 'amazing'. And so now Étienne had taken to attempting an English accent whenever he said 'amazing', which made Annie laugh because he sounded so comical, just like a plummy BBC news reporter from the 1950s.

Inside, and now with the beautifully bright Parisian sunshine beaming into the shop, Annie could really see its full potential. Imagining customers coming in through these doors, with the chandelier above the huge circular central display cabinet, the shelves set in a semicircle against the walls, giving the illusion of the whole shop feeling like a comforting cocoon. The floor felt soft beneath her sandals and, glancing down, she saw the remnants of a once sumptuously plush thick pile carpet, just like the one in the old department store she used to go to with her granny as a child – Carrington's, it had been called, and Annie remembered how springy the carpet felt as soon as she stepped inside, making the experience feel special and luxurious. And it seemed Trixie had created something similar here for her Parisian perfume boutique. There was even a china umbrella holder to the side of the door on the left and a little waiting area to the right, by the looks of the ornately carved wooden bench seat still in place behind a low coffee table. Taking it all in, Annie gasped.

'Are they magazines?' and she darted across the shop to take a closer look. They were. Picking one up she saw the distinct red lettering of the iconic *Paris Match* magazine cover and carefully brushed the dust away. 'Wow. Look at this,' she waved it at Étienne, 'it's incredible. Dated 1952. It's vintage. And there are more . . .' Annie marvelled, scanning the table. It was like a time warp. She picked up another magazine and another, *Vogue* this time, and dated 1991, so much more recent.

She wondered if it was around then when Trixie had closed the shop and retired, as it clearly hadn't been touched for decades.

'It's amazing!' Annie said without thinking, making Étienne shrug and shake his head in amusement, the corners of his mouth lifting as if he was trying not to laugh.

'Ahhhh, I really must stop saying it,' she sighed, clapping her hands over her mouth.

'Please don't, actually I like it,' and he gave her another one of his intense stares. 'It is . . .' He hesitated, as if thinking of the right word in English before settling on the French '*mignonne*' instead.

'Oh,' Annie said, not knowing what *mignonne* meant, but hoping it was good. There was a short silence, then Étienne lifted his hand up, he'd got the English word now. 'Cute,' he confirmed, lifting one shoulder and making her cheeks flush.

She looked away. She had never been called cute before; well, not since she was a child, and if anyone else had called her cute then she might have been a bit affronted, for she wasn't a little girl any longer, but the way Étienne said it in his French accent seemed OK. Appealing in fact. Sexy even. But she wished her cheeks would stop flaming, she could feel her neck tingling too and just knew that it would be blotchy by now. She busied herself with studying the magazine still in her hand, unsure of what to say. Was Étienne flirting? She couldn't be sure, maybe it was just his way. She had got the impression from Maggie that he wasn't your stereotypical Frenchman, suave and flirtatious, and in the time they had spent together he had been very professional, keeping the conversation wholly related to whatever task they were involved in at the time.

There had been a moment or two when their hands had brushed, he had passed a scraper to her in the bedroom, and it had felt like a bolt of electricity charging through her veins. And she had thought about it lying in bed last night, trying to work out if she was being ridiculous or not. Reading into it, romanticizing when she had no business in doing so. It wasn't as if they had actually chatted about themselves, their lives; in fact she knew nothing about him, other than that he wasn't married and, as far as Maggie was aware, he didn't have a girlfriend either. And he lived on a houseboat on the river Seine.

'You not like to be cute?' he asked, wandering across the boutique so he was standing opposite her.

'Oh, um . . . sure, it's . . .' She paused to swallow and put the magazine back on the table. 'It's nice. Err, thank you,' she finished, wishing he wouldn't fix his gaze quite so intently on her and wondering why it was so hot in here all of a sudden. She pushed the sleeves of her blouse up in attempt to cool down. After studying her for a few seconds, Étienne looked as if he was about to say something more but wasn't sure whether to or not, and so instead pushed a hand through his hair, the tendons in his muscular forearm flexing as he lifted his arm. The hem of his T-shirt riding up to reveal a tanned and very well-defined abdomen. Annie turned away, pretending to be fascinated by a collection of dusty old glass bottles on the windowsill, hoping he wouldn't notice her cheeks which were currently flaming like a pair of plum tomatoes.

'Come on, I take you to the garden?'

'Garden?' she echoed, wondering what he was talking about.

'Yes, is here. I see it from the bedroom window when I come here in the morning. Before you get here. Follow me,' and he actually took her hand, his fingers curling around hers and sparking an instant frisson of pure physical attraction to surge up her arm and straight into her heart. But before Annie could formulate her thoughts – for she had never experienced a feeling quite like it, the sheer magnetism of an incredibly attractive man she barely knew taking her by the hand in such a casual and confident way – they had left the shop through a door at the back and were now standing in a gorgeously pretty little paved garden. The early blooming honeysuckle gave the air a deliciously evocative scent of summer days and holidays, immediately making Annie feel light and lifted.

She looked around, taking in the small but perfectly formed garden, as Bijou bounced around enthusiastically, darting here and there, in and out of the hedgerow, having the time of her life. It was overgrown with weeds and wild flowers, which were sprouting from the borders and covering the brick-walled perimeter. A small stone-floored patio area was flanked on one side by a raised wooden-framed flower bed or, on closer inspection, perhaps it had once been a herb garden, as Annie could see coriander and mint leaves lingering in between the dandelions and daisies. She wondered if Trixie had cultivated the herbs and flowers especially for mixing into her perfumes and remedies. It seemed quite possible, and Annie thought of the letter from Paulette where she had actually listed out the ingredients; maybe Trixie was a connoisseur who took great pride in getting the right blend and advising her customers accordingly. How else would Paulette know the actual ingredients, or indeed make a point of mentioning them? When Annie bought a new perfume she had no idea what the ingredients were.

'Sorry, I . . . err,' she said, bringing herself back to the moment and realizing her hand was still inside Étienne's, which she gently let go. She then lifted her arms out wide and turned a full circle, delighting in the sight before her, marvelling that she was in such a glorious garden in the middle of Paris with a man so charismatic and attractive, when just last week she was sitting at home feeling dowdy and down about her 'basic life'. She felt so grateful to be here, to take some time out, to have this chance to change things for herself. Pleased too that she hadn't let Phoebe talk her into cancelling the trip . . . to live with regret was one of the hardest things to endure and with the benefit of beautiful hindsight she most certainly would have ended up doing exactly that.

'It's charming, yes?' Étienne said, unclipping his tool belt and placing it on one of the old, weather-worn wooden garden chairs before pushing his hand into his jeans pockets. The corners of his mouth turned up as he watched her twirl in delight.

'It sure is. And such a surprise. I wasn't looking for a garden as there was no mention of one in the paper-work, I'm quite sure of that. My friend, Joanie, would have said so otherwise and I would have checked outside to see the condition of it the first time I came here,' Annie said, coming to a standstill and making a mental note to ask Joanie to check the papers again, but still scanning and wondering if she might have time to tidy it up to make it look more presentable, if Joanie would like her to.

Annie enjoyed gardening, having spent lots of time in her own garden, where she always felt content and safe amidst her little haven of shrubs and colourful borders – she had even installed a water feature and a bird table and, after pruning and digging, found pleasure in sitting in the sun, reading and listening to the birdsong, completely content in her own company. But having now taken a leap of faith and ventured out on her own to Paris, she was starting to realize what she had been missing.

As if reading her mind, Étienne moved over towards a small ramshackle brick outhouse in the corner – it was covered in wisteria so Annie hadn't noticed it – and pulled open the wooden door.

'Ah, this will help,' and he lifted out a small spade, a shovel and a rake, 'for the tidy-up. Let's dig,' and he handed the small spade to her before putting the shovel back in the outhouse and lifting the rake over the worst of the overgrown weeds to make a start on pulling them all away.

'OK,' Annie laughed, lifting her shoulders and loving his spontaneity, 'why not?' and she set to work on sorting out the herb garden, figuring that it had been neglected for so long that if it turned out not to be part of Joanie's inheritance then the rightful owner surely wouldn't mind them having tidied it up. Plus, the opportunity to do a bit of gardening with an incredibly sexy French man didn't come along every day . . .

Ten minutes later, Étienne wandered over to where Annie was plucking weeds from around the base of a large lavender bush. She had almost finished tidying the herb garden and had been delighted on discovering mint, lemon balm, basil, wild garlic, lemon grass and even some strawberry and raspberry plants clinging on to life in amongst the weeds.

'How's it going?' she asked, looking up at him and using the back of her forearm to sweep away her hair that had fallen over the side of her face.

'Is going good, Annie, take a look.' And she turned around to see the paving slabs were now free of weeds and the nettles covering the back wall had been pulled down revealing lovely old stone brickwork.

'Wow, it looks great,' Annie smiled. 'You didn't have to do it, you know, but thank you.' She nodded.

'It's a pleasure. For a moment I was a boy again without a care in the world.' He waved a hand and laughed. 'But my grandmother would never have let her garden become like this.'

'Ah, I bet not,' Annie laughed too. 'Were you very close to her?'

'*Oui*,' he shrugged, 'for a while I lived with her. My father, he was a photo news journalist – of course he is retired now, but he used to travel so much around the world to many dangerous places to take the photos of war and horrible sights and my mother she like to be with him, so I stay with my grandmother for the school years.'

'How interesting! And after school?' Annie asked, keen to find out more about him.

'I stay here in Paris too. At the Beaux-Arts university, I study art before I start my career in finance.'

'You're an artist?' Annie was intrigued.

'Not so much now, but I enjoy sketching, Parisian street scenes, people wandering along the towpath by the river.' He lifted one shoulder as if it were no big deal at all. But Annie thought it sounded very romantic indeed and certainly different from any of the men that she had ever known before.

'And what about you, Annie? What do you enjoy?'

'Oh, well, I . . .' she started tentatively, tucking her hair behind her ears, not used to having this kind of conversation with an attractive man . . . it had been a long time. 'So home design is my passion. I like decorating and styling.'

'Styling?' he creased his forehead.

'Yes, making rooms look nice, cosy, and chic with different themes for Christmas and autumn, that kind of thing, and I like sewing, making things, cushions, curtains.'

'Ah, so this is why you help your friend with the apartment? The curtains. Is very kind, but fun for you too, *oui?*' A smile danced on his lips.

'Sure, and more fun having you here too.' And the second the words were out of her mouth, Annie felt an immediate surge of blood to her face, making it burn like a furnace. She immediately dipped her gaze back to the lavender bush as she gathered herself – she had just flirted with him! No doubt about it. It might have been a long time since she had remotely been in any kind of flirtatious situation with a man, but, as Beth would say, 'Annie Lovell: you still got it going on, girl,' with a whirling pointy finger, no doubt.

A beat of silence followed, broken only by the sound of Bijou's tail sweeping left and right on the paving slabs. She looked up at each of them in turn as if intrigued to see how this scene was going to play out.

'And fun for me too,' Étienne said, after what felt like ages for Annie, who could only muster a lame, 'Oh,' so maybe she didn't have it still going on, after all. But before she could say more, Étienne suddenly said,

'Are you hungry?' and gave the bottom of his T-shirt a quick flap around to create some air to cool him down in the warm midday sun.

'Err, yes,' she managed to squeak.

'Then let's eat. Annie, join me for lunch today, yes please?' and he moved closer, letting his T-shirt slip back down.

She stopped weeding and put down the little spade she had been using.

'Oh, err . . . are you sure?' she asked, using her hand as a shield for her eyes from the dazzling sun, but as soon as the words were out of her mouth she wanted to shove them back in. Why couldn't she have just said a breezy, 'yes please' or 'sure, my treat', for he had already done way more work in the apartment than they had originally discussed, with sorting out the double doors to the shop and now helping to clear the garden too, and he was refusing to accept additional payment. They had discussed it last night on the phone after Joanie had given the go-ahead for the shop to be sorted out too. Instead, she had her face screwed up and could feel sweat clinging to her top lip, and her fringe was now stuck to her forehead from working in the gorgeous suntrap of a garden. Annie pushed the chunk of hair away from her face and dropped her hand, wishing she had brought her sunglasses downstairs with her.

'*Oui!* Of course,' Étienne smiled, his eyes looking directly into hers as he thoughtfully stepped into the shard of sunlight so as to protect her eyes from the glare. 'Let me cook lunch for you . . . we can talk and I find out more about you,' he grinned, and for a moment Annie caught sight of a much younger man in his face, a glimpse of how he must have been in his early twenties, late teens even. Less experienced, shy, nervous of her potential rejection even, and it was very appealing . . . less daunting, and so she didn't feel quite so guarded with him. She took a breath and wondered if his invite constituted a date . . . possibly, and then, feeling herself relax further, she decided to go for it and ask him.

'Like a date?' She pressed her top teeth into her bottom lip, desperately willing herself not to look flustered, but she felt dizzy all of a sudden. Realizing she was holding her breath, she took in a big gulp of air just as he smiled, tilted his head and confirmed, 'Yes. A date, Annie.'

'Oh.' She felt like a bashful teenager all of a sudden. 'Great, I'll . . . um . . . well, I had better just finish off.' And as if on autopilot and for no good reason that she could fathom, she swiftly turned around, picked up the spade and pushed it once more vigorously into the ground. But instead of soft earth beneath the spade, it hit something hard, she lost her grip, and the spade catapulted from her hand. Étienne deftly caught it.

'*Wow, tu es si forte,*' then in English, 'so strong.' But before she could respond, something shiny caught her eye.

'There's something in here,' she said, feeling around in the mud where the sun was twinkling on what looked like a rock, or a piece of glass perhaps. Étienne moved closer to her and leant into the herb garden to take a look.

'Here,' he offered her the spade, which she took, and carefully scraped the mud away from the object.

'It's a jar!' she said, going to lift the object up. 'A jam jar by the looks of it.' They both inspected it, seeing there was something inside, newspaper or an old rag, it was hard to be sure, as the jar had browned with age and from being hidden in the mud. Annie tried to open the lid, but it was no use, it appeared to be rusted onto the jar. Étienne tried too, but had no luck, so he handed it back to Annie who placed it on the chair for safety. 'I'll take it back to the café and see if Maggie can let me have some olive oil or butter that might help to ease the lid off. I'm intrigued to see what's inside and I wonder why it was hidden away here in the garden?'

'It is a mystery,' Étienne agreed. Annie nodded before

glancing away from him. A short silence followed and then he asked, 'Are you OK, Annie?'

'Oh yes, I'm fine,' she lied, nerves and excitement at the thought of their impromptu date swirling around inside her, making it difficult to focus on the jam jar, or anything else for that matter.

'Are you sure? You seem distracted. You don't want to look at me?' He did a one-shoulder shrug, seemingly bemused, or maybe it was concern. 'Are you nervous to come on the date?' Annie opened her mouth to protest, wishing he wasn't so direct, but then hesitated, wondering why she felt embarrassed to admit, that yes, she did feel nervous. She hadn't been on a good date with a properly attractive man, in . . . well, ever, if she was perfectly honest. Of course she had been on dates, she had been married and had had several relationships, but not with anyone like Étienne. Nobody had ever made her feel the way she felt when she was around him. He was completely different to the men that she had known before. But then something else occurred to her . . . she was different too. Far different to how she felt at home. It was hard to put into words other than, since being in Paris, she felt as if she had become a better version of herself. Bolder. More alive. And so she changed her mind, figuring why lie? For the sake of saving face, stiff upper lip, keeping her guard up as she had done for far too long . . . or whatever it was, and so she told him.

'Yes. Yes, I am nervous.' She pushed her hair away from her face. 'It's been a long time since I went on a date and well, you see, I . . .'

And then everything changed.

Étienne stepped forward and murmured, 'There's no need to explain.' Annie could hear her own blood pumping in her ears, her stomach fizzing as the moment seemed to freeze-frame, his eyes searching hers, until—

'*Trixie, est-ce que c'est toi?*' And Annie instantly stepped back from Étienne, as an elderly man with a stoop and curly white hair appeared through the open shop door, his rheumy eyes looking fearfully at her and then darting towards Étienne as if he thought she were in danger. Then, after shuffling forward towards Étienne, he yelled, '*Éloignez-vous d'elle!*' and Étienne immediately moved right away from Annie and lifted his palms up and said something in French to the elderly man, and then to Annie, 'He thinks you are Trixie and has just told me to get away from you. I think he's scared I'm going to hurt you.'

'Oh no, he's clearly confused. I don't want him to be worried.' Annie walked over to where the man was still standing and held out her hand, intending to shake his and explain who she was and why she was here in the hope it might reassure him that all was well. But instead he yelled something more in French before lifting his walking stick and using it to point at the glass jar on the chair. 'Sorry, does this belong to you?' Annie asked him carefully, and then turned to Étienne, intending for him to translate, but to her surprise the man answered in perfect English with a soft French accent.

'Yes,' he said, pushing his chin out boldly, almost defiantly, and nodding slowly. Then he gave Annie a guarded smile, as if they were working together in some kind of secret and she was the one who was confused, his eyes constantly flicking towards Étienne and then back to her, before adding, 'I'll take it to the kitchen where it belongs, Madame Archambeau,' and then bizarrely he looked at Étienne and said something that sounded like German to Annie. The old man was laughing, as if Annie a.k.a. Trixie had done something silly, and he was appealing to Étienne to see that this was the case, almost like he was covering for her.

Annie shot a look at Étienne, who she could see was equally confused, but then he said something in German, and whatever it was the elderly man didn't like it one bit and tried to lunge forward to snatch the jar away, but instead toppled and – as he put his hand out to steady himself – the jar wobbled and fell off the chair, smashing down onto the concrete courtyard.

Annie went to help the man, but in his muddled state he shooed her away and so she immediately crouched down to gather up the contents – a piece of cloth wrapped around lots of little pieces of paper – before they fluttered away. Étienne took care of the shards of glass, using the old cloth to wrap them in. As this was all going on, a woman in a pink nurse's uniform came into the garden, and with a startled look on her face said something to the elderly man in French, before gently looping her arm though his and steering him back inside, saying, '*pardon*' several times over her shoulder to Annie and Étienne. They exchanged glances, each wondering what on earth had just happened. Why had the man thought Annie was Trixie? And why did he appear to think Étienne was German and was going to hurt her? Not to mention the glass jar: he was scared, genuinely scared of its presence there on the chair in the little courtyard garden at the back of Joanie's apartment in Cour Felice . . .

16

Later, on the deck of Étienne's glorious houseboat, Annie was still trying to figure it all out. The little pieces of folded-up paper had words written on them, names perhaps, it was hard to be sure as the ink had faded with age, but they were all now in a new jam jar that Étienne had found in the back of one of the cupboards in his galley kitchen, where he was currently preparing lunch and refusing to let her help. She had stowed the jar safely inside her handbag to properly look at the contents later when she got back to the café, figuring she could get Trixie's diaries out to see if any of the names that she had written about matched any of those on the pieces of paper. Annie wondered if Trixie had written notes to her friends, perhaps, and buried them, like a time capsule to be discovered in years to come, remembering how Phoebe had done something similar with an old biscuit tin in their garden under the apple tree.

Annie couldn't think why else anyone would bury a jam jar of notes wrapped in a piece of cloth, presumably for safekeeping to keep them dry. The same with the diaries in the wall cavity . . . they had been wrapped in a silk scarf and Annie presumed that Trixie wouldn't have had a plastic bag to use for waterproofing back in the 1920s, so had used the best materials she could find. That must mean that these things were extremely precious to her. Annie just needed to work out why.

She hadn't come across anything in the diaries yet of great significance or secret, other than about her close friend, Monty, being gay, which might have caused a scandal back then. But so why would Trixie write about him in the first place, and risk exposing her friend to potential harassment? It didn't make sense. So Annie was baffled and beginning to wonder if Madame Bardin and the old men in the café had been right and the secrets that Trixie had written about and then hidden away were because she didn't want her friends to find out about her relationship with the German soldiers – could that have been the secret she had to protect? If so, then she didn't do a very good job of hiding it, as Madame Bardin knew, and she even saw her brazenly laughing and joking as she gave the perfume to the German soldier. Plus it still didn't explain her link to Joanie! Annie hadn't yet read all of the diaries that she had found, although some of them were too damaged from damp and age to be legible in any case.

Letting out a long puff of air in an attempt to clear her head of the thoughts that swirled around and around inside her head, Annie sat back in the seat and surveyed the scene, thinking how marvellous it must be to live here on the river Seine. She could see people wandering along the towpath, hand in hand, some sitting on blankets sketching or writing, the sound of the bustle from the Parisian streets in the distance, the ripple of the water as a tourist boat chugged along on its way past.

The sky, the colour of periwinkle blue, smudged with streaks of white cotton candy, was mesmerizing, and she tilted her head back and drew in a breath full of the invigorating, light air. It seemed different here, cleaner and fresher, uplifting, or maybe it was just her mood which currently felt joyful and excited, full of possibility. Here she was enjoying Paris with a man, on his boat, and she smiled to herself, remembering how she had mused about this in the taxi as she had travelled along the Champs-Élysées on her first day here. It felt like a dream. Serendipity. Because that wasn't all. She had travelled here to Étienne's boat on the back of his scooter, Bijou in a little carrier box behind the seats, which had been the cutest thing Annie thought she had even seen.

But she had been unsure at first, when they had left the apartment and Étienne guided her to where he had parked the scooter under a tree in the courtyard. The two helmets linked together on the seat had made her smile, though, as he had clearly planned the lunch date after all. Throwing caution to the wind, Annie had straddled the scooter behind Étienne and wrapped her arms around his solid torso, just as he had instructed her to, urging her to 'hold me tightly' before he sped off. She had barely managed to squeak a 'yes' to his incredibly provocative instruction. And she had never felt so alive as she had in that moment, with the warm Parisian breeze wafting around her bare legs as her pink floral cotton sundress rode up to her knees, the citron scent of Étienne's aftershave lingering as the side of her face brushed gently against his shoulder when he took a particularly sharp corner.

She hadn't wanted the journey to end, as she took in the sights and scenery of the cobbled backstreets of Paris, past the flea market, skimming the perimeter of an immaculately cultivated public park, crammed with a rainbow of colourful flowers. Weaving in and out of cars as they rode past cafés and delis and boutiques with candy-coloured striped awnings, people sipping coffee and reading newspapers as if they had all the time in the world. She felt vibrant. And so very alive! And it had crossed her mind that Trixie might have felt the same way all those decades earlier, vibrant and alive, experiencing new things that she hadn't done before, like dancing the Charleston in sultry jazz clubs, having come to Paris to escape her boring life . . . And in a way that is exactly what Annie had done too. And she had never ridden on the back of a scooter either. Sure it wasn't the same as dancing the Charleston in a jazz club, but for Annie it had been just as exciting. And now here she was on the deck of a boat, about to have lunch with an incredibly attractive Frenchman.

Annie had offered to help make lunch, but Étienne had insisted on treating her, and suggested instead that she sit back and relax and watch everyday Parisian life from the deck.

'*Bon appétit!*' Étienne appeared on the deck beside Annie with two plates, which he placed on the table before sitting down opposite her. He had changed out of the white T-shirt and was now wearing a navy linen shirt with the sleeves pushed up, and the first few buttons undone, revealing a peep of a dark-haired chest.

Bijou came bouncing along and promptly sat on the deck between their two chairs, her little fluffy tail sweeping back and forth as she gave them each, in turn, a look of anticipation in the hope of getting some of the delicious-looking steak. Annie laughed and went to pat her head, but Étienne waved his hand. 'Please, we must not encourage her, she is a very spoiled dog.' And they both laughed as Bijou slid her front legs out in front of her, dipped her head on her paws and did a moany kind of growl, clearly put out not to have their full attention.

Étienne poured the wine and lifted his glass, Annie reciprocating, then he said, 'To us. Our date! Perhaps the first of many. *Oui?*' and lifted his eyebrows hopefully.

'Oh, err, yes . . . that would be nice,' Annie smiled, taking a quick sip of wine and willing her pulse to slow down. *Did he just say the first of many? So he's planning on us having more dates. But is he for real? Genuine? Or is this just some kind of holiday romance? Which, come to think of it, I might not actually mind at all. But what if I fall for him and make a fool of myself by thinking this is more than it really is? Or he breaks my heart? For all I know he could do this to all the women he meets, the forty-something single ones who come to Paris for a city break. To get away from it all, disillusioned with their life, and then fall for the first sexy French man they meet . . . it's such a cliché.*

Annie put down her glass and picked up the knife and fork, trying to keep cool, but it was hard when what she really wanted to do was laugh out loud at the surreality of the situation and pick up her phone right now instead to call her best friend, Beth, and say, 'You'll never guess what, but I'm literally sitting opposite the most incredibly sexy man, who I think is actually a really nice guy too, on his boat, in Paris, and he's talking like we are going out together – as in, you know, dating. He's just called it the "first of many" and I've only just met him and well, Parisian men sure are . . . different, but what if I'm being a fool and do you think I should ask him or will that make me look too keen and . . .?'

Annie took a breath and tried to get a grip; she could chat to Beth about it later, but her fingers were shaking as she sliced into the perfectly cooked medium-rare steak. The delicious waft of garlicky butter on the frites was making her mouth water, the rocket and vine tomato salad with slivers of shaved Parmesan was her absolute favourite meal. But how did he know? And then something struck her; she had never had a man cook a meal for her before, certainly not Mark, he would have balked at the mere idea of it, he'd always been backwards-thinking about that kind of thing and even saw eating out in restaurants as a waste of time and money. But as far as Annie was concerned, Étienne bringing her here to this pictur-esque location and cooking this marvellous meal for her was the most romantic, sexiest, most gentlemanly thing she had ever experienced. But rather than waste any more of the moment thinking about Mark, she looked at Étienne and said, 'Thank you, this is . . . amazing.' And as soon as the words tripped from her mouth, she shook her head. She had said it again. Étienne put down his cutlery and laughed, a proper belly laugh, and even that was very appealing, making it impossible for Annie not to laugh too.

After drinking more wine, Étienne leant forward and looked right into her eyes.

'So Annie, how do you like it in Paris?'

'I like it a lot,' she told him, 'it's certainly different from London.'

'You do not like London?' he asked intuitively, and she turned to look out across the water, unsure of how to answer him. 'Sorry, did I upset you again?'

'No, gosh, absolutely not.' She shook her head. 'Sorry, I'm not upset, and you haven't upset me. I just . . . it's the way I feel when I'm here in Paris.'

'Is it a good . . . feel?' he lifted his eyebrows, checking

to see if he had said the word in the right way. She smiled, thinking it sounded absolutely the right way.

'Yes. Yes it is. A much better feel,' she smiled. 'I love it here. Paris is such a wonderful place.'

'Then tell me please, why is Paris better than London? I'm listening.' And he carried on eating, but all the while looking at her curiously.

'Oh, well . . . I had got very . . .' She paused, searching for the best way to explain. She didn't want him to think she was a sad old sack who had no life since her best friend went to live in Australia, which – come to think of it – was probably a pretty accurate reflection of the truth. Beth had been an integral part of her life, plus wondering if Phoebe and Johnny were OK too, and apart from her love of home interior design TV shows, there really wasn't much else, other than a coffee and cake break with Joanie now and again so she settled on '. . . Set in my ways.'

'Like bored?' Étienne said, resting his chin on one hand as he took a sip of wine from the glass with the other. Annie laughed and nodded.

'Yes, I guess so!' she admitted, wondering where he was going with this, and her earlier concerns about being seen as a bored forty-something.

'And your job?' He tilted his head to one side. 'You not talk about it. Is this boring too?'

'Oh, yes,' and in that instance Annie realized that Phoebe had a point . . . about it being a boring office job. 'Accounting in an office. My daughter thinks I should go for early retirement.' Annie lifted her wine glass.

'Retirement? Like, um . . .' He paused, as if searching for the understanding, but before Annie could explain, he added, '. . . give up? Your daughter wants you to give up your life?' and his forehead creased in concern. She laughed.

'In a way, I suppose . . . yes she does.'

'But you are too young to give up. What would you do for the whole time? How old are you, Annie?'

'Oh, I'm forty-nine,' she said, tentatively, and then quickly, 'how old are you?'

'Thirty-nine,' he said, casually and without hesitation, and Annie was stunned as it sank in. Ten years younger! Oh God. And her invisible guard shot straight back up. She had guessed he might be a bit younger than her, but ten years . . . He was playing with her, surely. Why would he want to date a woman who was ten years older than him? With grown-up children too – she had told him back in the apartment on their first day working together that she had two adult children and he had politely asked their names and told her he had a daughter called Delphine. And that had been the end of the conversation as he had then busied himself by climbing up a ladder and scraping the top of the wall in silence. It had been a bit awkward after that, to be honest, as if the last thing he wanted to do was have a conversation about her adult children.

'Oh,' she managed, finishing the last of the steak and neatly placing her knife and fork on the plate. Bijou stirred from her watch post by the table leg and wandered over to sit nearer to Annie, nudging her little soft head into the side of her thigh. Figuring a stroke might be OK now, Annie ran a finger over Bijou's ear. Étienne had finished eating and was now topping up her glass. She put out her hand to stop him. 'I better not drink any more wine, I need a clear head for sewing the curtains when we go back to the apartment,' she grinned, immediately wishing she didn't sound like such a prude. A ten-years-older prude, too! She winced, wondering what he was thinking.

'Does it bother you?'

'My age?' she clarified, not really wanting to talk about it and potentially spoil the perfect moment. Right here and now with him on his boat in Paris. She wanted to store the memory, intact. Something to cherish when she returned to her 'basic life' back home. But then realizing that she was being dramatic – she had every intention of making changes when she got home – she picked up the wine bottle and topped up her own glass. 'A little bit more will be fine, I'm sure,' she smiled ruefully, and then, 'I don't feel old, if that's what you mean . . .' Étienne laughed and leant forward on his elbows.

'That's not what I mean. The question was for my age. Does it matter that I'm . . .' he paused and creased his forehead and then added, 'the toy boy?' with such a serious look of concern on his face that clearly showed he was clueless about the implication in English of what he had just said, making Annie almost splutter a mouthful of wine. She put down the glass.

'Well, I, err . . .' She shook her head and looked away.

'What is it?' and he genuinely looked worried now as he bent sideways and scooped Bijou up into his arms to give her a stroke.

'Sorry, I'm not laughing at you. It's just that "toy boy" isn't really how, err, what you . . .' She stopped talking to see him looking dismayed. How on earth could she explain this to him? And then she had an idea. Picking up her phone, she quickly found a humorous article that kind of explained it for her and so, after copying it into a translator app, she turned the screen towards him.

'Ah, Annie,' he started slowly, scanning the words. 'No, I not mean . . .' and he lifted Bijou off his lap and took Annie's hand in his across the table. 'I'm sorry. I not mean to be impolite. I like you and I want you to like me and not think I'm too young for you. What does age matter, eh? Is just a number. How you feel here in your heart is what counts.' And he tapped his chest with his free hand.

'Oh,' she squeezed his hand on the table, savouring the delicious tingle that his touch evoked within her, and leant forward. 'Well, I like you too,' she said slowly, throwing her earlier feelings of caution to the wind and lifting her eyes from studying the back of his hand to take a tentative look at his face.

'*Je suis heureux* . . . I'm happy,' he said, simply, as if that settled it then and there was nothing more to say. 'Come on, let me show you Paris! We work again tomorrow. But now I take you to the Paris I want you to see.' And before she could protest – not that she wanted to go back to the apartment now to sew curtains, she wanted to stay here with him – he stood up, lifted her handbag from over the corner of the chair and handed it to her, then took her hand and led her to the edge of the deck where he helped her step along the wooden board and onto the towpath. Bijou stood on the edge of the deck, her tail wagging and her mouth open as if joyfully wondering if she was joining them too. Étienne clicked his fingers and said, '*Viens*,' at which command Bijou leapt onto the board and then trotted down onto the towpath to jaunt along in front of Annie and Étienne, their hands linked as they strolled along the bank of the river Seine.

A little later, and as the sun was dipping down in the sky, creating a magical golden glow across the water on the horizon, Étienne let go of Annie's hand and placed his arm around her shoulder to guide her left into another street.

'This way,' he said, 'is for the best view.'

They had been walking for a while now, chatting and taking in the sights, and Annie was curious to find out more about him.

'So tell me about Delphine, do you have a picture of her?' Étienne fell silent and took his arm away from Annie's shoulders before pushing both hands into his jean pockets. 'What is it? You look sad . . .' she asked gently, turning her face sideways to see his. He stopped walking and Bijou instinctively turned around and trotted back to stand by the side of Étienne's leg, her little head tilted up to see what was happening.

'Is OK,' Étienne eventually said. 'Here, I show you a picture.' And he pulled his phone from his pocket and, after tapping the screen, he handed the phone to Annie.

'Oh, Étienne, she's beautiful,' Annie said, looking at an extremely photogenic little girl doing a big star jump on a sandy beach, her long black curls fanning out from her face, her dark brown eyes dancing with joy. 'Do you get to see her very often?'

'Err . . . *non*,' and taking the phone, he pushed it back into his pocket. They walked on.

'Why is that?' Annie asked tentatively, looking at him again to gauge his reaction, and inwardly hoping he wasn't another Mark, split up from Delphine's mother and having moved on without a backward glance. She found herself holding her breath in anticipation of his answer.

'Um . . .' he stopped walking and after taking a deep breath he told her, 'She died.'

Annie stopped walking too and let out a small gasp before covering her mouth in shock. The pain etched on his face making her heart ache for him. On seeing his shoulders taut and his head dropped, she instinctively put her arms around him, utterly lost for words. They stood together in silence for a short while, but it felt like an eternity, as if time had stood still, before Étienne took a step back and gently lowered her arms.

'I spoil the nice time?' he shrugged, kicking at a small piece of grit on the pavement.

'Oh no, not at all, Étienne, you haven't spoiled it,'

Annie pleaded. 'Please, I didn't . . . I shouldn't have . . .' She stopped talking again and then, on seeing a bench nearby, she asked if he'd like to sit for a while. It didn't feel right to just keep on walking. She wanted to at least give him some time to contemplate, some space with his thoughts. This moment needed to be given the gravitas that it deserved.

After a while of them sitting together in silence – Annie felt it only right to keep quiet until he felt able to talk – with Bijou at their feet, Étienne slipped his arm back around Annie's shoulders and pulled her into his chest and told her what had happened. His precious daughter, Delphine, and wife, Brigitte, had died in a car accident four years before. They had been on holiday in St Tropez, travelling to the airport to pick him up to join them for the rest of the holiday, and a truck had turned the wrong way onto a motorway. 'It was sudden and they did not suffer in the pain,' he finished telling her, quietly. And Annie swiftly brushed away the solitary tear that had trickled from her chin and landed on the back of her hand.

'Étienne, I don't know what to say,' she started, feeling heartbroken for him and ashamed of herself for assuming the worst of him, that he was like other men that she had known. No wonder he had fallen silent that time in the apartment when he had spoken about his daughter. It wasn't a lack of interest in her grown-up children. But it had never crossed her mind that his own child was no longer here. And losing his wife too. Annie assumed she must have been young, in her thirties also, like him. And suddenly their conversation on the boat about age seemed utterly irrelevant and pointless. At the end of the day, all that really mattered was the moment. The being here and loving and feeling and living. Life was so precious. And Étienne, more than anyone, knew this.

'There is nothing to say,' he said, leaning his head on hers as they both looked at their hands in their laps. 'My life changed in an instant . . .' He started, leaning forward to give Bijou a pat. 'But I am living again now. For a time I didn't do it and then I quit my work and sold my house and I come to Paris to live on a boat and do a simpler life. I like the decorating and to paint the people I see and the scenery, for it helps my mind to be happy and calm. Always the rushing in my past work, like the traffic in the city . . .' He sighed, lifting his head away from hers.

'What work did you do?' Annie asked, sensing that he wanted talk about it.

'A bank. Buying and selling the trades,' he sighed and then added, 'my father, he prefer it to me being an artist. Yes, I earn lots of money but lost my family for it.'

'How come?' Annie said softly, looking at him to check she hadn't overstepped the mark.

'Is why Delphine and Brigitte come to the airport. I not finish work to travel to St Tropez with them at the start of the holiday. I make them wait because I am working,' he paused, and Annie gently brushed the back of his hand.

'Please, you don't have to tell me if it's too painful.'

'I want to. Annie, I thought my work was everything. Too important.'

'Oh Étienne, I'm sure you love and care deeply for your family, then and now and always . . . we do what we think is best at the time,' she soothed. A short silence followed. 'And please don't ever feel that you have to say sorry for talking about your family when we are together, not ever. They are a part of you and I want to get to know all of you.'

'Oh, Annie, you are so . . . cute,' he paused and gave her a tentative look, she smiled to indicate it was OK to say, 'and kind. Such a good friend – Maggie told me you come to Paris to help your friend with the apartment. And thank you for being my friend tonight.'

'Always,' she said, puzzled why he was thanking her. Surely it was the least anyone could do to listen to a man talking about his deceased wife and child. 'Why wouldn't I?'

'Not all the women like to hear . . .' His voice tailed off.

'Is that why you apologized?'

'*Mais, oui,*' he nodded. 'My last date, she say it in the past and too sad for us to talk about. It was last summer and so I stay on my own until . . .' he turned to look at her. 'Until I meet you. And you not like the other women. They flirt and they not like my boat and say I should live in a house.' He shook his head, the corners of his mouth lifting into a wry smile.

'Oh Étienne. Well, then it's for the best you stay on your own and not be with a woman who doesn't want to acknowledge your past, or wants to change how you live . . .' She stopped talking, not wanting to criticize other women as it wasn't really her style.

'So what is best for you, Annie?' he asked, changing the subject.

Silence followed as she considered his question. It was way too soon for her to suggest that meeting him might possibly be the best thing that had happened to her in a long time, even though she was very attracted to him and liked him a lot, but they barely knew each other, and she didn't feel it appropriate given the conversation they'd had about Delphine and Brigitte, so she told him about other parts of her life.

'Well . . . certainly not my job,' she told him. 'But

that sounds ungrateful as it enabled me to stay in my home and look after my children after my marriage fell apart.'

'When was this?'

'A long time ago.'

'And now?' he turned to look at her.

'And now, I want to try something else . . . I don't know what yet, but I know I want to make changes in my life.'

'Then you must do the changes! Life is too short for regrets,' he said, letting his voice fade in contemplation.

'Yes,' she agreed, quietly, thinking of his daughter and wife.

'OK, now I show you this beautiful City of Light!' And he let go of her hand, pressed both palms onto his knees, as if to signify a line under the conversation for now, and then he stood up, put his hand out for hers and led her on through more cobbled streets of Paris.

'Here, you like to see pretty colours?' Étienne said as they turned a corner and on into another narrow alleyway.

'Sure,' Annie said, looking around to see what he could be referring to.

'Come, it's not far.' They were practically running now, with Bijou up ahead, her little tail swinging from side to side, seemingly full of glee as she came upon a crowd of pigeons in the middle of the pavement, making them all flutter and disperse up into the sky as she bounced along and then bobbed up and down, as if trying to take off with them. It was exhilarating to see and Annie could feel her spirits soaring too as she savoured the moment, feeling carefree and happy with Étienne as her personal Parisian tour guide. She glanced sideways at him, happy to see him smiling and taking pleasure in showing her around his magnificent city.

Taking Annie's hand, he steered her around the corner and then stopped moving, turning to look at her, eager to see her reaction. Blinking, she caught her breath and stopped moving too. The sight before her was enchanting. A narrow, cobbled street crammed full of pastel painted houses – powder pink, yellow, blue, green with brightly contrasting coloured wooden shutters. Tall, lush green plants in pots lined the pavement on both sides, the streetlights – majestic white globes on black-painted posts – a pleasing contrast to all the colours. The rhythmic sound of a saxophone swinging in the warm breeze gave the atmosphere a sultry, decadent vibe.

'This street is incredible,' Annie said, dropping Étienne's hand and turning a full circle as she drank it all in. 'Imagine living here,' she laughed, thinking how uplifting it would be to come to this every day after work. It was stunning.

'Is good, yes?'

'Yes, yes it is, and thank you for showing it to me.'

'Come on, there's more. Are you hungry?'

'Um, well, not really . . . but . . .' She stopped talking, keen to know what he had in mind next.

'You won't be able to resist these. Let's go,' and Étienne took her hand again. After strolling along the most gorgeously colourful street Annie thought she had ever seen, they crossed the road and came upon a big, white marquee with lines of easels spanning the perimeter, displaying a vibrant selection of water-colour paintings. The air was infused with the sweet scent of sugar and spice and yes, definitely, all things nice, were her immediate thoughts as Étienne led her into the marquee.

'Oh my word,' Annie beamed, as Étienne scooped Bijou up into his arms.

'Is best this way so she doesn't try to steal the pastries or batons of bread. It's happened before.' And he laughed, giving the top of Bijou's head a little stroke and a kiss.

'And who could blame her? This is heaven and impossible to resist,' Annie said, trying to take in the array of sights and smells all around her. They were in a market packed with stalls selling bread, ropes of garlic, chillies, cakes, cherries, pastries, macarons, fruit, fish – she could see oysters nestling on trays of ice, wheels of cheese piled up in tall Jenga towers, the market traders ready with platters, offering delicious-looking slivers of tasting samples. To her left, a florist's stall caught Annie's eye with buckets of pink peonies on tiered wooden shelves mingled with sprays of lavender and yellow roses, creating another burst of vibrant colour. Étienne headed towards the flower seller and, after chatting in French, he plucked a small posy of peonies from a bucket and handed it to Annie.

'To match the pink of your dress,' he shrugged, smiling easily, as if it was the most obvious thing in the world for him to do such a thing. But for Annie, it was an amazing gesture, and not one she was used to experiencing with a man.

'Thank you, they're beautiful,' and she leant into him to plant a kiss on his cheek, thinking how wonderful he made her feel.

'Now, we eat cake,' and he led her to a tiny stall at the far end of the market, where an elderly man was sitting behind a table full of sugar-dusted seashell-shaped madeleine cakes. The man stood up and greeted Étienne with an enthusiastic hug and a quick kiss on each cheek before turning to Annie and saying something fast in French.

'Ah, *pardon*,' she tried to apologize for not speaking French as he offered pieces of a madeleine to try, refusing to take any money as Annie quickly found her purse, looking to Étienne to ask how much to pay.

'*Pour mon ami – bon appétit!*' the man said, and Étienne thanked him and handed a piece of a madeleine to Annie who was delighted to feel that it was still warm.

'Mmm, this is delicious,' she said in between bites, as the buttery soft sponge melted in her mouth, the lemon-flavoured sugar dusting sticking to her lips.

'Is the best you tasted, *oui?*' Étienne said, his eyes dancing enthusiastically on seeing her delight. He devoured some too before breaking off a small piece and treating Bijou to the rest.

'It definitely is,' she nodded, licking the sugar from her lips.

'Come, there's more.'

Moments later, and Bijou was again leading the way, trundling along as fast as her little legs would go as they climbed up a steep cobbled hill, the view of Paris getting more and more panoramic, the streets smaller and more winding with traditional shops – a *boulangerie* with piles of baguettes in the windows, a *boucherie* with hams hanging on hooks. Cafés with tables outside and people drinking coffee and glasses of Ricard, pouring water from little glass jugs into the golden liquid to turn it cloudy white. Higgledy-piggledy houses and tall pink cherry blossom trees lined the pavements as they reached the famous La Maison Rose restaurant on the corner at a crossroads.

'You like to take a picture?' Étienne turned to Annie.

'I'd love to,' she grinned, taking in the cute, iconic sugar-almond-pink building with its green wooden shutters and wreath of green vines tumbling all along and up the side of the building. Annie lifted her phone to take the picture, but Étienne gently took it from her, swivelled her around until she was standing with her back to the pretty café and, after moving in close beside her, he lifted the phone up high and took several selfies of them laughing and smiling. Bijou circled their legs, clearly keen to get involved too, and was scooped up into their arms, where she sat upright and cocked her little head to one side. And Annie wondered if she dared lift her left hand into a half-heart shape, remembering her musing in the taxi when she first arrived here in Paris, for this really was a picture-perfect moment that she had never envisaged ever happening.

Stars glittered in the now night sky, the air still warm,

infused with the scent of coffee and floral notes from the flowers in the pots on the pavement as they passed by another bistro on their left. Turning right, and after wandering hand in hand through more pretty little streets and passages, Étienne stopped walking at the foot of a metal staircase running up the side of a building.

'Follow me,' he said with boyish enthusiasm, the excitement evident in his voice.

'Are you sure we can go up there?' Annie looked at the steps which appeared to be some kind of fire escape.

'*Oui*,' he grinned, scooping Bijou into the crook of his elbow and reaching for Annie's hand, 'this apartment up there,' and he motioned to the third set of windows at the front and side of the building, where there was a large wraparound balcony with a black wrought-iron balustrade, a small gate to the side leading directly off the metal steps. 'Is belonging to me!'

'Oh,' she said, surprised, and then as if he had read her mind, wondering why he lived on the boat in that case, explained, 'My friends, I let them rent it, but they are away and they don't mind me coming here.'

And so they climbed up the steps and, after opening the little gate, went onto the balcony. Étienne carefully placed Bijou on the floor of the balcony and quickly moved behind Annie, gently lifting his hands around her head until he was covering her eyes. 'Is OK, I look after you,' he whispered, carefully motioning for her to take a few steps sideways, guiding her around the corner of the building until they must have arrived in the perfect spot because, when Étienne took his hands away, Annie blinked and then gasped, momentarily stunned by the sight before her. The whole of Paris dazzling in front of her eyes.

'Oh Étienne, it's magical,' she managed, gazing all around. She felt as though she was on top of the world.

And then, like a burst of beautiful fireworks, it came to life.

The Eiffel Tower.

Shimmering as if sprinkled in gold dust, sparkling and luminous against the inky velvet night backdrop. An illuminated carousel of painted wooden horses dancing up and down at the base of the tower. People, lovers, hand in hand, kissing and looking up in awe. The atmosphere was electric, and Annie felt delighted and touched that Étienne had brought her to this vantage point where she could see the Eiffel Tower in private, away from the crowds. Their very own special viewing. A memory she would cherish for ever.

Étienne slipped his arms around her back and under her elbows into a warm, comforting cuddle, his face nuzzling the side of her neck. Annie brought his hands up to her lips and gave each of them a soft kiss before holding him tightly as they stood together in silence, content in each other's company, contemplating and enjoying the gloriously breathtaking and iconic Parisian view.

17

'Morning!' Maggie beamed, standing up as Annie came into the café and made her way towards the table where Kristen was sitting with a coffee cup in one hand and a *pain au chocolat* in the other.

'Hi Annie, I can't wait to hear all about your evening,' Kristen said, beaming too as she patted the chair beside her. Annie had stayed the night on Étienne's boat. By the time they had finished admiring the Eiffel Tower and had meandered hand in hand back through the cobbled boulevards of Paris together, Étienne had invited her back onboard. They had drunk coffee and carried on their conversation and had ended up chatting and putting the world to rights until the early hours of the morning, wrapped up in cashmere blankets with lantern lights twinkling and Bijou sprawled across their laps to keep them warm. It had been blissfully indulgent and quite romantic and Annie felt floaty and excited at the prospect of seeing Étienne again tomorrow at the apartment.

'Would you like a coffee, Annie?' Maggie asked, not waiting for her to reply as she set the coffee machine into action with a big scoop of powder placed in the handle followed by the whoosh of the steamer in a jug of milk. Annie helped herself to a *pain au chocolat* after Kristen motioned to a plate piled high with every kind of delicious-looking pastry possible. It was early Sunday morning and the café wasn't open until later, so they had the place to themselves and with the weather a little cooler today, Annie was grateful for the cosy air radiating from the bread oven where Maggie had opened the door to warm the café up ready for when the customers arrived later.

'Thanks, Maggie,' Annie said, stirring the coffee in the cup that Maggie had placed in front of her.

'So, come on, we are both excited to hear all about it. How did your date go?' Kristen said, giving Annie a gentle nudge. 'Did you have sex with him? Was it out of this world?'

'No!' Annie laughed, shaking her head as she leant sideways and put an arm around her friend's waist to give her a quick affectionate hug. She had become so fond of Kristen in the short time they had known each other, and now couldn't imagine not having her in her life. Annie loved her effervescent nature and her forth-right personality, always straight to the point; it was liberating, and Annie thought she could learn a thing or two about honesty from Kristen too, vowing to be more like her when she returned home. Less reserve and more openness, with an excitement for life too, something that had been missing for Annie until she came to Paris. And Kristen had been through a tough time with the relentless rounds of IVF, seven in total, she had told Annie, and then for her husband to move on with her best friend who was now pregnant . . . well, Annie reckoned Kristen was remarkably resilient and pretty incredible to have dusted herself down and come to Paris to put herself back together again. Always with a smile and a sense of hope for what a new day would bring, Kristen was one of the strongest women that Annie knew. 'Oh Kristen,' Annie sighed, 'so sorry to disappoint you. There was no sex. We talked, that's all.'

'Talked? What about?' Kristen polished off the last of her pastry and did a petulant pout. Annie shot a glance at Maggie, wondering if she knew about Étienne's wife and daughter, but figured she didn't as surely she would have mentioned it. She took a sip of coffee and gently told them, taking care to be sensitive and not dramatize the details in any way.

267

'Poor Étienne,' Maggie spoke first. 'This explains it all. He's always been reticent. I put it down to him being reserved, or shy perhaps. And since Sam died he has become even more so . . .'

'Is it any wonder with so much tragedy? Losing his wife and child, and then his friend, Sam, your husband, Maggie. That's a lot of loss,' Kristen said, shaking her head, a look of sorrow on her face. 'I so shouldn't have flirted like that . . . what must he have thought? The poor guy putting up with me being so crass. Just goes to show, doesn't it? That you never really know someone else's story. I'm glad you guys had a nice time together last night though.'

'Ah, don't be too hard on yourself, Kristen,' Maggie said, 'you weren't to know and I'm sure he wouldn't have really minded a bit of flirtation from you.'

'I agree, Kristen. You're gorgeous, and I'm sure Étienne was extremely flattered,' Annie smiled, remembering Étienne's comment about women flirting, but Kristen didn't need to know that, there was no point in hurting her unnecessarily, and besides, she had been playful not predatory.

'OK,' Kristen agreed, 'but please, at least tell me you had a kiss, surely you did?' and she opened her eyes wide in anticipation of hearing all about it.

'Sorry to disappoint you, Kristen, but it really isn't

like that. We cuddled and did the usual kiss on each cheek when he dropped me back here and said goodbye, but that's all. It's more of a friendship than a romance,' Annie told them. And she felt content with that. The evening had been about so much more than physical attraction, and for once in her life she was enjoying getting to know a man properly before moving on to more. Although she had an inkling that sex with Étienne would be incredible and mind-blowing, if that's how things developed between them, and she really hoped they did, but only when the time was right and last night had not been that time.

'I think that sounds utterly romantic,' Maggie sighed. 'And was the steak and frites good?'

'Oh yes, it was delicious,' Annie told her. 'My favourite.'

'That's right,' Kristen said. 'I was here when he asked Maggie what he should cook for you.'

'Really?' Annie turned to Maggie.

'Yes, that's right,' Maggie confirmed. 'He called in when you were upstairs in your room and so I told him – I remembered when you first arrived, you said steak and frites was your favourite and it's an easy dish to make – he mentioned that he wasn't a very experienced cook. He seems very smitten with you, the most animated I've ever seen him. He seemed very keen to make the lunch date just right for you.'

'Thank you, Maggie. And how kind of him.' Annie grinned, inwardly glowing at his thoughtfulness.

'You held hands though, yes?' Kristen tried again, so keen was she to hear how far things had progressed between them.

'Yes, we did.' Annie laughed.

'I can picture it now,' Kristen continued, looking into the distance, 'the boat all lit up in the dark and having a lovely cuddle and chat.'

'It sounds very romantic, I think I would prefer it to sex!' Maggie said.

'What do you mean?' Kristen exclaimed, horrified as she swivelled in her seat to stare at Maggie.

'Sex is so overrated,' Maggie chuckled and sighed. 'Sam and I used to go a long time without sex because we were both exhausted from working in the café until late into the evening. But there was always comfort and affection and holding hands and saying, "*je t'aime*" in the dark before we went to sleep every night. And that's one of the things I miss the most about him not being here, to be honest.'

'Ah, Maggie, that's so beautiful. Chad was all about the sex, right from the get-go. Not that I'm complaining, I love sex but it sure would have been nice to have had what you had with Sam too. And you know what, I did feel pressured sometimes, like if I didn't make out then he would grow bored and find someone else . . . which he did in the end anyway,' she shrugged, pulling a face. 'I hope I find someone to just "be" with one day. I want to grow old with a man who I can sit up all night with, just chatting and putting the world to rights. A man who is content with holding hands in the dark. And not always having to end up in us having sex.'

'You will find what you are looking for, I am sure,' Maggie said, kindly. 'When the time is right, you will meet the right man and it will all fall into place . . . you will see. Just give yourself time, you are still healing . . .' Kristen leant across and gave Maggie a kiss on her cheek.

'I love you, Maggie! And you too, Annie,' she added, giving Annie's hand a squeeze. 'You're the very best kind of women and I am so damn happy that I came to Paris and found you both.'

'Ah, and you too, Kristen,' Annie said, a surge of gratitude rising within her on having her two gorgeous new friends. 'And you, Maggie.' She took a sip of coffee and, after a couple of bites of a croissant, she added, 'Right, now that we've had our morning love-in, can I show you something? I'd love to know what you think about this!' And reaching into her handbag, Annie found the new jam jar, into which Étienne had transferred the pieces of paper, and put it on the table.

'What's that?' Maggie asked, picking the jar up.

'We found a jar in the garden yesterday, buried in an overgrown old herb garden,' Annie explained. 'That one broke but we transferred it to this one. If you open the lid you'll see there are lots of little pieces of folded-up paper with words on. Perfume recipes, I think, in French . . .'

'How intriguing,' Kristen said, peering into the jar that Maggie was holding up to the light now. 'Let's open it.' After finding a big bowl, Maggie unscrewed the lid and tipped the papers into it. 'Wow, it's like a lucky dip.' Kristen took a few of the papers and started unfolding them. 'Ooh, this one says, Rose, Aniseed, Clover, Hawthorn, Echinacea, Laurel, and then a space with some more ingredients after that but the words are too faded to read.'

'Oh, that's a strange concoction for a perfume, aniseed and clover are very strong smells,' Maggie said, and the other two women nodded their agreement. Kristen unfolded another piece of paper.

'This one sounds a bit nicer. Juniper, Elderflower, Rosehip, Evening Primrose, Myrrh and Ylang-Ylang.'

'Yes, it sure does,' Annie said.

'And this one, I adore the scent of rose, and patchouli, so this one could smell good,' Maggie smiled, unfolding another piece of paper and reading the recipe aloud, 'Patchouli, Indole, Echinacea, Rose, Rose de Mai and Eucalyptus.'

'What is it, Annie? You look like you're miles away, deep in thought.' Kristen looked at her.

'The names of the ingredients . . . they sound familiar,' Annie said, pondering. 'The letter we found in the basement room! The one from Paulette with the perfume recipes listed out. Didn't one of those have two lots of rose in it?'

'*Oui!* That's right,' Maggie agreed, 'the rose de Mai.'

'From the French Riviera, with the Mediterranean sea air. I remember now,' Annie said.

'How glam!' Kristen said. 'No wonder Paulette listed the ingredients out, most likely couldn't believe her luck on receiving such an exotic perfume during wartime.'

'But still strange to list all the ingredients when she could have just written her thanks and mentioned that one of the phials didn't make it,' Annie said.

'True. And now we have a whole jar of papers with odd combinations for perfumes or potions,' Kristen said, 'and it's a bit weird . . . to stick them all in a jar and bury them in the garden.'

'But we don't know that they were buried on

purpose,' Maggie said, diplomatically. 'Maybe the jar just got left in the garden and forgotten about. It's possible that Trixie was tending to her herb garden and writing down combinations of ingredients and—'

'Oh no!' Kristen interrupted, shaking her head, 'I prefer the weird option,' she laughed, widening her eyes dramatically. 'What if it's some sort of secret code! You never know, it was wartime after all, and I read somewhere about people doing all sorts of stuff in the war to bury secrets . . . literally, in this case.' She laughed.

'It's possible!' Maggie joined in. 'And I read about coded information being passed on by very extraordinary means – perhaps these papers were messages and the jar was left in the garden to be collected by someone.'

'The Germans!' Kristen said, sitting upright with an agitated look on her face. 'Annie, didn't you say that the old man in the garden thought Étienne was German?'

'Yes, but he was scared,' Annie told her. 'He seemed fearful of Étienne seeing the jar so that doesn't make sense.'

'Then maybe the jar of papers were coded messages meant for the other side,' Kristen suggested. 'The French Resistance?'

'OK, let's not get carried away,' Annie said, picking

up her phone where she had a photo of the letter from Paulette to Beatrice, as she had since replaced it back inside the book in the basement. 'OK, so here's the letter from Paulette.' And she showed them the picture of the letter which Maggie read aloud in English, translating it from French.

> *My dearest Beatrice*
> *I write to thank you for the perfume. The phial containing the scent made up of Patchouli, Indole, Echinacea, Rose, Rose de Mai and Eucalyptus has arrived safely and is quite the sweetest fragrance yet. Sadly, the herbal remedy accompanying it made up of Juniper, Elderflower, Rosehip, Evening Primrose, Myrrh and Ylang-Ylang was less fortunate, the body of the glass bottle damaged beyond repair. I trust that you will send a suitable replacement in due course.*
> *Until we meet again.*
> *Your friend,*
> *Paulette*

'I knew it!' Kristen could contain herself no longer. 'There's no way that's a coincidence.' She tapped the screen of Annie's mobile. 'The letter must mean something . . . a secret message, why else would Paulette specifically list out the ingredients and then the very same ones appear in a jar in the herb patch?'

'But what could it mean?' Annie said, racking her brains to see if Kristen's suggestion had legs. Surely not, it couldn't really be some sort of code, could it? All this talk of passing messages to the Germans – or to the Resistance – was muddling her thoughts. Surely there was a simpler explanation.

Silence followed as the three women pondered on the possibilities until Maggie quietly said,

'Rachel.'

'What's that?' Kristen asked.

'Here, on this piece of paper.' Maggie tapped the first paper that Kristen had read out. 'See, the first letters of each ingredient, Rose, Aniseed, Clover, Hawthorn, Echinacea, Laurel. Put them together and they spell Rachel.'

'Oh my God, they do,' Kristen near screamed in excitement at the possibility of her secret coded messages theory being plausible. She was bobbing up and down now in anticipation of discovering more.

'And this one,' Maggie picked up another piece of paper, 'Fennel, Rose, Indole, Daisy, Arnica, Ylang-Ylang spells Friday and there are numbers on the back,' she turned the paper over so they could see 2100 was written there.

'Friday 2100,' Annie said, thinking that perhaps it could mean Friday 9 p.m.? Her thoughts were racing now: was it really possible that the jar she had found in Trixie's garden was full of coded messages? And if so, what did this mean? Was Trixie a traitor? Passing messages to the Germans? She was seen publicly colluding with the head of the Gestapo, shaking hands with him, after all. Her picture was on the front of the newspaper! It's one thing selling perfume to German soldiers, normal French citizens wouldn't have been able to avoid trading with them, but to publicly show conviviality and pose for a photo is a different matter altogether. But then why was the elderly man so clearly scared of the jar being discovered? Was it because Trixie wasn't a traitor at all, and instead she was actually working for the Resistance? Passing messages to them . . . If indeed, the jar was even hers, although it seemed highly likely as the handwriting on most of the papers was the same as that in her perfume ledger and diaries . . . but not all of them, some of the papers had different handwriting, smaller and less flowing in style than Trixie's, suggesting that another person was involved. Annie made a mental note to scrutinize the rest of Trixie's diaries to see if she could find anything to substantiate these seemingly far-fetched notions.

'OK, so now we go through all the papers and see what they say,' Kristen clapped her hands together, interrupting Annie's thoughts.

A while later, the three women had gone through all of the pieces of paper and discovered that they did indeed reveal a list of names and messages, varying in days, possible times, and even a few places too, such as rue de Passy and Avenue de l'Opéra.

'And the two recipes listed in the letter from Paulette spell out Pierre and Jeremy,' Annie said, pulling her pad out from her bag to make a note, figuring these names might be of more significance given that they were also in the letter.

'And here are the two pieces of paper with the same ingredients as in the letter – Jeremy and Pierre,' Annie said, looking at all the pieces of paper in front of her as if they held the key to some sort of puzzle.

'Look, this one has more ingredients on the back,' Kristen said, turning over the piece of paper that spelled out 'Jeremy' and quickly read out the first letter of each ingredient.'

'Sutherland!' Annie said. 'That's very English-sounding.'

'And there's more on this piece of paper,' Kristen said, and Annie wrote the letters down: SQN LDR. 'Oh, well that's not a name!' she added, petulantly.

'But hang on,' Annie said, it might be a code for something, and she quickly did a Google search on her phone to see if the letters meant anything. 'Ah, here we go, they mean squadron leader, a commissioned rank in the Royal Air Force.'

'Wow! As in an English pilot?' Kristen clarified.

'Maybe there is more to this letter after all,' Maggie nodded slowly.

'Well, the letter was sent during wartime,' Kristen pointed out.

'Yes, true,' Annie said, 'so I wonder if Paulette was saying that Pierre, as in the first bottle of perfume, arrived safely. But the other perfume bottle, a.k.a. Jeremy, didn't.'

'Arrived where?' Kristen said, her forehead creasing as she seemed to be trying to work it out.

'That's the mystery,' Annie said, 'but let's not forget that this could be pure speculation.'

'But hang on,' Kristen grabbed a piece of paper. 'This one, the Pierre one, has more ingredients on the back.' She read out the names and Annie wrote down the first letters, Aniseed, Uva, Magnolia, Oregano, Nutmeg, Turmeric.'

'A-U-M-O-N-T,' they all said in unison.

'Aumont,' Annie said, then repeated slowly, as if she was having a light-bulb moment. Kristen smoothed the piece of paper out on the table so they could all see it clearly. A short silence followed. And then, 'Are you both thinking what I'm thinking?' she asked, looking first at Maggie and then to Kristen. They both nodded.

'Monsieur Aumont! The *avocat*,' they all chimed.

Annie rummaged in her bag to find the lawyer's business card and sure enough his initial was P. She hadn't realized as he'd been very formal in all his dealings with her and Joanie, introducing himself as Monsieur Aumont, never Pierre.

'Well, this is very intriguing!' Annie shook her head, trying to work it all out. 'Of course, it could just be a coincidence.'

'*Mais oui*,' Maggie interjected. 'Pierre is a very common name in France.'

'But then again,' Kristen said, pursing her lips and drumming her fingers on the table, 'maybe not. I mean, why would Trixie put these pieces of paper in the jar and hide it in the back garden? If not for some very good reason . . . It would be a bit odd to just write random names and messages for no reason at all, and if you look at the rest of these pieces of paper,' she paused to pick up a few more to show them, 'they are mostly names, days and times, and mostly French, but this one sounds British. Look, see here, this one spells out "Monty Franklin".'

'Monty? He was Trixie's friend,' Annie said, 'we read about Monty, do you remember? He was the English soldier that she first knew from Étaples and then met up with again in Paris. She cared deeply for him from what I can gather from the other diary entries I've read so far.'

'OK, so we are getting somewhere now . . . for sure, we know that Monty was important to Trixie, she wrote about him, and worried about him in the diary, so if our theory is right and she was passing messages on, then I don't believe she would give Monty's name to the Germans,' Annie said, convinced of it. 'It's more likely that she would have protected him!'

'Good point!' Kristen said, 'and what's the betting that cranky Monsieur Aumont knows much more than he's made out?'

'Ah—' Maggie started.

'Oh, come on,' Kristen was fired up now. 'He was positively dismissive when Annie tried to find out what he knew about Trixie. Rude even! He's hiding something, I guarantee it. I bet he and Trixie were friends.'

'But hang on.' Annie was thinking. 'How old do you reckon he is?'

'Eighties perhaps. And, I mean, he's pretty old to still be working as a lawyer, so maybe he just got involved because she was a personal friend, a favour maybe . . .' Kristen puffed.

'Maybe,' Maggie said, 'but I'm not sure he came out of retirement just to deal with Trixie's inheritance. Although he still does the tracing work.'

'And there's no way he could have been an adult in the 1920s and therefore part of Trixie's gang of friends. Not like Monty, who we know was definitely Trixie's friend,' Annie nodded. 'And there's no mention in the diaries I've read so far of a man called Jeremy, or even a woman called Paulette.'

'Hmm,' Kristen sighed. 'He could still know Trixie. Certainly more than he's letting on. And it was weird the way he carried on, almost like he was scared to tell us about her.'

'But let's think this through . . .' Annie said. 'If Monsieur Aumont is the same Pierre that Paulette writes about in the letter dated 1944, and we reckon he's in his eighties now, then he would have been a young child back then.'

'Well, I guess there's only one way to find out.' And Kristen picked up Maggie's phone from the table and handed it to her. 'Let's call and ask him.'

18

Monsieur Aumont hadn't answered Maggie's call, so now the three women were standing outside his office just a few streets away from Trixie's apartment on Cour Felice.

'We can't just barge in without an appointment,' Annie said, placing her hand on Kristen's arm as she went to press the button beside his name on the doorbell.

'Of course we can!' And before Maggie or Annie could stop her, Kristen had her index finger pressed firmly on the bell. A few seconds later, a buzzer sounded to signify for them to pull open the door, which they did.

Inside, and with Kristen leading the way, the three women went up the stairs and into the office. Monsieur Aumont was sitting at his desk with a startled look on his face.

'Bonjour, Monsieur Aumont,' Kristen said, attempting to be polite, but then ruined it by dumping her oversized tote bag on top of a pile of files and planting her hands on her hips so he was in no doubt that she meant business.

'Mesdames,' he stood up, his eyes darting from Kristen to Annie and then to Maggie, 'what is the meaning of this intrusion? I tell you, there is nothing more to say about Madame Archambeau,' he declared, holding up his palms and flashing a look at Annie who was standing behind Kristen. 'My instruction was to find the beneficiary only, the Englishwoman, Joan Smith, and I have done this.'

'So why is your name inside this jar found buried in Beatrice Archambeau's garden?' And Kristen took the jar from the top of Annie's open bag looped over her shoulder, and plonked it on the desk next to her own tote bag. She then unscrewed the lid and took out a few of the pieces of paper and read the names aloud, starting with his. Then Monty's. And a few more. Even mentioning Paulette's letter again. Annie was horrified.

'What are you doing, Kristen? This isn't what we agreed.'

'But he knows more than he's letting on,' Kristen claimed, 'I'm sure of it. Why shouldn't he help you? Is it really that big a secret to know how Trixie is connected to your friend Joanie? He's playing with you and it's not right.'

'And this isn't right either. Please, Kristen, stop it,' Annie pleaded, knowing that they weren't going to get any help badgering the man like this. Turning to Monsieur Aumont, Annie apologized and, pointing to the jam jar, she tried to explain.

'We just wondered if you might know who these people are, and if you could tell us why your name might be on this piece of paper inside a jam jar buried in Beatrice's back garden.'

'I, err . . . *je ne sais pas. Je n'ai jamais vu ce pot.*' And he pointed at the jar.

'He says he's never seen the jar.' And, seeing the panic in his eyes, Maggie swiftly stepped in and spoke to him in French, her voice sounding soft and sincere, to which he replied with much shrugging and animated gesticulating while Kristen and Annie looked on, trying to understand what was being said. But whatever it was, Annie could see that his defences were down now and he looked genuinely fearful, deflated, tired even, of whatever it was that seemed to be haunting him, and she instantly regretted their decision to visit him. If she had known Kristen was going to carry on in this way then she would never have agreed to them coming to see Monsieur Aumont in the first place. It wasn't right to turn up unannounced, and it sure wasn't right to put such fear into a person. An elderly person. And then she realized . . . the look right now on Monsieur Aumont's face, she had seen it before. The haunted eyes, the dart of panic flitting across his face, it was familiar. The man in the garden. He had also been frightened by the sight of the jar. What did these two Frenchmen know about the jar full of names, dates and times? And, more to the point, what secrets did it hold to make them react in such a way? But then something extraordinary happened. Kristen grabbed another piece of paper and blurted out, 'Squadron Leader Jeremy Sutherland. Ring any bells?' and raised an eyebrow as if testing Monsieur Aumont for a reaction.

And she got one.

He sank down into his chair and dipped his head into his hands, muttering something over and over in French. Words that sounded as if he was in physical pain, or troubled by a memory perhaps. As if he had the weight of the whole world hanging from his sagging shoulders. For a moment, Annie thought he might actually be crying.

Maggie took Kristen's arm, and after picking up the jar and handing it to Annie, who instantly thrust it into her bag, she propelled them both from the room. Then, when Kristen and Annie were through the doorway, Maggie turned back and said in a quiet, consoling voice.

'*Je suis vraiment désolée,*' and then in English, 'I'm so sorry, we won't bother you again.'

Outside, and the three women stood in silence for a while, with Maggie shaking her head as if trying to formulate the right words to say to Kristen without losing her temper. Annie intervened as Maggie started pacing up and down, barely able to look in Kristen's direction.

'What were you thinking?' Annie asked Kristen, frustrated with her, but keen to work out what had just happened.

'I . . .' Kristen started. Then, after letting out a long puff of air, she lifted her hands up in an open gesture and said, 'I'm sorry. I don't know. I just saw red, I guess, I wasn't thinking . . . I wanted to help you, Annie. You've come to Paris to help your friend and he's sitting there looking smug and refusing to cooperate. It's—'

'*Tais-toi!*' Maggie spluttered. 'Be quiet, Kristen, you have no clue what this man has gone through . . .'

'What do you mean?' she asked.

'If you had stopped for *un moment* to let me talk to him, calmly and politely, as we agreed on the way here, then we might have found out more. Did you not see how distressed he was?' Maggie asked, almost

287

shouting as she pointed towards the door of the building they had just left. 'The man was in pain. Real pain.' She was pointing at Kristen now and tears were pooling in her eyes.

'Maggie, I'm really sorry,' Annie started, hating seeing her friend upset and angry like this. She went to place a soothing hand on Maggie's shoulder, but instead Maggie leant into Annie and gave her a quick embrace.

'I'm fine. Please . . .' Maggie then said, stepping back and wiping her eyes with the corner of tissue that she had pulled from the pocket of her dress.

'Maggie, please. I feel terrible. I didn't mean to upset you,' Kristen murmured, holding her clasped hands up under her chin with a worried look on her face. 'But I'm confused. What did he say?'

'Not now, Kristen,' Annie jumped in, keen to defuse the situation, and dismayed at how only an hour or so ago the three of them were marvelling over how wonderful their new friendship was. But now . . . well, Maggie was very evidently upset and frustrated. And she too still felt annoyed with Kristen.

'It's OK, Annie,' Maggie said, 'I'm overreacting. It was painful seeing him genuinely upset. He said the pilot, Jeremy Sutherland, saved his life and . . .' Maggie's eyes filled with tears again. Annie steered her towards a nearby bench, and they sat down, with Kristen next to her.

'Did he say any more?' Annie asked, gently. 'What is it that's made you this upset?'

'Maggie, I truly am sorry,' Kristen said, patting the back of her hand in reassurance. Maggie carried on talking.

'Oh Kristen, I'm sorry too. I shouldn't have taken it out on you. I know you were only trying to help Annie get to the truth for her friend, Joanie. I'm sad because I'm concerned . . . that the truth is uglier than any of us could imagine.'

'In what way ugly?' Annie persevered tentatively, keen to know what Monsieur Aumont had revealed, but not wanting to upset Maggie further.

'He confirmed that it is his name on the piece of paper in the jar. And the pilot helped him escape from the Nazis when they occupied Paris in the war when he was a child. He also managed to tell me that he was one of the Jewish children in the orphanage in Cour Felice! And that's as far as we got . . . he seemed in such anguish at recalling the events from his difficult childhood, an orphan who I imagine would have been terrified and traumatized by having to flee for his life, that I told him it wasn't necessary to say any more and that we were all extremely sorry to cause him anguish,' Maggie said softly.

'Oh God. I never learn! Me and my big mouth and bull-in-a-china-shop approach,' Kristen said. 'First the flirting with Étienne and now this. I must go and apologize properly to Monsieur Aumont right away. I'm appalled with myself for causing him to have to remember even a moment of that terror. No wonder he didn't want to be in Cour Felice on that day to hand over the keys. Why would he want to revisit the very place where he had experienced such pain all those years ago! The truck turning up and the soldiers taking all the children away. And oh my God, what if he won't talk about Trixie because she was in some way involved in his horror? We know that she was friendly to the German soldiers. Maybe she betrayed him in some way. Along with the other names in the jar.'

'But Trixie's dear friend, Monty, was named in the jar too, so we mustn't jump to conclusions,' Annie reminded them all. 'That could have been for any number of reasons . . .' Her mind was working overtime, frantically trying to find a plausible explanation, something to make sense of it all because it just didn't add up. Not from what she knew about Trixie so far. And she also knew that Joanie would be absolutely horrified if it turned out that Trixie had been involved in any way with the children in the orphanage being taken away by the Germans. And then she remembered the letter. 'Trixie can't have had anything to do with causing harm to Pierre!' Annie stood up and started pacing the pavement, nodding silently and resolutely as she recalled the details in the letter from Paulette, listing out the ingredients in the perfumes, that they'd found in the basement, sensing that she was getting closer to the truth.

'How do you know?' Kristen asked, hopefully.

'OK, let's think about it . . . the letter we found was addressed to Beatrice, telling her that the perfume – a.k.a. Pierre – had arrived safely to wherever Paulette was writing from. She even wrote that it, "*has arrived safely and is quite the sweetest fragrance yet.*"'

'*Ah, oui!*' Maggie nodded, 'and the "sweetest one yet" could be words used to describe a child.'

Silence followed as the three women contemplated the possibilities.

'But it still doesn't change the fact that there's a person up there in that office sitting with a painful memory, the same painful memory my Polish ancestors endured . . . and I made him bring that memory to the forefront of his mind when I had no business doing so.' And Kristen went to stand up. Annie took her hand and gently pulled her back down.

'No, I think it's best we leave him in peace now,' Annie said, swallowing down the knot that was forming in her throat, deeply regretting the intrusion into Monsieur Aumont's office and the horrible reminder of a past he clearly shouldn't be forced to relive. 'I'm going to carefully go through all the other diaries and letters and see if there's any mention of Paulette, the pilot, Jeremy Sutherland, and what happened to him if he didn't arrive with Paulette in one piece, or more information about Monty and what happened to him too – to shed some light on why his name was in the jar.'

'And we will help you!' Kristen said, and Maggie nodded in agreement.

'Thank you. If you're sure?' Annie asked, 'I don't want to take away from your time here in Paris, Kristen, and I know that you're busy in the café, Maggie.'

'But we want to help,' Maggie assured her.

'Yes, it's what friends do,' Kristen nodded, vehemently.

'But you must enjoy your time here in Paris too,' Maggie said. 'With Étienne. Take a chance on romance with him, Annie. I know you said it isn't like that . . . but I think for him it is exactly like that . . . for you too. The romance comes in so many ways. You'll see . . . he has been hurt too, in a different way to you and it takes time. He still loves his wife, I'm sure, and always will, so he has to find the right place now in his heart for her, so that he can let you into another part. And he wants to, I'm convinced of that . . . men don't go to the trouble of finding out what their date's favourite meal is just for anyone, you know. You're special, Annie.'

And Annie gave her friend a hug, no words needed in that moment.

'And then when he's found your place in his heart . . . well, he'll be all over you and I want to be the first to hear about the incredible sex. I bet he'll make love to you in French. Oh God, imagine that,' Kristen grinned, pointing her fingertip in the air and giving them both a cheeky look to see if she was going to get away with the comment. Fortunately for her, they both laughed.

'What do you mean, in French?' Annie spluttered.

'You know!' Kristen's eyes widened, 'he'll say sexy stuff in French. *Je m'appelle Annie* or whatever.' And she clasped a hand to her chest in a dramatic way while doing kissy lips at Annie.

'Sexy stuff?' Maggie howled. 'You just said, "my name is Annie"!' And the three of them fell about laughing.

Once they had all composed themselves, Kristen picked up another piece of paper and, with a serious look on her face now, she said, 'So I reckon we should make a list of all the other names in the jar, too. I have a feeling it's important to know who these people are.'

'Yes, I agree,' Annie said, followed by, 'and see if we can find out what Trixie really did during the Second World War in Paris, instead of relying on hearsay. I don't believe she put those names and dates in a jar because she was a collaborator. I just don't.'

19

Back in the Odette café, upstairs in Annie's bedroom, having sifted through the pile of diaries – the three women having each taken a couple of the eligible ones, undamaged by damp and age, to read through for clues – they came across one written during the Second World War and dated 1940.

My dearest husband, Jacques, is never coming back. I can't bring myself to write the actual word of his passing, for it is so final and my heart is shattered all over again. The news came on the tenth anniversary of our wedding in Monte Carlo in 1930, a glorious affair with all our dear friends there. Even Queenie – my dearest childhood friend – made the journey from Tindledale to be my bridesmaid, although we have lost touch so I haven't seen her since the wedding and she hasn't answered any of my letters since war was declared in 1939. I often think about her and wonder how she is keeping, fondly recalling the time we spent together as children when she was brought in from the village each day to be taught French and German with me. The rudimentary foreign language conversations we had were quite jolly at times, although Queenie was always a much faster learner than I was and picked it all up in next to no time!

But the anniversary of my wedding day is now tainted for ever more. I knew as soon as the post boy pushed the shop door open and asked for Madame Archambeau, removing his cap as he did so, before placing the cable on the counter and leaving swiftly, on to deliver the same crushing news to another wife or mother, no doubt. I hesitated at first, desperate to delay the moment of knowing for sure, my heart suspended in time, but it couldn't last and so I closed the door and turned the sign to Fermé. Then, sitting in the little waiting area, clearing a space on the coffee table, I placed the envelope there next to the magazines heralding another happier time long past that now feels like an eternity ago. Moments later, I could put it off no more and my worst fear became a cruel reality. Jacques, shot by the German Wehrmacht near Maginot. In this dreadful war, the second of its kind, *but we are here again. Did they learn nothing from before? Men, from all countries, hundreds of thousands of them dying senselessly. I recall the last moment I saw Jacques, the scent of his hair oil and tobacco smoke still lingering on my blouse as he glanced over his shoulder and blew me a kiss. His conker-brown eyes twinkling bravely, his beautiful cheekbones lifted in a grin. I had wanted to go after him. To envelop him in my arms one more time. Younger than me, I always thought he'd be the one growing old without me . . . certainly not this.*

After reading the words on the cable over and over through tear-filled eyes, I gathered myself and went in search of Maurice, next door. My dear friend, Maurice, my companion from the jazz days, too old for the French army, mercifully, took my hand in his as he always does and, after planting a kiss, he pulled me to him and let me sob against his chest for the rest of the day and night until we woke to the dreadful sound of the loudspeaker hailing from the motor-car cavalcade of grey-uniformed Nazis invading the streets of Paris. The flag bearing the swastika flying above the Eiffel Tower. The shrill German voice informing us of the curfew. Nobody to be outside in the night-time and through until the morning.

Paris belongs to the enemy now. The ones who took my darling Jacques from me. My first love, Bobby, and my dear brother, Edward, too. And I fear so dreadfully for Monty and his Jewish lover, François, what will become of them? I know what I must do to protect them . . . and what I have always done. I shall endure. I will mix up more potions, perfumes and soothing balms for the people of my cherished gay Paris, suffering at the hands of these devils, and I will carry on. In plain sight as I have always done . . . working with Maurice to do whatever it takes to thwart the enemy.

'Oh Trixie,' Maggie said, a quiver to her voice as she put the diary down on the table and took a sip of her French 75. They were sitting on the balcony, with the view across the cobbled boulevards, enjoying cocktails in the evening sunshine. The faint sound of the accordion floated up to give the moment a truly melancholic feel.

'What is it?' Annie looked up from the diary she was reading, dated 1928, with more about Trixie and the gang still enjoying the roaring Twenties, dancing and hanging out in the jazz clubs where Maurice was dazzling them all with his trombone playing. Monty had been staying with his lover, François, in a hotel for the weekend, and dining in a restaurant together in public for the first time, albeit with Trixie covering for them by posing as Monty's wife when checking into the hotel, with François his 'brother' in the adjoining room.

'Trixie's husband has been killed and the German soldiers have arrived in Paris!' Maggie turned the diary around so Annie and Kristen could see for themselves. Both read in silence – Annie shaking her head, Kristen biting her bottom lip. Maggie went to turn the page.

'Wait!' Kristen suddenly leant forward and tapped the corner of the page. 'Maurice! See this line here . . .' She carefully hovered her finger over the words. 'Next door! Do you think Trixie means the apartment next to hers? There was another bell in the hallway, wasn't there?' And she went to stand up.

'*No!*' Annie and Maggie quickly exclaimed. Then, 'We are not going there and making that mistake for a second time today,' Annie said, firmly. 'Besides, the man who lives in the apartment next to Trixie's can't possibly be the same Maurice that she writes about in her diary – he's elderly but he's not that elderly. She first meets him in a jazz club in 1926, when presumably he's an adult, and that was nearly a hundred years ago!'

'OK, you got me,' Kristen said, her American accent

suddenly sounding stronger. 'I never was any good at math in school.' She shrugged and smiled wryly. 'But he still might have known Trixie . . .'

'Yes, he might, but he was very distressed when he saw me with Étienne in the garden, so the last thing we need to do is upset him too. I will try to chat to him when I'm back at the apartment tomorrow.'

'I'd offer to come and help translate but I'm going to be flat out here in the café tomorrow with a birthday lunch for thirty people,' Maggie said. 'Will Étienne be there to help?'

'Yes, he will, although Étienne's presence in the garden seemed to scare the elderly man, but he has a carer so we'll speak to her first and see if she can broach the subject of Trixie with him,' Annie said.

'Good idea,' Maggie nodded.

'And I guess we can definitely assume that Trixie wasn't in cahoots with the German soldiers and didn't betray the people whose names are in the jar,' Annie pointed out. 'Not after reading this last section of her diary. Poor Trixie, she sure suffered terribly in her life . . . such a lot of heartbreak.'

'And, I'm afraid there's more!' Maggie said, turning towards the end of the diary. 'Here,' she showed them by carefully pointing to a passage about Monty.

A Postcard from Paris

Dearest Monty, I worry he cannot bear much more of the fear he and François endure. Monty is constantly afraid to be heard speaking on the street in case his French is marked out as foreign. Queer. And an Englishman. The enemy. And the soldiers take him away. Maurice and I have taught him to perfection so Monty sounds like a genuine Frenchman now, and with none of his gentle tendencies, so the Wehrmacht have no reason to mark him out for checks and humiliation, but still he is fearful. Maurice has acquired the correct papers for Monty to pass as a French citizen, at great risk to himself, for he would surely face torture and execution if caught resisting the Germans in this way. But Maurice is passionate about defending our beloved Paris, as I am too. So I have assured Monty that he will be safe, even though in my heart I am constantly on alert for him.

His body is so thin now, with the food shortages and lack of daylight from hiding away in his apartment; he is a shadow of his former flamboyant self, scared after hearing the stories of what happens to men like him and François, taken away to the camps to be humiliated with pink triangles pinned to their jackets and cruelly used as target practice for the German soldiers, experiments as well to 'cure' them of their sexual persuasion. Monty and I have spoken about an escape plan for him and François, but they fear being captured with the road blockades and train checks at every point from Paris to the coast, making it impossible to find a way for them to reach England, and Monty cannot bear to try to escape on his own and leave François behind, for fear he will be caught in the next round-up of Jews. Monty says he wishes never to return to England where he is sure to be vilified again as he was all those years ago. He still cannot be free there, for relations with a man are unlawful, but his life here is a prison too, so it is hopeless for him. I continue to pray for him every night, as I did in the field camp at the start and end of every shift. It is the only way. Please God, let it be over soon so Monty and François can live freely in peace without fear of persecution.

'It's so dreadful, I can't even imagine having to live in such fear,' Annie muttered, scanning the pages for more, but the rest of that year's diary was ominously empty. But she was sure her hunch was right now, after reading the bit about Maurice obtaining fake papers for Monty . . . Trixie and Maurice were working with the French Resistance.

'And no wonder Trixie hid the diaries away inside the wall,' Kristen puffed, her nostrils flaring in indignation, 'I would have as well, if I had been living here in Paris during the German Occupation, because I too would have wanted to make damn sure there was a record for someone to find in years to come. What's the point of staying silent? To stay silent in the face of injustice where children are carted off in trucks – people persecuted for their sexuality – and then to do nothing, not even record that it had happened, is . . . well, it makes you complicit as far as I'm concerned! Hell, I would have written down every single detail. Oh yes!'

'I agree, plus Trixie would have been scared too, surely, of being exposed as an Englishwoman, given that Britain was at war with Germany,' Annie said.

'Yes, it must have been terrifying for Trixie and her friends. She actually mentions teaching Monty how to talk in French like a native, and we know that she spoke German too, so maybe she was able to blend in and not draw attention to herself. She was Madame Archambeau, after all,' Maggie added. 'What we still don't know is why she gave the perfume to the head of the Gestapo and allowed herself to be photographed for a newspaper fraternizing and shaking his hand?'

'And how she's connected to Joanie, the main reason

for my being here,' Annie sighed, fearing that they might never know.

'Are there any more diaries?' Kristen asked, helping herself to another almond croissant.

'Afraid not,' Annie replied, despondently. She was just about to take a second croissant too when her mobile rang. 'Ooh, it's my friend, Beth,' she told the others brightly, wiping her fingers on a napkin before picking up her phone. 'Mind if I take this?' And she stood up.

'Of course not. Go ahead, I'll make us some more coffee and give you some space,' Maggie smiled, picking up the empty cups before bustling over to the kitchen.

'I'll give you a hand,' Kristen said, carrying the croissant in her mouth as she tidied up and then took plates and cutlery to the kitchen too.

Annie mouthed her thanks as she tapped the screen and then heard her best friend's bubbly voice talking all the way from Australia, instantly transporting her back to a few months ago when they were seated side by side on her couch together, sharing a bottle of rosé and having a laugh as they put the worlds to rights. Annie still missed her so much, but felt happy that she was living her dream . . .

20

'Beth, how are you? How is Australia treating you? Is the weather still amazing?' Annie said, conscious that she was babbling, but she couldn't help it, she was keen to have a good catch-up. The last few times Annie had tried to call Beth, she hadn't answered, or if she had, she had quickly said that she couldn't talk and would call back in a bit, but hadn't done so. And Annie hadn't wanted to badger her. She knew Beth was incredibly busy with singing at the opera house every evening, and with the time difference it was tricky too. But in the back of her mind, Annie had started to wonder what else was going on as it was unlike Beth to be distant with her. Yes, she was on the other side of the world, but she hadn't responded to the WhatsApp messages Annie had sent to her in the last couple of days, even though Annie could see from the blue ticks that they had been read. So she hoped everything was OK and it was a relief to hear from her best friend.

'Yes, it's all good here. How are you?' Beth answered brightly, but Annie immediately sensed something else in the air. Or could it be that Beth was in a hurry? Maybe she had a rehearsal or something to get to.

'I'm great, thanks. Beth, are you definitely OK?' Annie found herself feeling tentative, a little awkward even. Beth was usually really chatty and would have launched into an extremely effervescent account of what she had been doing by now or would have asked to hear more about Paris or what was happening with Étienne, but now she seemed uncharacteristically flat.

'Yes, I'm fine, thanks.'

'Great,' Annie repeated, instinctively knowing something wasn't right. 'Is everything OK between us?'

'Oh yes, I err . . .' A short silence followed. 'But, there is something actually, Annie,' Beth said, hesitantly.

'Oh?'

'Yes . . . it's Phoebe.'

'What do you mean? Has she been in touch?' Annie asked, and wasn't quite sure how to feel about it if she had, as the last few times Annie had tried contacting Phoebe she had either not answered or had responded to a message with a very short reply.

'Yes. Yes she has, and she wants to come and visit me in Australia, which is fine, of course. I've missed her, but—'

'Did she say when?' Annie jumped in.

'Right away, which is why I am calling you as she seemed very keen. Almost like she couldn't wait to leave England and get away . . . It set off an alarm bell, if you know what I mean?'

'Well, yes, sure, I do know what you mean as she told me she couldn't get away at the moment – that she was too busy with her classes,' Annie started, feeling confused, 'this was when I asked her to join me here in Paris. I thought a change of scenery might do her good.'

'Ah, yes, she mentioned that.'

'Oh! What else did she say?' Annie asked tentatively, wondering what was going on.

'Well, she said that she wasn't sure you really wanted her there with you in Paris, which I thought was a bit odd as I couldn't imagine you feeling that way.'

'How strange. Of course I want her here!' Annie said, her voice jumping an octave. 'Why wouldn't I?' Another silence followed as Annie tried to think why Phoebe would feel this way. 'Has she split up from Jack? Is that why she wants to get away? Maybe I should go home and see if she's all right. I shouldn't be here going on dates and such like, and trying to work out how complete strangers are connected to Joanie, it's not right, not if Phoebe needs me, I should—'

'Annie, hang on a second! Please, just listen for a minute . . .'

'What do you mean? Maybe just tell me what's really going on,' Annie suggested, a swirl of worry in the pit of her stomach now.

'OK,' Beth took a big breath, followed by a long sigh. 'Right. Well, probably best if I just come out with it . . .'

'Yes,' Annie said, with more conviction than she actually felt.

'Right, OK, so here goes . . .' Annie heard Beth clearing her throat, as if preparing herself to impart bad news, but before she could hazard a guess as to what it might be, Beth told her: 'Phoebe has asked me to tell you that she has an eating disorder and took an overdose and wants to come and stay with me in Australia.'

'What?' Annie gasped, completely stunned, clasping a hand to her throat as she felt all the air whoosh from her body. A million thoughts suddenly hurtled through her mind, making her feel light-headed now. Why? How? When? No. No. No. And most importantly, why didn't she know? Her own daughter was ill. Suffering. And she hadn't even noticed. What kind of a mother did that make her? And a wave of guilt made Annie feel physically sick now. She reached for a glass of water and downed it in one. She stood up and began walking towards the kitchen, but Maggie and Kristen must have gone outside or upstairs as they weren't there. Annie went back to the table and sat down, took a deep breath and willed herself to try to think straight.

'Annie, are you still there?'

'Um, yes,' she managed after a few seconds.

'I'm so sorry,' Beth said, quietly.

'Oh Beth, I don't know what to say or do,' Annie said, her mind still boggling 'Please, tell me what exactly did she say?' And Annie burst into tears. The news was devastating. She couldn't hold her emotions in any longer. She felt ashamed. That she hadn't noticed. That she hadn't heard Phoebe's cry for help. It made sense now, Phoebe asking Annie to retire and move in with her. She must have wanted her close by. And how long had she been feeling this way?

'Annie, darling, please don't cry. God, I wish I wasn't here. Miles away when you need me most.'

'I have to go home!' Annie managed in between sobs. 'I need to see Phoebe. I'll get a train today, or a flight, and can be in Yorkshire by,' she glanced at her watch, it was lunchtime now, 'later tonight.'

'Annie, please. Listen to me. Phoebe is already on her way to the airport.'

'But she can't be. She needs me. I need to find a

hospital. A specialist clinic to help her. I have to do something. She tried to kill herself!'

'Annie, please, listen . . . I need to reassure you and it's important you hear this . . . I've spoken to her at length. She called me a few days ago and we talked for a good few hours, and we've spoken a few more times since then. The overdose was a cry for help, she recognizes that – it was paracetamol and some vodka and then she stopped, realizing that she needed help. Jack was in the house and he took care of her. He wanted to call you right away but she pleaded with him not to – I've spoken to him too.'

'OK,' Annie said, her panic subsiding slightly.

'Annie, it's a good thing that Phoebe's facing this.'

'How do you work that out?' Annie said, a little more aggressively than she meant to.

'Because if she recognizes the issue for herself then it's far easier for her to get the help she needs in order to get better.'

'But I only spoke to her a little while ago and she said everything was fine, that I didn't need to worry, in fact.' Annie remembered the conversation clearly; she had asked Phoebe about the Instagram post with the ice cream.

'Yes, she mentioned that. I think she . . .' Beth paused as if keen to pick her words carefully. 'Well, I got the impression that she felt she might have been getting a telling off!'

'Oh . . .' Annie had a strange feeling, like sand trickling through her fingers and she couldn't do anything to stop it. 'But I wasn't . . . I was just worried. You see, I knew there was something up. Something bothering her. I thought it was me. She seemed annoyed with me when I didn't want to move up to Yorkshire.'

'And why would you? Phoebe can't expect you to uproot your whole life for her.'

'But I'm her mum, I should be there for her,' Annie sniffed, the tears still flowing.

'And Phoebe is an adult. You have to let her take responsibility for herself, Annie. You are a wonderful mum. You've given Phoebe everything in life. And most of all, you've given her love. Lots of it. In fact, I'd go as far as to say that Phoebe hasn't wanted for anything!'

'Then why is this happening? Why does she have an eating disorder? Why would she contemplate taking her own life, if only for a moment? What did I do wrong?'

'You didn't do anything wrong,' Beth said, gently. 'And please don't drive yourself mad thinking and analysing about everything that's been said or done in Phoebe's life. She told me the therapist has been—'

'Hold on. The therapist? She has a therapist?' Annie couldn't keep up. But she felt rubbish on realizing that she had been having the time of her life in Paris, making new friends, riding around on the back of a scooter as if she hadn't a care in the world, eating steak on boats and marvelling at the Eiffel Tower bathed in glitter, while the whole time her own child had been suffering.

'Yes, she's been seeing a therapist for a few months now, apparently. And please, don't chastise her for that. She's taken responsibility.'

'But why didn't she tell me? I'm hurt that she couldn't confide in me,' Annie said, instantly regretting the sound of self-pity, for this wasn't about her, she got that, but still . . . it was painful to feel shut out like this.

'She didn't want to let you down,' Beth said, gently. 'And sometimes it's hardest of all to talk to the ones who are closest to us.'

'Oh God,' Annie cried, and her mind went to all the times Phoebe had irritated her with her need for control. How she had lectured Annie over her alcohol and food choices, not to mention the work ethic, how she set impossibly high standards for herself. And how Annie had laughed it off or had been flippant, judgmental in return even, in saying Phoebe should relax a bit. She had even implied that Phoebe should maybe lighten up with Jack when they had split up that time. Had she somehow made her daughter feel that she wasn't enough? Inadequate? No wonder Phoebe had shut her out when that had happened. It was as if a new light had been cast over the events and Annie could see them differently now.

'And Phoebe didn't want you to blame yourself. I know you will,' Beth said, as if reading her mind. 'But please, Annie, lots of how Phoebe feels is to do with image and the impossibly unrealistic expectations these days for young people to look a certain way. And then there are the issues with Mark.'

'Mark?' Annie asked, wondering for a moment if he had been in touch with Phoebe after having drifted away for practically her whole life. And a sudden surge of panic mingled with fury charged right through her. Had he said something to Phoebe? Something to hurt her? Had he let himself be influenced by his wife, yet again? Why would he keep doing that? Couldn't he see what he was doing to his daughter? The damage and hurt he had caused her . . .

'Yes, I know you did everything you could to make up for his failings as a dad, giving her and Johnny as much love as you could, so, again, don't blame yourself,' Beth told her. 'It was clear from talking to Phoebe that she has low self-esteem and she feels angry with Mark. She mentioned not even really knowing her dad or if he even "gives a shit about her", to put it into her own words. I guess she's been dealing with those strong emotions for a very long time.'

Letting the news sink in, Annie found a tissue in her pocket and used it to dry her face. After taking a deep breath she swallowed hard and forced herself to get a handle on the situation. To figure out what was best for Phoebe because that's what mattered most right now.

'Beth, please, tell me what I need to do?' she asked her oldest friend, the person who knew her best and who she trusted with her life. 'I'm scared, and I need to get this right.'

'Let her go! Jack is coming with her so she isn't travelling alone. And when they get here, I will spend some time with her. I've already found a fantastic clinic here in Sydney where she can stay for a week and—'

'But what about your work? Your singing? And the cost? The clinic will be expensive. And the gym? Phoebe has worked really hard to make it a success. What will happen to that? No, I really should come home. Maybe I should move to Yorkshire after all.' Annie was figuring it all out as she spoke. She had some savings, and she could always sell her house and move in with Phoebe to look after her. The proceeds of the house could pay for her treatment.

'Oh, Annie, I don't think you need to do that. And

please don't take this the wrong way, as it's only natural that you want to do everything you can for Phoebe, but she has said this is part of the reason she hasn't been able to talk to you about it.'

'What do you mean?'

'Um, well . . . I don't want you to feel hurt any more than you already do right now by saying this . . . but she feels that you're a bit intense.'

'OK, did she say more? In what way?' Annie asked, pushing her own hurt feelings aside to listen to why her daughter felt this way, so that she could try to understand.

'That you've always gone over and above for her – with the cheerleading, the tournaments, the costumes, the extra tuition. And I know you've always had her best interests at heart . . . but that's a lot of pressure too. A pressure that Phoebe has then put on herself . . . and well, look, let's not analyse and speculate on this. Let's deal with this together so we can support her, what do you say?'

'I say, thank you.' And Annie could feel the tears pricking in her eyes all over again. Her dear friend wasn't judging her. Blaming her. She was helping. Keen to do whatever it took to make sure her daughter was going to be OK. And what did it matter that Phoebe had turned to her godmother for help, instead of her . . .?

Surely what mattered most was that her daughter had found the strength to ask for help in the first place . . .

'Darling, you don't need to thank me. It's what we do, we've always done . . . we're in this together. You've always been there for me. It's my turn to be there for you this time and I know there will be other times when it will swap over again. Back and forth, that's how the best friendships work.' Annie could see in her mind's eye, Beth tilting her head and doing that thing she always did when they had a heart to heart – she'd be flapping a hand in front of her eyes so as not to ruin her immaculate eye make-up when the tears of emotion came. And sure enough, as if right on cue, Beth sniffed and added, 'God, I'm going to cry now.'

'Oh, don't, or you'll set me off again,' Annie said, feeling a little lighter as the fear lifted further. There was a long way to go, but she knew that Phoebe would be in safe hands with Beth, and with Jack to support her too. It was time to step back and let her daughter be the strong, independent, resilient woman she knew that she was and would continue to be.

'And don't worry about the gym – Phoebe has a manager in place to run things while she is away.'

'OK, well that's good,' Annie said, pleased that Phoebe was able to do this. Surely this was a positive sign. 'I'll pay for the clinic though,' she quickly added, keen to do something, not yet quite able to take a full step back.

'Phoebe has that covered too,' Beth said. 'Honestly, Annie, she really is dealing with this. And she is sorry that she hasn't talked to you herself about it yet . . . she promised she would though, after I had spoken to you. And I'm actually really looking forward to having her here, I've been feeling lonely . . .'

'Oh Beth, why didn't you say so? Let's try to chat more.' Annie shook her head, 'I've missed you too.'

'Sorry I haven't made as much effort recently as I should have,' said Beth. 'I've seen your messages and then, well . . . I've been distracted and I guess I was also avoiding having to tell you about Phoebe, as I knew it was going to hurt you and that's the last thing I would ever want to do.'

'I understand. It's a difficult situation to be in,' Annie said. 'And you've had a whole new life to set up on the other side of the world.'

'And the time difference is taking some getting used to; there have been moments when I've wanted to call you to share a laugh or my excitement about something that has just happened, but then I realize it's the middle of the night and that you're most likely fast asleep.'

'Oh, Beth, I have too!' Annie said, remembering the moment on Étienne's boat.

'We need to get ourselves organized and sort out a regular phone call or a Zoom chat. A weekly date, at least.'

'I'd love that,' Annie said, her heart lifting.

'Me too. Annie, I have to go now but let's talk later and sort it out properly.'

'Sure. Take care, Beth. I love you.'

'I love you too, Annie. And thank you for trusting me to take care of Phoebe. I said I would, without hesitation, when she called, but only if you agreed. I want you to know that, and I know she's my goddaughter, but I would never take over without talking to you first. Phoebe knows that she and Jack would be turning right around and going back home if you weren't comfortable with her coming all this way to me in these circumstances.'

'Oh, Beth, of course I agree. I'm pleased and relieved that she turned to you. But she is an adult and I can't, not that I would, stop her, so thank you for considering my feelings. And for helping me understand,' Annie told her best friend.

'Always, Annie, you know that. It's hard to take a step back sometimes and see what's happening . . . especially when it's your child.'

'Yes. Yes it is!' Annie agreed.

After ending the call, Annie took a moment to let

it all sink in. She felt as though she was agreeing to the hardest thing she had ever had to when all her natural instincts were making her want to go straight to Phoebe and look after her. But who better to be there for her daughter, when she needed it the most, than Annie's best friend who had been like a sister to her. And Beth was right . . . it was time for her to let Phoebe grow up. To trust that she had brought her daughter up as best she could, as fully equipped as possible to deal with all the adversities and challenges that she would inevitably face in life. Annie knew that she had to take a step back and let Phoebe go in the hope of her coming back to her.

She placed her phone on the table and took a moment to gather herself. Inhaling through her nose and out through her mouth, her hands pressed on her thighs, she momentarily closed her eyes and willed her daughter to be OK. To get better and be happy and to have hope for a brighter future. Annie also wished that she could hold Phoebe, stroke her hair and tell her she loved her, just as she had when she was a little girl. And then, as if some special kind of intervention had read Annie's thoughts, her phone buzzed. She turned the phone over so as to see the screen. And there she was. Her daughter. Annie quickly pressed to answer.

'Hello, Mum.'

'Hello, Phoebe, sweetheart . . . how are you—'

'Mum,' Phoebe cut in. 'I'm at the airport, but Aunty Beth just called me and so I wanted to call you to tell you that I love you.'

'I love you too, darling. Very, very much.' Annie blinked back tears and she scanned Phoebe's face, searching her eyes for a sign, something to show that her daughter really was going to be OK, that she was going to get through this. Then, as if reading her mind, Phoebe told her.

'I'm going to be fine, Mum. I promise.'

21

The following morning, after a restless night's sleep, Annie got up and sat on the balcony of her bedroom, at around four thirty, to see the plump golden sun rise over the roofs of Paris. As she bathed in the beautiful sight set out before her, the pink cherry-blossom trees amid the soft-grey-slate-topped roofs, the shuttered windows and burst of colourful, tumbling geraniums, she reflected on the phone call from Beth and how the sun brought a sense of renewal. This was the start of a fresh day, with a fresh set of opportunities and moments for her to see things in a different way. To try to trust that Phoebe was going to get well. Annie felt as though she had been so focused on her own life and the changes she wanted to make that she had inadvertently taken her eye off the ball with her children. Yes, they were grown-up now, but that didn't mean they didn't still need her. All that had been going on with Phoebe had happened right in front of Annie, literally, with all the FaceTime calls, and she hadn't noticed enough. Not properly seen her. Of course, she had known something was going on for Phoebe, but she also knew that she wanted to do better from now on. Pay more attention. So, after breakfast, she had called Johnny, and at first he had been worried to hear from her.

On answering the phone he had asked whether something had happened. He then remarked that it was unlike her to call him . . . and this had been a stark wake-up call that her son's perception was that he never heard from his mum. But then when she explained that she missed him and just wanted to chat and see how he was, he had been thoroughly happy to hear from her and had even said that he missed her too. But he didn't want to bother her with phone calls or visits as he knew how busy she was with work! And to think that she had always presumed it was the other way round. He also explained that he had only said to Phoebe that her suggestion about Annie moving up to Yorkshire was a good idea, because he thought it might bring the three of them closer together. With his university in Sheffield, it would mean that he could come home more often and not just for Christmas. But then later, having thought about it, Johnny had decided to take up the chance to spend his next year of university on the exchange programme at an affiliated campus in Arizona, where he could travel around America and study the meteor craters in exciting places like the Grand Canyon. Annie was thrilled for him having such an exhilarating opportunity, even if it did mean that he wouldn't make it home for next Christmas. But there would be more Christmases and this was a once-in-a-lifetime opportunity, he had said, and she had firmly agreed that he should go for it. She didn't want Johnny to miss his chance, as she had with her dream of having an interior design business all those years ago.

And now, Annie had just arrived in Cour Felice to work on getting the curtains finished. Keen to keep busy, at least until Beth called to tell her Phoebe was with her and where she knew that she would be OK, Annie figured it was the best course of action. Maggie and Kristen, after asking her about the phone call, had both offered to come with her to the apartment so she wouldn't be on her own with her worrying thoughts – Étienne was arriving after lunch as Bijou had a trip to the vet already scheduled for her booster vaccines. Maggie had even offered to swap her shift with the café manager so she could join Annie after all. But Annie was looking forward to the sewing, to feeling the fabric beneath her fingertips. The monotony of it was soothing, she found, and she was also looking forward to spending time alone with Trixie, which she knew sounded a bit daft, but Annie could feel her presence there. And it was calming. Refined, and bold too, it gave Annie a sense of clarity, being in Trixie's apartment enabled her to properly think.

By lunchtime, Annie had finished the curtains and had just plugged in the old electric iron that she had found in Trixie's kitchen cupboard, when her phone rang. It was Joanie. After unplugging the iron, Annie went into the sitting room and sat down on the window seat so she could look at the Parisian view as she chatted to Joanie.

'Hello love, it's me,' Joanie said as she always did to start a conversation, and Annie liked the familiarity of it. 'How are you?'

'Oh, hi Joanie, I'm fine,' she said, deciding not to tell her about Phoebe. It would only worry her. 'It's lovely to hear from you, how are you? Is everything OK?' Annie asked, as it was unusual for Joanie to call her; she wasn't one for chatting on the phone and only switched her mobile phone on when she was expecting a call and happened to be away from home, which was hardly ever.

'I'm very well, and I have a bit of news for you,' she said, excitedly. 'I'm just getting my pad so I can tell you all about it. Are you OK to hang on for a bit?'

'Sure, take your time, Joanie, no rush,' she smiled, intrigued to know what Joanie was excited about. Plus it gave her a few seconds to drink in more of the glorious view – the cobbled streets and the tall, majestic buildings leading down to the Eiffel Tower on the horizon. Annie had grown to love this view, having sat here several times now, contemplating and daydreaming and wondering what Trixie had been thinking about when she had done the same. Did she sit here and muse over her exhilarating nights with her friends in the jazz clubs? Plan her wedding in glamorous Monte Carlo? And grieve for poor Jacques and worry about her dear friend, Monty, and his lover, François, which got Annie thinking about the names and messages in the jar again, figuring there must be more hidden in the apartment. Something else, another diary, a letter, a clue of some kind as to what happened next. Why is Monty's name in the jar? Pierre's too, and the pilot's? The others as well. Annie, Maggie and Kristen had counted twenty-seven names in total. But were still no nearer to discovering the truth.

'Got it, duck. And sorry, I should have got myself organized before I phoned you. Now, are you still there?' she puffed, presumably from the exertion of bustling around her front room and easing herself into the comfy chair by the fireplace. Annie could picture her doing so, just as she had always done for the decades that they had been friends.

'Yes, I'm still here.' Annie turned her attention back to Joanie.

'Right. Well, I want to tell you about my trip. Sandra and I had a lovely drive out with her daughter and her fiancé – did I tell you Sandra's daughter is getting married next month?'

'Yes, you did,' Annie reminded her, wondering where this was going.

'Oh, yes. That's right. Silly me. I'd forget my own name some days,' and she chuckled. 'And he's a lovely fella. Very clean, you know, as in polished shoes, you don't see that much these days, and none of that bushy beard they all have, and a nice white collar, and perfect manners too. He opened the car door for me and gave me his elbow to help me out from the back seat when we stopped to have a spot of lunch in the lovely pub there. Gorgeous it was. Right on the village green. And with a splendid duck pond. We even had a little mooch along the high street and I treated them all to a cream cake in a quaint teashop with those cute little round mullion windows. A proper café too, it was, with table-cloths and teapots. Not like you get in the supermarket café or the garden centre.' She paused to draw breath and Annie took the chance to ask where it was that she had visited. 'Tindledale!' she said, as if it was obvious, and Annie smiled, keen to hear all about it. 'I told Sandra what you had found out in Trixie's diary and she was ever so intrigued. I was too, so we thought we'd make a day of it and get her daughter, Laura, to take us there so we could see for ourselves. And you'll never guess what?'

'What's that?' Annie asked, sitting upright, excited to know.

'Well, we saw the name of Trixie's brother, Edward, on the war memorial. Bold as brass it was, right there near the top . . . with it going in alphabetical order and his surname being Crawford and all.'

'Really?' Annie was amazed. It might seem like just a small detail, but it somehow brought him alive. An actual real person, in the English village where he had lived, and not just an old black-and-white picture with a stuffy, serious, unsmiling face from a past long gone, or a name in an old diary.

'Yes dear. And thankfully, there wasn't a long list of names – about twenty or so – still, far too many young men to have sacrificed their lives for us. And it's a very small village so it would have been a huge blow to have lost that many young men,' Joanie sighed, and Annie could hear her turning the page on her pad. 'And that's not all.'

'Ooh, tell me, Joanie, I'm intrigued, did you find out about a connection, something linking you to the Crawford family?' Annie asked, momentarily holding her breath, not even daring to ask if she had found something that connected her directly to Trixie in case she hadn't and they would never know . . .

'Well, I got chatting to a very nice old lady in the tearoom. The Spotted Pig it was called. Fancy that, it's a funny name for a café, isn't it?'

'It is a bit,' Annie agreed.

'Hettie she was called, the old lady. And she's retired now, of course; must be in her eighties, at least, or even ninety, as she was quite frail, but sharp as a pin. She has a haberdashery shop there and I said what a shame it was that we weren't staying in Tindledale for longer than the afternoon as I would have liked to have visited her shop and stocked up on my knitting supplies. But I've promised to pop back another time. Anyway, I'm digressing, dear. So, I told Hetty about Trixie, Beatrice to be exact, and she said that she knew the name. She had definitely heard of the Crawford family – a very well-to-do set, aristocracy, and there had been a rumour of a wayward daughter who had run off to Paris to work as a topless showgirl in the 1920s but it was all hush-hush and this had been a very long time ago, certainly before Hettie was even born. And she had a vague memory of when she was a child and the adults were talking about Beatrice's stepmother, Mrs Crawford, dying, this would have been around the start of the Second World War. Lily, she thought she was called, or possibly Iris – definitely a flower, she said.'

'Yes, that's right!' Annie jumped in excitedly. 'She was called Iris, and Trixie wasn't too fond of her from what I've read in her diaries. Iris sounds like a bit of a harridan, to be honest, who criticized Trixie all the time.'

'That sounds about right, as later on when Sandra persuaded us to have another pot of tea – it's what she's used to, you see, dear, in the luxury place where she lives – they come round and just top you up whenever you want more,' Joanie said, sounding very impressed, and Annie hoped they would manage to sell the Parisian apartment and shop for enough money so that Joanie, in her late seventies now, could have her dream home too. Although Annie had grown so attached to Trixie and her lovely little apartment on Cour Felice that she wasn't sure how she was going to feel about Trixie's beautiful belongings being packed up or sold at auction, the apartment emptied and strangers moving in with no idea or interest in the woman who had spent the majority of her life living within it.

'A friend of Hettie's – Marigold – came in the café, and she said that she remembers her mother saying good riddance when Iris passed, and that she wasn't a patch on the first Mrs Crawford. A proper gentle-woman she was, apparently. She adored her daughter and was often seen out in the fields picking flowers and waving with a jolly smile whenever anyone rambled across their land. Whereas the other wife would bellow at them to stop trespassing or she would set the dogs on them.'

'Wow, it sounds fascinating,' Annie said, taking it all in and loving hearing the little snippets of detail from living people who actually knew of Beatrice's family all those years ago.

'It does, doesn't it? Anyway, I gave my phone number to Hettie and she said that if anything else comes to mind then she's going to give me a call, which was very nice of her indeed.'

'It sure was, Joanie,' Annie said.

'Well, I'll say goodbye now, lovey, and not take up any more of your time.'

'Oh, you're not, it's lovely to talk to you,' Annie assured her. 'And I've almost finished the curtains. I'll send you a picture when I've hung them up.'

'Thank you. You're a treasure, dear, and thank you for doing this for me – getting the flat and shop spruced up and finding out what you can about Beatrice's life. It's all been so fascinating hearing about her in the 1920s and her friends, Queenie, Monty and Maurice. But I hope you've managed to have a bit of a holiday too while you're there?'

'I have. It's been amazing. And thank you for asking me to come and take a look at the apartment. For giving me the nudge to venture out, literally, of my comfort zone.'

'Oh, don't be silly . . . you're a marvellous friend to help me out with it,' Joanie chuckled.

'Well, you've always been a marvellous friend to me, Joanie. And coming to Paris was just the thing I needed . . . I've realized that even more since being here.'

22

The next day, and Annie and Maggie were waiting by the door in the hallway as the elderly man they had met in the garden had left a message, written in French, in the mailbox for them to call in. The note had been signed by a woman called Ingrid, his carer perhaps . . .

'Do you think we should go? Maybe the carer isn't there and the man can't make it to the door – I don't want to antagonize him further,' Annie said. 'He was ever so distressed in the garden that last time.'

'Maybe we can leave a note . . . to thank him for the invite and we are sorry to have missed him on this occasion, but can come back another time,' Maggie suggested, fishing inside her bag for a pen. 'Do you have any paper, or something I can write on?'

'No, but upstairs in the apartment, Trixie has a notebook on the counter in the kitchen,' Annie said, remembering seeing it there – sadly it hadn't any writing inside – no more clues about her life and connection to Joanie. 'I could get it.' But just as Annie went to leave, the door of the other apartment opened and the elderly man was standing there with a confused look on his face which broke into a wide smile when Annie turned back around.

'*Trixie! Ma chère amie, où étais-tu?*' and he shuffled forward with his hands outstretched as if to clasp hers. Annie looked at Maggie.

'He thinks you're Trixie,' she said, subtly out of the side of her mouth as she leant into Annie and translated, 'my dear friend, where have you been?'

'Oh, I'm sorry, I—' But before Annie could say anything else, a younger woman, in her sixties or seventies perhaps, with warm brown eyes and black curly hair swept up into an elegant chignon, came to the door and said something in French. Maggie replied and then translated for Annie to explain that the woman was his daughter visiting from her home ten miles away in La Varenne-Saint-Hilaire. On hearing Maggie translate into English for Annie, the woman then put out her hand and introduced herself directly to Annie in perfect English.

'Hello, I'm Ingrid. Come in, my father is very pleased to see you. He says you are friends, how do you know each other?' she smiled warmly, shaking Annie's hand and then Maggie's.

'Well, we don't exactly know each other, we met just recently in the garden . . .' Annie explained, as she and Maggie followed Ingrid into a lovely bright room with the same floor-to-ceiling windows as Trixie's apartment, but sadly without the view of Paris. The view here was of the garden with glass doors leading directly out to it. Presumably the doors that the man had appeared from when Annie had been tidying the herb garden. 'You see, I'm looking after the apartment upstairs, Trixie's old apartment,' she clarified. 'My friend, Joanie, in England has recently inherited the apartment and the shop below and so I'm here to help get it ready for sale.'

'Ah, yes, Father said that you were in the garden and that he wanted to talk to you, this is why I left the note for you. And my grandfather was friends with Trixie for many, many years,' Ingrid told them over her shoulder as she helped settle her father into an armchair with a lovely, sunny view of the garden, and then to Annie and Maggie she said, 'Please, take a seat.' She then said something to him in French and Annie heard her mention Trixie so assumed that she was explaining who Annie was. But the man appeared to get upset, shaking his head and saying, *'Non, non, ce n'est pas possible,'* over and over again. His rheumy eyes were watering and his papery hands twisting together in distress.

'I'm so sorry, I didn't mean to upset you . . .' Annie started, going to lean forward to offer a soothing hand to the man. But instead he leant forward and whispered something to her, placing his hand covertly to the side of his mouth as if not wanting Ingrid or Maggie to hear what he was saying. He then tapped the side of his nose and winked at Annie. She glanced at Ingrid who subtly shook her head and smiled sadly.

'My father, he gets confused, it's the dementia,' she said, looking at her hands folded in her lap. 'He is convinced you are Trixie; maybe it is the English you are speaking as Trixie was English, although she rarely spoke in English, mostly French, but she used to help me with my studying . . . this is why I learned English so well.' And she did a little laugh, lifting her eyes as if recalling fond memories.

'So you actually knew Trixie?' Annie asked, astounded, and feeling a little foolish for not coming to talk to them sooner. She could feel her heart rate quicken in anticipation of finding out who Trixie really was, and hopefully the connection to Joanie too, who would be over the moon to finally know.

'Ah, yes, of course!' Ingrid shrugged. 'She live here a long time and was very kind to my father. Especially when his mother died in the war, she took care of him as her own child and then also took care of me when my own mother died too.'

'I'm sorry to hear that,' Annie said.

'Thank you. It was a very long time ago. My mother died in 1964. But Trixie made sure we were OK; she looked after me when my father was working at night in the theatre – he's a pianist. Not that he's played for a long time now.' And she smiled over at him. 'A musician like my grandfather. Trixie always used to say that nobody played the trombone better than Maurice.'

'Maurice!' Maggie said at the same time as Annie. The two women looked at each other.

'Yes, that's right. My grandfather, he is Maurice . . .'

'Wow!' Annie was dumbfounded. She had read about Maurice, the trombone player who had dazzled Trixie in the jazz club when she'd first met him in 1926. And now here they were meeting his son and granddaughter. 'I've read about Maurice, your grandfather, Trixie and he were very close . . .' She quickly stopped talking, suddenly wondering if she had said too much. And what would Ingrid think of her going through Trixie's things? 'I, I'm sorry, I . . . I found some old diaries in the apartment and was keen to learn about Trixie's life and how she is connected.'

'It's good,' Ingrid waved a hand. 'It is quite right to want to know about Trixie. She was a wonderful woman. Kind to me, and courageous too, from what my father has told me. Although she never spoke about her life before I was born but I know she did remarkable things in the war. She helped people. She gave this apartment to my grandfather too. The whole house was hers, from her family, I believe, and she had this section downstairs made into a home for my grandparents when my father was just a young boy – the garden was a place for him to play – this was before the Second World War in the 1930s. You see, my grandparents didn't have a home of their own and nobody would rent a place to them – my grandmother was white and Maurice, my grandfather, black.' And she turned to her father and spoke to him gently, patting the back of his hand for reassurance as he was becoming agitated again. After a few minutes, he looked at Annie and then at his daughter, and said something in French, something alarming as Maggie gasped and put a hand to her chest. Something about Monty and François, the only words that Annie could understand. The old man said the words several times, with fear in his eyes and then tears which he tried to wipe with a tissue he plucked from a box on the coffee table nearby. But his hands were trembling and so Ingrid had to help him.

'I'm so sorry,' Maggie said, softly, and then turned

to Annie to explain what Ingrid's father had been saying. 'He is worried about the man who was with you in the garden . . .'

'Étienne?' Annie confirmed.

'Yes, he says you must not trust him because he saw the jar of messages,' Maggie continued, looking at Ingrid for confirmation who nodded for her to continue. 'My father said you must be careful as he will take you to the camps . . . like they took Monty and François! They were betrayed by a neighbour, a villainous collaborator,' she finished quietly.

The three women fell silent.

Annie swallowed and blinked a few times. The camps! Oh Monty. And Trixie. Annie had read of Trixie's worry for her dear friend. She would have been devastated and terrified for him and François, after having been taken away, presumably to their deaths in one of Hitler's evil hellholes.

'You know of these people?' Ingrid asked gently, looking at Annie.

'I read about Monty – Trixie and he were friends. From England, they came to Paris in the 1920s, having first met in the fields of France in the First World War. And François was his partner.'

'Ah, I see,' Ingrid shook her head sadly, and went to say something else, but her father was talking again.

'Paulette?' Annie had suddenly heard, then, 'Sorry for interrupting . . . did he say Paulette?' she looked at Maggie and then to Ingrid and explained about the letter she had found from Paulette to Trixie, containing the code disguised as perfume ingredients.

'Ah, yes. Paulette was Trixie's friend from Switzerland. She had been Trixie's governess, I believe, when she was a child growing up in England,' Ingrid confirmed. 'My father took my grandfather, Maurice and Trixie to her funeral when she died in 1974 . . . I remember it well as my daughter was born a few days after and we all celebrated the new life coming so soon after Paulette's passing.' She smiled wistfully. 'I'm sorry I do not know about the connection to your friend, Joanie, how she inherit the apartment and the shop, but it is nice you want to learn about Trixie,' Ingrid added. 'She was a special person.'

'Thank you for speaking to us, and to your father too,' Annie smiled at the elderly man, but he seemed far away now, his eyes staring ahead as if deep in thought, his hands together making a steeple with his fingers.

'It is a pleasure. Is there anything else we can help you with?' Ingrid offered, standing up. Annie and Maggie stood up too, taking it as their cue to leave. 'I think my father must rest now, he usually sleeps at this time, but do come and visit again. I am here every weekend and on Wednesday too, when Michelle, his carer, can't come to look after him. My father is a stubborn man,' she laughed gently, shaking her head, 'so many times I ask him to live with me, but he say *non*, is not possible. He must stay here. He only agree to leave on his ninetieth birthday, a whole year ago. He finally say it is time. Yet he still not do it. I think this is why your friend receive the apartment now . . .'

'Ah, yes, the caveat,' Annie said, remembering Joanie telling her about the paperwork detailing that Beatrice Archambeau had died many years ago, yet the inheritance had become due only when the other occupant died or chose to move elsewhere.

'So I tell the *avocat*, Monsieur Aumont, my father is ready now, and then he contact your friend and so it is my father must make the move to live with me. It is not safe for him here on his own any more – the carer tell me he wanders into the garden and I worry in case he has a fall and nobody is here – and he will be happy with his grandchildren to fuss him, yes? Is better for everyone.' Ingrid nodded, resolutely, clearly having made the decision for her father with the best of intentions.

'When will your father make the move?' Annie asked, making a mental note to talk to Joanie about the contents of Trixie's apartment. 'Would he like to have something of Trixie's to take with him? A memento?' she offered, knowing Joanie would insist on it as soon as Annie explained about the friendship the family had spanning almost a hundred years from when Trixie and Maurice first met in that jazz club in the 1920s.

'Oh, is very kind of you, but we have many artefacts and special items that Trixie left with us. Jewellery and trinkets. She already gave me some scrapbooks – beautiful pressed flowers collected as a child with her mother – I cherish them. And her diaries from the war years . . . although she tells me there are more diaries but she forget where she hid them. I remember asking her why she hide them and she say it was to protect her friends from the Germans.'

'Ah, yes, I found them, hidden in the wall,' Annie told Ingrid.

'A very good hiding place . . .no wonder she forget them,' Ingrid said, tilting her head to one side. 'And she ask me to take great care of the diaries she gave me and read them only after my father passes. I think she not want my father to know about the love affair with my grandfather, Maurice.' Ingrid leant towards Annie and smiled covertly. 'Is true, Trixie and Maurice become lovers after Trixie's husband, Jacques, died in the war. I'm a curious person and so I already read only one of the diaries to discover this news and then I stop when I remember her wishes.' Annie's mouth opened but she couldn't bring herself to ask. Sensing her reserve, Maggie stepped in.

'Ingrid, would you mind if we take a look at the diaries? Annie is very keen to learn more about Trixie and there may be a clue within the pages for Annie's friend, Joanie. It would make all the difference to her to know how she is connected to Trixie . . . she never knew her family, you see. So it really would make a difference. And we promise to be discreet.'

A short silence passed as Ingrid seemed to consider the request. Then her smile widened, she lifted her shoulders and said, 'Sure . . . Trixie not say the friend of the new owner of her apartment could not read them! I bring them tomorrow for you.'

23

Paris, France, July 1942

Beatrice woke with a start to the sinister rumbling sound of a truck convey coming into the courtyard. Fear tightened its grip around her heart, making her breathing shallow and rapid as she put her hand on Maurice's shoulder to wake him from his slumber in the bed beside her. Immediately, he was sitting up and pushing his feet into the boots he kept by the bedside to access at a moment's notice. Sleeping in his trousers and vest, he pulled a shirt on, looped his braces over his shoulders and reached for his gun stowed under the mattress.

In silence, with only a mere wisp of light from the early morning sunrise coming from around the sides of the blackout boards, he motioned to Beatrice to go to the shop and carry out the usual morning checks.

Nothing must arouse suspicion if the Wehrmacht were approaching to carry out another of their terrifying round-ups. Last week they had taken Henri and Estelle, their three young children too – they owned the boulangerie around the corner near the café Bastille, but an order had come from officials for them to board up the shop and cease trading. Jews were no longer allowed to own a business. The family had limped on, sustaining themselves with food parcels from friends, Beatrice herself discreetly leaving a pail of milk by the door each morning and giving a swift tap-tap on the boarded-up window to notify them it was all clear to take the milk inside. Maurice and the other Resistance fighters were keeping watch over the courtyard and the surrounding streets from the windows high up that had clear views of the streets of Paris. Until the first round-up came a few weeks later, a rough-handed Nazi shoving Henri and Estelle, together with their children, onto the back of a truck, never to be seen again.

Moving swiftly, having already swapped her night-dress for one of the day dresses she wore for working in the perfumery, Beatrice left the bedroom, hastily tidying her hair as she went. She made her way into the shop, preparing to give the appearance of a typically busy day where she would serve the officers and the traitors who courted them – young Frenchwomen, German mistresses, members of the English aristocracy too.

It is barely daylight as I unlock the door and make a fuss of tweaking the window display. Picking up and polishing each of the glass bottles, allowing me to look along the length of the courtyard outside. The rumbling sound having stopped now as two trucks come to a halt outside the orphanage at the opposite end of the courtyard. I can barely keep my eyes open, terrified to witness the horror that I know is to come. Young children still huddled in the blankets from their beds standing mute and terrified, barefoot on the cobbles before being lifted onto the back of the trucks. I manage to count twenty-five boys and girls, two women as well, too stunned and scared to do anything other than comply with the orders being barked at them from the malicious men in their grey uniforms and black boots. Guns at their hips poised to shoot should anyone dare to disobey.

Ten minutes is all it takes for the young lives to be over, for that is what will happen when they reach the camp. I resist the urge to gag as vomit rises in my throat. My hands are shaking with shock, rage and fear. Praying helps to calm me so I mutter the words through a false smile as one of the soldiers, who I have seen before in my shop, smiles and tilts his hat in recognition as the truck passes by. I allow myself a moment of release, letting my breath stream out as I sag into the chair by the table of magazines, my prayers turning to Maurice standing guard behind the door of the cellar below, with his gun cocked, ready to protect our friend hiding in there, who will be moving on tonight. They brought him here from the American hospital in Paris where he was first taken after his aeroplane crashed, to convalesce and avoid capture while fake papers were prepared.

The arrangements are made now for his journey to the border, where Paulette will meet him in the forest, ready to escort him through to Switzerland and safety, as she has done eleven times before. Each journey riskier than the last. And with our friend still recuperating from the fractures to his arms, sustained on the sudden impact of the hard landing when his parachute got tangled in the trees near Boulogne, his journey will be the riskiest so far. Last time it was easier. A small child able to hide and stay quiet underneath the crops as the farmer trundled into the countryside unchecked, despatching the girl to his mother, who took her in as her own until she was well enough to travel on to Paulette in the forest. I think again of my dear friend, Monty; there has been no word of him, or François, now for what feels like an eternity, and so I can only pray that their end was swift and not drawn out with torture, hard labour and the minimum of rations. I venture back to the window, checking to see if the courtyard is clear now and, on seeing that it is, I move swiftly to the shelves at the back of the boutique to give the signal to Maurice. My hand is poised on the perfume bottle hiding the button to open the secret door when a sudden noise startles me. A cat perhaps. Mewing and wailing as if injured. I hurriedly dash back to the window. And gasp. A thin, young boy is standing bewildered by the water pump. His hunched shoulders covered in a blanket, his fingers clasping the corners, and tears are trickling down his cheeks. He is turning in circles. Looking and looking and not knowing what to do.

I see a curtain twitch at a window opposite. They have seen him too. But nobody comes for him. My heart pounding and my palms tingling with the sweat of fear, I slip the latch back on the door and flick my eyes up at the twitching curtain. It has fallen still now. But do I dare go and get the boy? What if the soldiers check the numbers of boys and girls in the records and then, on discovering that one is missing, come back for him? What if they search all the buildings looking for the missing boy? What if they find our friend, the pilot? But what is the alternative? The boy is taken to his death with all the other children from the orphanage, for I presume this is where he has come from. Hidden away somewhere out of sight when the raid took place. And now he is all alone. Petrified.

I make the decision and open the door. Five seconds is all it takes for me to dart out and snatch him up, his tiny body weightless as I swiftly fold him into the blanket until he is fully covered, bundled into my arms and back inside the shop with the front door firmly closed and latched. Moving fast, I run around the circular counter to the shelves and lift the perfume bottle, immediately depositing the boy behind the secret door as it opens, Maurice standing at the top of the stairs, his gun lifted and a look of astonishment mingled with fear on his face. He immediately knows from my frightened, urgent eyes – no words needed – and grabs the bundle from me and bolts back down the stairs.

I push the secret door back, replace the bottle

and turn around to tend to the shop as I do every day. A few hours later and a soldier and his mistress are strolling along by the tree in the courtyard. Her arm looped through his and they are headed towards me. Forcing myself to regulate my breathing, I smooth down my dress and make a fuss, once again, of sorting the window display, giving them a cheery wave as the soldier laughs and plants a kiss on the woman's cheek as she giggles and simpers and holds up, first two fingers, then three, saying she wants deux flacons . . . non, trois flacons! *He calls her a tease before telling her in German she can have two, three bottles, she can have them all to wear for dinner tonight. I open the door, hoping they don't notice me slide the latch from its closed position after bringing the boy inside, as nothing must arouse suspicion by seeming out of the ordinary . . .*

Annie looked up from the page of Trixie's diary and saw Maggie and Kristen staring at her, hanging on to her every word, their eyes wide, their foreheads creased in concern. She had been reading aloud from Trixie's diary, the third one that Ingrid had shared, and so they now had a vivid insight into who Trixie really was. Ingrid's grandfather, Maurice, the jazz trombone player from the 1920s, too. Annie's suspicion had been confirmed beyond doubt: that Trixie and Maurice worked for the French Resistance in Paris and bravely put their own lives at risk to save others. But there was still nothing to connect Trixie to Joanie.

'Are you OK, Kristen?' Annie said, suddenly noticing a tear trickle down her friend's face.

'Yes, please, carry on. I'm fine,' she said, brushing the tear away. 'It's just so sad, but important too that we discover the truth. It's history!' She reached for her coffee and took a big swig. They were sitting in Trixie's apartment, now Joanie's, figuring it a fitting place to find out what really happened here in Cour Felice all those years ago. Plus Ingrid had asked that the diaries not be taken away just in case they got lost or damaged, which Annie thought very fair indeed given their significance in history. She wondered if in time Ingrid might pass them on to a museum, as they really were a remarkable personal account of life in in occupied Paris during the Second World War.

'And now we can put Madame Bardin right, and the rest of the men from that night in my café!' Maggie said, resolutely.

'Yes, good idea. And Joanie will be fascinated, and relieved too, to discover what an exceptional, brave woman her benefactor was,' Annie said, having already chatted to her about the discovery of the new diaries.

She had promised to take pictures of the most important pages to share with her when she got home.

'So, what happens next?' Maggie asked, helping herself to one of the delicious pastel-coloured macarons that Annie had bought from a gorgeous little patisserie near the café Bastille this morning on their way to Cour Felice. A box for Ingrid and her father, too, as a small gesture of thanks for sharing the diaries.

'Yes, I need to know for sure who the boy is . . . although I'm guessing that it must be Pierre and the friend is the pilot, Squadron Leader Jeremy Sutherland,' Kristen said, taking a macaron too. 'And the letter we found in the basement was most likely smuggled back from Paulette to Trixie by one of the Resistance fighters . . .'

'It sure looks that way,' Annie said. 'But remember all the names in the jar, far more than the eleven that Trixie mentions here.' And she tapped the page of the diary.

'We must read on and see if Trixie reveals more,' Maggie prompted.

Annie turned the page and immersed them all once again in Trixie's words.

Busying myself behind the circular counter, having long since removed my perfume recipe ledger to safety on a ledge that Maurice created inside the old chimney breast in the basement, I wait for the soldier and his mistress to come into the shop, for I know they will, they always do. The soldiers like to treat the women they keep company with.

Forcing my eyes downwards, I put on my white gloves and polish the glass top, needing something to occupy and disguise my trembling hands. Moments later, the door springs open and the soldier strides in, the high shine of his black leather boots sparkling in the light from the crystal chandelier, the woman demurely following behind him. It is only when she emerges to stand next to him at the counter, that I freeze, momentarily, before dropping the cleaning cloth in my shock. It flutters to a landing point on the floor beside my feet. Bending to scoop it up and sneaking a second to gather myself, for I can't be sure, I stand up and hastily remove the gloves before walking around the counter to greet them, as is the custom. The soldier has come to buy perfume before, of that I am sure, although the woman I have never seen. But at the same time I am convinced that I have seen her many, many times before. Queenie. The woman standing before me is my oldest and dearest friend from England, my childhood friend. Or is she? The tumble of auburn curls are now sleek platinum-

blonde movie-star waves and her lips are coated in crimson, giving her an alluring air that many of the soldiers' mistresses have. But her eyes, now boring into mine, are the same impish green as my Queenie's. The Queenie who came to my wedding, which was the last time I saw her, many years ago. But, how can it be? Surely I am mistaken? My own eyes must be playing tricks. Perhaps it is the fear of being found out. The boy in the basement, who Maurice told me mere moments earlier is called Pierre, is only 6 years old! Our friend too. I have to protect them . . . to protect myself. Maurice too, who is standing guard down there behind the basement door. For the two souls are now hidden away in the space beneath the shop floor where the soldier's boots are pacing up and down as he picks up bottles and lifts a lid here and there to see if the scent appeals to him.

The woman is by the soldier's side now, her manicured hand touching the uniformed sleeve covering his forearm, as she purrs to him in French, her Parisian accent perfect. So I assume I must be mistaken. Queenie can speak French, of course; she was a fast learner when Paulette taught her alongside me, but not to the standard she is talking now. And for a fleeting second, as the soldier comes back

*to the counter having selected three bottles for her,
I am convinced there is a dash of recognition, but
how could she be here with a German soldier? She
knows what they did to my dear brother, Edward,
and my darling Bobby. Her own brother, Stan, too!
But it is hard to know anything as her blank stare
instantly moves back into place and her eyes bore
into mine once again, as if looking right through
me. Willing me not to challenge her, almost. And
then I know. She is talking in German now,
conversing fluently, and the soldier is laughing, but
there is a tension around her jaw. A whiteness to
her knuckles as she clasps her handbag closer to
her coat. She is scared. Scared of me. Hence her
not daring to see me. She is scared of making proper
eye contact, of making a visible connection. Could
it be that she is scared I will betray her? Blow her
cover, if that is what this is, for many people must
hide their true identity from the Nazis for lots of
different reasons, as must I. But I can't be sure!
What if I have it all wrong? Here I am fawning
and making small talk in my own fluent German
as I help the soldier choose a remedy for his aching
feet. He is telling me about the problem, but I'm
not fully listening as my mind is muddled from
panicking and praying that Queenie won't betray*

me as being an Englishwoman and not Madame
Archambeau, the Parisian perfumier who performs
every day as a friend of the soldiers she serves!

The transaction is completed and the soldier hands
the gift bag containing the perfumes to Queenie, and
goes to leave. Queenie follows. They have just reached
the door when there is a sudden roaring sound,
followed by screeching tyres on the cobbles. Then
silence. An eerie silence. Then hammering on the
door of the orphanage. I don't need to see it to know.
More hammering on more doors, and coming closer,
until I know they will be here any second searching
for the missing boy. The soldier has left the shop
now, only to be replaced by another, younger soldier,
who storms inside almost knocking Queenie over as
she tries to step aside. He stops, apologizes and
stretches out his hand to steady her. She accepts the
hand and flutters her impish green eyes before
coquettishly accepting his apology in perfect German.
There is a moment of silence as they exchange flirtatious glances.

Suddenly a thud can be heard from underneath
the area around my counter! My heart jerks in fear.
A trickle of sweat snakes a path down my back,
all the way from the nape of my neck to the base
of my spine. The soldier doesn't appear to have

heard the sound but he snaps back to attention and shouts, 'Ein Junge wird vermisst' . . . a boy is missing! I reply in German asking what does the boy look like? The soldier stalls, for he doesn't know, but says he is a filthy Jew from the orphanage and must be found. He then glances around the shop as I inwardly pray for him to leave. Another thud. I instinctively bang my foot as hard as I can on the floor, hoping to alert Maurice to the soldier's presence as I let out a scream and shout, 'Maus! Es ist eine maus!' and run around the counter, as if trying to shoo away the imaginary mouse in my shop. Suddenly, Queenie sees me – properly sees me from the position of relative safety behind the soldier's back as he strides around as if looking for the imaginary mouse. The moment is brief, but I'm sure I spot it in her eyes as she also screams, a shrill, ear-splitting scream followed by a faint-like stumble into the door frame.

The soldier, driven by vanity I assume, swiftly bolts back to the doorway to loop his arm around Queenie's shoulder, one hand on her elbow to steady her as she staggers some more, begging for air as he leads her outside to where her more senior soldier friend is tapping his watch impatiently. Seeing Queenie being manhandled by another soldier, he instantly snaps to attention and orders the younger, lower-ranking soldier to remove his hands from her immediately. Calling her Chantal, he bats the younger soldier aside and leads her away, yelling for him to leave at once and get back to his duties somewhere else. But he hesitates and turns, as if to head back into my shop. Seizing the moment, I grab a phial of perfume and, after pulling the shop door shut firmly behind me, again to alert Maurice to the danger, I dash after the soldier and hand him the phial, saying in German, 'For your wife, thank you for saving us from the mouse.' And to my immense relief he smiles, takes the perfume and stuffs it into his pocket before clicking his heels together and striding off back to his black motor car parked outside the orphanage.

I turn to walk back into the shop but there is more commotion now. More black cars are arriving, an open-top one with flags displaying the swastika, a soldier standing, scanning the street with an imperious look on his face as the other soldiers salute him with raised, outstretched arms. He is yelling, 'Halt, halt' and the car stops to allow him to get out and walk around. And my blood turns to ice.

It is Kurt Lischka, head of the Gestapo, I recognize him from the pictures on the front of the *propaganda papers glued to the lampposts in the streets. He is striding towards me with an inane smile on his face. Another uniformed man appears by his side now with a camera. I freeze, unsure of what I should do, but the decision is made for me as the man with the camera lifts the brown box as Kurt Lischka puts one arm around my shoulders and lifts my hand to shake. His inane smile widening as he tells the cameraman to make sure he includes the chic Parisian perfumery in the picture, as my own face moves into a smile to mask the sheer terror and revulsion swirling around inside me.*

I will myself to stay standing for my legs are trembling. From the corner of my eye, I see Monsieur Bardin and his young daughter walk past, both giving me looks of disdain, and I want to tell them. To assure them I am not one of the collaborators, but I daren't, and so I stay rooted to the spot while the men sicken me further with blatant flirting and false platitudes, thanking me for my participation in their staged welcome in Paris. As they leave, I retreat swiftly back inside the shop and once again make a fuss of the window display until I am sure all the motor cars containing the real enemy have departed. As my breathing intensifies to force the bile back down inside me, I dust the bottles and tweak their positioning, and Chantal – or is it really Queenie; I'm convinced of it now – turns her face sideways as she walks away past the shop window, swinging her gift bag gaily and catching my eye with the briefest of glances and the slightest incline of her head. And never have I been more grateful for our enduring friendship spanning all these years . . . we lost touch over a decade ago and I do not know what she is doing back here in Paris but today has shown me that true friendship can stand the test of time . . . I will never forget my dear friend, Queenie, for not only saving my life, but also that of my beloved, Maurice, and the British pilot Jeremy Sutherland and the young Jewish child Pierre hidden in the basement below.

24

Four days later, having taken Maggie's advice and spent some time having fun in Paris, meeting up with Étienne and sightseeing with Maggie and Kristen, Annie was back in Cour Felice, having just enjoyed lunch on her own at the café around the corner. Étienne had wanted to get the last of the wallpapering finished and so she had brought back his favourite lunch, a Parisian sandwich – a baguette stuffed with ham and butter, or *jambon* and *beurre*, as she had managed to ask for in perfect French. She had loved strolling to the café in the glorious sunshine, feeling like a proper Parisian, as she'd bought a newspaper on the way and then enjoyed the most delicious croque monsieur with a refreshing, fizzy glass of Kir Royale as she had sat outside, trying to read the news in French, in between watching the people of Paris.

It had felt like such a treat to stop for a moment and just sit and relax and contemplate all that had happened. So much seemed so different now. She felt different too, and the most remarkable thing was that she felt closer to her children than she had in a very long time. She had enjoyed a few more lively conversations with Johnny, thrilled that he was involving her in his exciting plans for the future. And Phoebe was doing well, always keen to chat about all kinds of things. Fun things, like a new bubble bath or make-up range, only available in Australia, that she had tried and loved, or a boxset she had watched and thought Annie might enjoy too. The control and scrutiny to which Phoebe had subjected Annie's life had dissipated also, and now Phoebe seemed genuinely interested in hearing all about Paris and the extraordinary life of Beatrice Archambeau. It was as if the distance had somehow given them space and yet to grow closer . . . in a different way. And Jack seemed happy too, he'd even come on the phone one time and spoken candidly to Annie about Phoebe, saying that he wanted to reassure Annie that her daughter was having a great time, was relaxed and seeking out all the help she needed – the break away was doing her the world of good.

Back in the apartment now, and Annie was directing Étienne on where to gather the curtains beneath the pelmet so they hung beautifully and perfectly.

'Is good, *non?*' Étienne said from the top of the

ladder, laughing over his shoulder before shrugging and shaking his head, clearly bemused by Annie's insistence the curtains must be exactly right.

'If you can just tweak that section by your right hand, please?' she said, pointing to show him where, before standing back across the room to get a good look. Satisfied that the curtains were precisely how they should be and how Trixie would have wanted them, if the other curtains in the sitting room were anything to go by, she thanked Étienne and said that he could come down now. 'See how marvellous they look,' she beamed, lifting her hands out wide to showcase them for him as he came to stand beside her.

'*Oui, magnifique*. You have a gift, Annie,' he told her, putting his arm around her shoulders.

'Thanks, I've really enjoyed making them,' she said, 'I'd love to spruce up other parts of the apartment also – the curtains in the sitting room are faded, and there are stains on the walls in the kitchen, the beautiful fleur-de-lis tiles cracked in places too. I'd love to source some replacement tiles or, better still, have a go at restoring the original ones.'

'Then why don't you?' He folded his arms and gave her one of his curious looks.

'Oh, well, I . . . you know, I have to go home soon,' she said, hardly able to believe that she had been in

Paris for twelve days now. She'd had the most wonderful time, seeing the sights and spending time with Maggie and Kristen, not to mention Étienne. They had enjoyed several more lunches on the deck of his lovely boat, dinner too one evening when they had finished working in the apartment very late and so had taken a picnic of gooey cheeses, cold meats and crusty baguettes, grapes and garlicky olives with a bottle of red wine and sat on the grassy bank of the Seine in a secluded spot that only Étienne seemed to know about, as they had the area to themselves. The air had been warm, the dark sky studded with silver stars as they had lain back, his arm around her shoulders as she had rested her head on his chest, soothed by the rhythmic rise and fall of his breathing as they chatted and put the world to rights all over again.

Annie had talked to Étienne about Phoebe, and how she had arrived in Australia with Jack and seemed different already, lighter somehow, more vulnerable, but in a positive way, as if she was showing herself properly for the first time without the barriers of control and criticism that she used to hide behind. Étienne had suggested that perhaps she felt free and more relaxed to be away from the stress and expectations of running the gym and having to look a certain way. And Annie had loved the interest Étienne had shown, genuinely keen to find out about her family and be a part of her life, it seemed. They had talked as well about Delphine and Brigitte and the dreams and aspirations that they'd had. Étienne had spoken honestly too about Brigitte's personality, her flaws and attributes, explaining that he never wanted her to be put on a pedestal as some kind of untouchable saint. That she was only human and, by being honest about her, he also kept her memory alive. Apparently, she had had a fiery temper and they would often fight, but she could also be gentle and kind, especially with Delphine, with whom she had endless patience, even the time when she had drawn a picture in black permanent pen on Brigitte's expensive new handbag. Étienne had been cross and had yelled at Delphine – something he regretted deeply – but Brigitte had been philosophical, saying the squiggles added character, making the bag unique and special just like her funny, sweet girl. And Étienne had kept the bag as a reminder to see the gifts in life, the positive moments always . . .

Annie had cried when he had told her about the bag, thinking how poignant it must be for him to look at it now. He had assured her that it was a comfort, a lesson that had helped release him from being materialistic and greedy. Annie was surprised because this didn't seem to be the same Étienne she saw now, who lived simply on his boat with very few belongings. So he had explained how, after studying art and then bowing to his father's wishes with a career in banking, he had then got swept up in the world of finance, always chasing the next big deal, revelling in bigger bonuses and prizes until his world imploded on that day on the way to St Tropez when everything changed.

'But why?' Étienne asked, nudging her arm playfully and breaking her reverie. 'Why do you have to go home if you want to stay here and refurbish the apartment?'

'Um, well . . . I have to go back to work for starters. They are expecting me.' Annie looked away, not wanting to think about leaving Paris just yet.

'But the job is boring you, yes?'

'True.' Annie nodded.

'Then maybe Phoebe is right . . . you could take a new job to refurbish the apartment.' Silence followed as his words sank in.

'Oh, Étienne, I wish it was that simple, but I need to earn an income, I have a home, a life in England,' she said, even though she felt as though she'd had more of a life here in Paris the past twelve days than she'd had in months back home. And with Beth and Phoebe away, Johnny too . . . what was really stopping her? Annie let out a long puff of air before wandering over to the window to tweak the curtains and secure them in the matching tie-backs that she had made.

Moments later, she could feel Étienne's arms around her back, his fingertips on the side of her neck, gentle as he lifted her hair away and rested his face by hers, wrapping his arms around her.

'I'm sorry, Annie. I shouldn't put ideas into your head. To tease you, to tempt you to stay . . . it's not fair. But I will miss you. And I think you will miss me, yes?'

'Yes, you're right, I will,' she murmured, wishing it could be different. 'I'd love to stay in Paris, but it just doesn't seem possible,' she added, not even allowing herself to dare to dream of making that big a change to her life. She was determined to make things different, but moving to another country was a whole type of different. Where would she live for starters? Where would she work? Not to mention the legalities of it all.

'Is certainly possible. You can stay with me . . . on the boat,' Étienne suggested softly, shrugging his shoulders in the casual, easy-going way that Annie had become accustomed to. 'Or I find us a proper house if that's what you like more.'

And she turned around to look into his kind, soulful brown eyes.

'But, I . . . no, please don't do that,' she said, glancing away. 'I couldn't, I wouldn't . . . you love the boat. I love the boat!' She paused, swallowed, and used the moment to gather her thoughts. This was insane. Here she was talking to a man who she had just met only a week or so ago about living with him. 'We've only known each other for a short time,' she settled for, searching his eyes for a sign that he really knew what he was saying, that he wasn't playing with her and, more importantly, that he wasn't wishing for this because he was vulnerable, still grieving and missing the love he had with his wife. Of course, he would always grieve, but Annie felt it was important that he was sure. And she needed to be too. They simply needed more time . . . certainly more than the two days she had left in Paris.

'Annie, I never feel this way with a woman,' he said, as if reading her mind. 'We know each other a short time but we talk like old friends. Please stay longer. I want to kiss you . . . I not kiss you yet because I don't want to like you more and then you go away . . .' And he dipped his forehead onto hers, his lips close to hers. And Annie could hear the sound of her own blood pumping in her ears. She longed for the kiss, the connection. She wanted it too. But she sensed that he needed to go at his own pace. He had already told her there hadn't been another woman since Brigitte so the moment was special. It had to be. For him. And for her also.

And then, before she could question or doubt or second-guess any more, Étienne's lips were on hers . . . kissing her gently, tenderly, passionately, intimately. And the feeling she had inside was like nothing she had ever experienced before . . . like a bath bomb landing and sending an exquisite, fizzing swirl all around her and on into her heart. The intensity making her feel giddy and light, as Étienne swept her up into his arms, one hand on her bottom, the other at the nape of her neck as she instinctively looped her legs around his hips, all the while still kissing, faster and even more intensely now. Soon they were sitting on the window seat, Étienne with his back to the view, Annie with her arms around his neck, savouring the sizzling sensation of his fingertips stroking her thighs before moving up and under her floaty cotton sundress to caress the small of her back making her arch in pleasure.

When the lingering, passionate kiss eventually ended, Étienne gently lifted her chin and, as he moved a stray tendril of hair away from her face, he kissed the bridge of her nose and smiled.

'Um,' Annie managed, barely able to talk, her breathing still fast.

'Is good?' Étienne asked, perfectly seriously, keen to be sure, making Annie smile.

'Yes. Is very good,' she nodded and laughed.

'So you promise to come back to Paris?' and his eyes tentatively widened in anticipation of her answer.

'I do. I promise,' and she kissed him right back, knowing that she had never felt more certain of anything than she did right now . . .

25

Greenwich, England . . . One month later

'How about I make us a nice pot of tea?' Annie suggested, surveying the pile of boxes and old suitcases that she had brought down from Joanie's loft. 'Then we can go through this lot and see what you want to take with you and if there's anything that can go into the charity shop pile.' She glanced at the growing mountain of books, shoes, blankets and items of clothing dating as far back as the 1970s with their bold, swirly flower patterns, all stacked up in the corner of her front room.

'Oh yes please, Annie, dear. And why don't you slice us both a big piece of the Victoria sponge that I baked fresh this morning.'

'Good idea. If you're sure it won't spoil your lunch?' Annie teased with a wink, knowing how partial her friend was to cake. And why not! It was an exciting time for Joanie. A cause to celebrate as her dream of luxury living with her best friend, Sandra, was about to come true.

After assembling the tea and cake on a tray, Annie placed it on the coffee table and sat down in an armchair opposite the sofa where Joanie was sitting.

'Have you heard any more from Phoebe, dear? How is she getting on down under in Australia?'

'Ah, yes, I called her yesterday and we had a lovely chat . . . it's so very nice to hear her happy,' Annie said, pouring tea into a china cup with a matching saucer, just as Joanie liked it.

'Well, I'm very pleased for her. And you too, lovey. She's sure been a challenge over the years, that child . . .' Joanie laughed, affectionately and without any trace of malice, 'but she's turned out to be a super girl who deserves every happiness. Does she know about the ring yet? Has her young man popped the question?'

'Not yet,' Annie smiled, stirring milk into the tea and handing it to Joanie. After making a cup of tea for herself, she sliced the cake onto plates and placed one on the lamp table nearest to Joanie. 'Jack is going to propose tomorrow evening at sunset, so that will be morning time for us. Beth also called yesterday and said that it's all arranged. She's going to set up the camera on her phone so we can see it as it's actually happening on the beach.'

Annie couldn't wait, knowing that Phoebe was going to be over the moon. Jack had picked out exactly the right ring, having called Annie to get her input, and had even sneaked one of Phoebe's other rings into the jewellers there in Sydney to have the size checked so the engagement ring would be just right to pop onto Phoebe's finger. Annie was so delighted for her daughter, who had worked extremely hard on her recovery, the therapy sessions having been a great success.

Annie had called the therapist, with Phoebe's consent, to chat through some of the issues that had come up around Annie's ex-husband Mark not making as much effort as he should have done for Phoebe. It was clear that Phoebe had ended up believing that she was to blame. This had manifested over the years into Phoebe feeling inadequate and in turn her need for control to feel secure had spiralled, culminating in her determination to succeed with her gym business being a positive factor in her life, but her obsession with her image leading to the distorted eating patterns. Annie had learnt that Phoebe had been mostly surviving on protein shakes and the occasional salad when her natural need for actual food had kicked in. It was a balance that had gone awry for Phoebe, but she was now working hard to find a harmony that worked better for her. Learning how to care for herself and nourish her body and mind. And Annie couldn't be prouder of her daughter for facing her fears and emerging stronger than ever.

'Well, fancy that,' Joanie said, giving her tea another stir with a little silver spoon. 'All those miles away and it will be like we're actually there with the lovebirds on the beach.'

'Yes,' Annie mused wistfully, wishing that she really could be there in Australia, but Phoebe and Jack would be back soon and so they would celebrate together then.

'And how are you, dear? How is that handsome Frenchman of yours?' Joanie asked with a twinkle in her eye.

'Ah, Étienne is wonderful,' Annie said, in a dreamy voice, the memory of his incredibly sexy kiss still fresh on her lips. She hadn't seen him since coming home from Paris and missed him a little more each day. 'We talk all the time, and it's marvellous getting to know him, but . . .'

'Well, hopefully you'll get to see each other again very soon,' Joanie said.

'Yes, I hope so,' Annie smiled, thinking about her plans to return to Paris. She missed being there. Missed the feelings she had when she was there. And she missed Maggie and Kristen. The three of them spoke regularly too. Kristen had more or less moved in permanently at Maggie's place, with no plans to return to New York any time soon, and had even managed to persuade her boss at the fashion magazine company where she worked that she could do her job just fine from Paris. And so that's what she had been doing ever since Annie had returned to England. 'And I'm so sorry, I couldn't find out why Trixie left the apartment to you.'

'Ah, as I said before, dear, there's no need to fret about it. We have to accept that we may never know. It's the only way. I accepted a very long time ago that I have no family . . . I had to, otherwise I would have gone a bit doolally, driving myself mad with wondering and looking. I used to do that, you know – when I first left the children's home, I would scan people's faces as I walked along the street, just in case they had similar features to me, because you never know, I might have been related to them. I guess I was looking for answers . . . a place to fit in.'

'Oh, Joanie, that must have been very hard for you,' Annie said.

'It was!' she nodded. 'But not any more. I made my peace with it. And I have friends. Some really wonderful friends, like you, my love, and Sandra of course. She's been my friend since we first met in our twenties in the office where we worked in the typing pool, and I have to say that she's been like a sister to me. Always there through thick and thin . . . yes, we've had our clashes over the years but we always make up and I know she'd do anything for me, as I would for her. So who's really to say if blood is thicker than water . . . I don't know, Annie . . .' She paused to shake her head. 'Personally, I'd say it's just a different colour! Friends have always been my family. The extra-special one that I got to choose.'

'Well, that's a lovely way to think about it,' Annie smiled. 'And I have the same with Beth. She's been like a sister to me, and I still miss her so much.'

'Of course you do, love. But no matter how far away she is, you still have her close to you in spirit. I know it's taken you a bit of time to adapt to her being in Australia, but she's still there for you.'

'Sure.' Annie pondered for a while as they ate cake and drank some of their tea. 'But it would have been amazing to know why Trixie left the apartment to you . . .'

She couldn't help wondering and had considered all kinds of theories, the obvious one being that Joanie was Trixie and Maurice's secret love child, born out of wedlock. But then Joanie knew that she had been born in London in 1944, and if Trixie had been eighteen in 1916, as Annie had discovered in one of her earlier diaries inside the writing slope, then she would have been forty-six in 1944, so was it likely that she would have travelled to England during wartime to have a baby, leaving her to grow up in a children's home? Annie thought it extremely unlikely. Besides, she thought, Trixie was in Paris, saving children and pilots from being taken to the death camps! Plus Joanie knew her parents, even if she didn't ever have the chance to get to know them.

'But look what you did find out,' Joanie said, interrupting Annie's thoughts. 'A fascinating insight into the life of a top-drawer lady who knew her own mind and stood true to her word. Loyal and fearless. And Trixie didn't accept her lot in life. No, she walked her own path and did it her way,' Joanie added proudly, having read through most of Trixie's diaries now, right back to when she had written about being a debutante but not wanting to marry the man of her parents' choosing. Wanting a different life, free from the constraints of her aristocratic background.

'Yes. And what a woman!' Annie said.

'And you met a marvellous man, love, who you are enjoying getting to know, not to mention a couple of smashing new friends, and things with your Phoebe and Johnny are better than ever,' Joanie smiled. 'So maybe that's why a seemingly complete stranger left me a lovely apartment in Paris . . . it was so all these wonderful things could happen! Think about the impact it has had on all of us. Not only have we got to find out about Trixie's extraordinary life. We've changed our own lives too – you with Paris and your new friends there and I've got my lovely luxury living lifestyle that I've spent the best part of the last year dreaming about. You know they say things happen for a reason . . . and you were stuck in a bit of a rut, if you don't mind me saying so, love.'

'Not at all, Joanie,' Annie smiled at her friend, thinking how she was going to miss having her living next door. 'I can always rely on you to tell it how it is.'

'You sure can. Ooh, will you fetch my phone, please dear?' Joanie asked on hearing it ring out in the hall. Annie dashed to pick it up and passed the handset to Joanie who mouthed that it was Hettie's friend, Marigold, who she had met when she went on her day trip to Tindledale.

'Oh, yes, thank you very much,' Joanie said, followed by, 'how kind of her,' and then, 'really? Well, that's fascinating . . .'

Annie tried to be polite as she listened in on Joanie's conversation, keen to know if Hettie and Marigold had managed to put together any pieces of the jigsaw and had found out something more about Trixie. 'Right you are . . . shan't be a minute.' Joanie put her hand over the phone and reached for her pad and biro from the coffee table. Then, turning to Annie she told her, 'Marigold is saying that Hettie's friend, Sybil, who runs her haberdashery shop in Tindledale, is going to email something over for us to have a look at. Would you mind popping your email address on the pad for me, love, as I don't have one myself. And then I can read it out to her?'

'Ooh, yes of course,' Annie said eagerly, taking the pad and pen from Joanie and quickly writing her email address down.

'Thank you.' And as Joanie returned to the phone call, Annie mouthed to her that she was just going to pop back next door to fetch her laptop ready to receive the email.

Moments later, when Annie returned, Joanie was still chatting on the phone with a curious look on her face. She motioned for Annie to come and sit next to her. Eventually, having ended the call, Joanie put the phone on the armrest of the sofa and turned to Annie.

'You'll never guess what!' she said. Annie's eyes widened in anticipation. 'Well, Marigold has just told me that she was chatting to a friend of theirs from the knit and natter circle that they all belong to about my visit to Tindledale, and how I was asking about Beatrice Crawford, a.k.a. Trixie, and she remembers her mother talking about Trixie and knowing her friend, Queenie. They were best friends, apparently, the mother and Queenie – the mother is dead now – but the knitting friend says that she has a book that was her mother's and she thinks it originally belonged to her friend, Queenie. The book has got Queenie's name in the front of it, you see, and she thinks Queenie lent it to her mother the last time she saw her. It would have been around the end of the war, she can't remember when, exactly. Anyhow, she says that it will all be in the email! That it's easier to write it all down rather than tell us on the phone as it's a bit long-winded.'

'It sounds fascinating. I can't wait to find out more,' Annie said, opening her laptop and logging in to her email. 'Did she say when Sybil was going to send the email?'

'Right away, dear. I think they had it all ready to send. Marigold had written it in a letter that she was going to post to me – that's why she was originally phoning – to get my address. But then Hettie said that she shouldn't bother with all that and just email it over. That's when Sybil came on the line and asked for my email address. The marvels of modern technology, eh? I can see the letter right away instead of waiting for the post. You know, they are going to take a picture of the letter and attach it to the email?' Joanie marvelled, making Annie smile.

'Ooh, looks as if it's arrived,' Annie said, suddenly seeing the 'new mail' notification. She clicked to open the first attachment, a letter written in beautiful flowing cursive handwriting, and turned the screen towards Joanie.

'Will you read it to me, dear? My eyesight isn't so good these days.'

'Sure, here goes.' And Annie started reading.

Dear Joanie
It was such a pleasure to meet you and Sandra in the tea shop and I hope your journey back to London was a comfortable one. Please forgive me for talking about your interesting story re. the flat in Paris, I'm not one for gossiping, but I was rather keen to see if I might be of help in solving your mystery. As it turns out, a few of our older knitting circle ladies remember the Crawford family; they were very well-to-do and lived in the big manor house by the old water mill, surrounded by fields, with many of the villagers working in service for them back in the day. More interestingly, Valerie says her mother was friendly with Beatrice

Crawford's young companion, Queenie, and lived next door to her in Pear Tree Cottages many moons ago in the Thirties.

They lost touch briefly during the Second World War when Queenie went away to work in Oxfordshire for the Land Army – with her being a country girl, it was a good fit for her, you see. Although there were rumours in the village of her being a spy!!! But Valerie says her mother was never convinced of it as she saw Queenie briefly near the end of the war and said she seemed perfectly normal to her, just like her old self. Mind you, she said Queenie would have made a good spy as she was very quick-witted and a fast learner and that's why she was picked to be Beatrice's companion back when she was a young girl. After our conversation, Valerie went home and found the book that had been her mother's, originally belonging to Queenie, and there was an old postcard from Beatrice, who went by the name of Trixie, inside it. I've enclosed a photocopy of the postcard for you and will keep the original safe until you are able to visit Tindledale again. I trust the postcard is a comfort to you and helps explain why Trixie remembered you in her will.

Yours truly,
Marigold

Annie felt her pulse quicken as she went to click on one of the other attachments, then hesitated as the letter was addressed to Joanie after all and so she should be the one to read it all first.

'Sorry, I was getting carried away . . . it's so exciting,' Annie said, turning sideways to see Joanie's reaction.

'Oh, don't be silly. Open it up, dear, or whatever it is you have to do so we can see the postcard,' Joanie said, giving Annie a quick nudge, clearly keen to find out too.

'Ah, look, it's a postcard from Paris,' Annie said, as the glorious black-and-white picture of the iconic Eiffel Tower appeared on the screen. 'Are you ready to see the other side?' she asked.

'Oh, yes. I can't wait!'

And so Annie clicked on the attachment.

'Ooh, it's from Trixie, I'd recognize her handwriting anywhere,' Annie noted, clicking to enlarge the picture so she could see the words, which were very small, faded and faint.

'Can you see what it says?' Joanie leant in closer to Annie.

'I think I can, just about.'

Annie read the words aloud.

A Postcard from Paris

To my dearest friend Queenie,
I write with congratulations on the birth of your
dear daughter, Joan. I'm sure you and your husband
are delighted. Such marvellous timing that he was
able to be back for the birth and thank you for
getting the picture of the three of you to me. I shall
treasure it. Much love to you all. I am forever in
your debt, my dear, after saving me from the mouse!!
Your friend always.
Trixie x

Both women sat in silence for a while staring at the screen. Annie opened her mouth, took a deep breath, and then closed it again. She was stunned. She tried again to talk but Joanie beat her to it.

'Whatever does it mean?' she turned to look at Annie with a puzzled expression on her face.

'Well,' Annie started gently, 'I think it means that Trixie left the apartment to you as a thank-you gift in recognition of Queenie playing along in the shop that time when Trixie was trying to distract the German soldiers. You remember I told you how she pretended to have seen a mouse?'

'Yes, that's right, you did, dear,' Joanie said.

'So, Queenie's quick thinking saved Trixie from certain death, because if Trixie had been caught harbouring a missing Jewish child in her basement she would have been arrested for sure. Not to mention if they'd found the British pilot, Jeremy Sutherland, who was sheltering in the basement as well. Pierre told us it was the pilot who took him as a little boy to Paulette in Switzerland, though the pilot was killed before he could cross the border. So this means, Joanie, that Queenie was your mother!'

'Oh no, dear, that can't be right!' Joanie chuckled. 'It must just be a coincidence that Queenie had a daughter called Joan. You see, my mother was called Enid! That's what they told me at the children's home. Her name, Enid Smith, is on my birth certificate.' More silence followed. And Annie felt deflated. Then, as she was trying to figure it all out, another email pinged into her Inbox. 'What does it say?' Joanie said, keenly.

'Oh, it's from Sybil this time.' Annie read the email out to Joanie.

Dear Joanie
Coincidentally, Valerie has just popped into the haberdashery shop to buy some wool and says she forgot to mention that she is friends with Kathryn, who lives in Stoneley, not far from Tindledale, and to tell you that Kathryn is Stan's granddaughter. Valerie says she is very sorry it slipped her mind

and that she has spoken to Kathryn who would very much like to call you, if that's OK? Shall I give her your number?

Thanks

Sybil

'Oh yes,' Joanie said quickly, looking at Annie. 'Let her know it's OK, so we can get this all cleared up.' And so Annie typed an email giving Joanie's consent.

Moments later, her phone rang. 'I'm going to pop it on the loudspeaker so you can hear too,' Joanie said, leaning forward in anticipation.

'Hello, is that really you, Joan?' Kathryn said, sounding as if she was welcoming Joanie like a long-lost family member. Joanie gave a tentative, 'Yes.'

And then Kathryn explained that her dad was Harold, who was the son of Queenie's brother Stanley, making him Joanie's cousin. That meant Kathryn and Joanie were second cousins. But then Joanie interrupted with an abrupt, 'I'm sorry, dear, but you have the wrong person. I can't be your second cousin. My mother was called Enid—'

'That's right!' Kathryn jumped in, excitedly. 'Dad told me that his father Stanley, who died in the First World War, had a sister called Enid. But their dad always called her Queenie, as she was his little queen, with her being the first girl born after five boys. And so the name stuck. Stanley was the youngest, the other four sadly died of TB in childhood.'

Annie stole a look at Joanie who was sitting in silence, her mouth open and her hand clasped tightly around the phone that was held out in front of them.

'I see,' Joanie said, seemingly in shock as she glanced at Annie. She blinked a few times before lifting her eyebrows in amazement. 'And did your dad say what happened to my mother, Enid . . . or Queenie, as she was known?'

'Yes, yes he did. I'm so sorry, but she died in a London bombing raid, in Mile End,' Kathryn said softly, her voice full of empathy. 'He also thought that she'd had a baby called Joan, who grew up in Suffolk, perhaps, where it would be safer from the bombs. That she lived in a children's home for a while and might have been adopted—'

'I wasn't adopted,' Joanie cut in, before falling silent for a moment. But then added, 'I did grow up in a children's home in Suffolk though.'

'Ah, he was a little patchy on the details as it had been passed down the family and things can get a bit muddled, so I'm sorry if I've remembered it incorrectly. But I've been looking for you, Joan, ever since I did the family tree for Dad's eightieth birthday back in 1999.'

'Really?' Joanie managed, followed by, 'well, I never . . .' and a shake of her head.

Annie placed her hand over Joanie's free hand, which was trembling now on top of her leg, then gently took the phone from her as she sniffed and dipped her head, clearly emotional as she took it all in. After a few seconds of stunned silence, Annie rubbed the back of her friend's hand and quietly asked if she would like her to talk to Kathryn. Joanie nodded and smiled and so Annie explained who she was and that her dear friend, Joanie, was overwhelmed at this surprising news.

After ending the call, and with a promise of speaking again soon when Joanie had digested all this new information, the two friends sat together and reread the words on the postcard.

'Are you OK?' Annie ventured as Joanie smiled and shook her head, letting out another sigh of disbelief.

'Yes, I think so, dear. I'm stunned, and well, to be perfectly honest, I feel quite delighted too,' she paused to tap the screen of the laptop where the image of the postcard was still displayed, 'and fancy that . . . discovering the truth of my inheritance, right here . . . on a postcard from Paris.'

Epilogue

Paris, France . . . One year later

To get everyone's attention, Annie tapped the side of a champagne glass with a small silver spoon from the sumptuous buffet that Maggie had created especially for the occasion, and took a look around the stunning design studio that she had created in Cour Felice. The glass-topped circular counter had been beautifully restored now, and was perfect for showcasing her interior design ideas for the discerning residents of Paris who flocked here to put their names on the waiting list for their chance to have Annie create her magic in their home, just as she had in her own, upstairs.

After being in back in England for a few weeks and missing Paris far too much, Annie had made the life-changing decision to come back here for good, and so had resigned from her job, sold her house and bought Trixie's apartment and beautiful little boutique. The last year had been spent restoring the apartment so it now resembled a timelessly elegant home that Annie was sure Trixie would have approved of. Having paid particular care to source such things as the original kitchen tiles to replace the broken ones, Annie had left no detail untouched. She had even thought to recreate the glorious herb garden and had figured out, from Trixie's old perfume ledger, how to create a small selection of home fragrances in authentic glass bottles that sat on the display shelves – lavender pillow spray, lemon grass livener, as she called it, used to freshen up laundry, and a choice of mint, basil and bay handwashes – with plans for a Christmas range coming soon.

Now that she had everyone's attention, Annie officially opened the memorial event by thanking them all for being here.

'Beatrice, or Trixie as she preferred to be called, was a truly remarkable woman who left a lasting legacy that I know some of you here today are personal testament to . . .' She paused to tilt her glass in Monsieur Aumont's – Pierre's – direction. He was standing stoically by the shelving unit that led down to the basement, with his wife beside him and his three grown-up daughters and all their children. After Trixie's diary had revealed the truth of that terrible day for Pierre, the little Jewish boy from the orphanage, Maggie had written to him, asking if he would meet up with her, Annie and Kristen. Pierre had met the three women in a quiet restaurant, where over a long lunch he had gradually opened up and quietly spoken about his escape. He told them how Jeremy Sutherland was indeed the pilot in the basement who had taken him to Paulette in the forest so that he could escape over the border to safety in Switzerland where Paulette lived. Pierre remembered Jeremy telling him to run for his life into the arms of Paulette, who scooped him up just as the gunfire came. He remembered hesitating and trying to run back to see if he could help the man who had risked his own life for his, but Paulette refused to let him, saying it was too dangerous, and so the last he had seen of Jeremy was of him falling down dead, the scarlet of his blood stark against the white of the snow on the ground where he lay.

Years later, Pierre had returned to Paris and had looked after all of Trixie's legal affairs from then on, saying that she was an extremely modest woman who relished her privacy, and everything that she had done for him was still very painful to talk about. With Annie's help, while she was in England, Pierre had managed to trace Jeremy Sutherland's son, who had travelled here today, grateful for the opportunity to see his father, whose story he hadn't known, be honoured and celebrated for his bravery in taking a child to safety, and to recognize Trixie for the enormous risk she took in hiding him. There were also relatives of some of the other people who Trixie and Maurice had helped, after Pierre had managed to trace a family connection for every one of the twenty-seven coded names in the glass jar buried in the garden, so they could be remembered as Trixie had always intended. A record of those events in history. Pierre had also listened to Kristen talk of her Polish grandparents before accepting her apology for the way she had behaved in his office that day.

Annie went on to talk about Queenie too, who it turned out had indeed been a Special Operations Executive in the Second World War, having been noted for her quick wit and fast learning, not to mention her flawless French and German language skills.

'So, I would like us all to raise a toast to two very courageous women, Beatrice Archambeau and Enid Smith, or Trixie and Queenie as we know them, for their fearless determination, endurance, courage and unwavering friendship that lasted a lifetime, and beyond. Our thanks and debt of gratitude to two women who came from very different starts in life, but who always had each other's backs and knew the true meaning of friendship.' Annie thought of her own friend Beth, as she waited for Maggie to translate for the elderly men and Madame Bardin from her café, who had come along to commemorate Trixie too, before raising her glass. Beth had decided to extend her stay in Australia; her singing career was soaring and she had met a marvellous man who she was enjoying getting to know. So Annie was thrilled for her friend and always looked forward to their weekly online get-togethers.

Stepping aside, Annie listened as Ingrid spoke about her grandfather, Maurice, the talented jazz trombonist who had fought fearlessly as part of La Résistance. Her father too, who, only a young teenager during the Occupation, had known about the glass jar used to communicate coded messages and then when the dementia had developed in later life, he had regressed and taken it upon himself to fearlessly guard it, having also been bravely involved in some of the clandestine activities that had gone on in Cour Felice to save those being persecuted.

As Ingrid finished speaking, the celebrations moved outside, where the Mayor of Paris was waiting to unveil the commemorative plaque on the wall beside the door to Trixie's shop, Annie took another look around, her heart swelling on seeing all the familiar faces of family and friends. Everyone was here. Even a radiant Phoebe and her new husband, Jack, had come all the way back from where they lived now, with Beth in Australia, to see Annie and to join in the celebrations. Joanie too, had ventured through the Channel Tunnel, with Sandra – her son-in-law chauffeuring them door to door from Tindledale.

That's right, Joanie and Sandra had decided to live their luxury life in the brand-new retirement complex that had just opened on the outskirts of Tindledale. Having discovered her mother, Queenie, had come from the village, and her brother Stanley was remembered on the war memorial in the village square, Joanie had decided it was the perfect place to be, not least because she finally had the chance to get to know her extended new family. Kathryn had five daughters and numerous grandchildren, so Joanie now had a lovely large family, which she was enjoying being a part of. She was also delighted that the luxury living complex had its very own minibus, with gold lettering down the side, that did a twice-daily run into the village, so she and Sandra could meet up with their new friends, Hettie and Marigold, in The Spotted Pig café and teashop. As Joanie had said herself, when Annie had had a quiet moment alone with her earlier: she was having the time of her life!

While the party was in full flow, Annie wandered through the studio, stopping to shake hands and have a catch-up with everyone before slipping upstairs into her apartment, wanting a moment to herself to contemplate all that had happened since that day back in Greenwich when she had fallen off the ladder and fractured her foot. She looked around the drawing room, resplendent with its spruced-up décor and redesigned gallery of pictures.

When she had been renovating the basement, Annie had found an old suitcase belonging to Trixie, that had been hidden on a ledge up high in the chimney breast. Inside the suitcase, there had been a small brown envelope with a selection of black-and-white photos, with Trixie's now familiar cursive handwriting on the back. And so now Annie had a fantastically atmospheric and poignant picture of Trixie herself, wearing a beaded flapper dress, a feathered headband and long satin gloves up to her elbows. On one side was her friend Queenie, on the other her dear friend Monty, with a flamboyant silk scarf draped around his shoulders, dazzling and loving life. And Annie felt grateful that he'd had that moment in time, here in Paris in *Les Années Folles*, to be free to live his life in the way he chose. She reached a fingertip out to touch the glass covering their smiling, happy faces, before turning to see Étienne coming into the room. Taking her hand, he greeted her with a kiss on each cheek before leading her over to their favourite spot by the window seat.

'How do you feel?' Étienne asked, wrapping his arms around her back and resting his head on top of hers as she gazed out of the window where Trixie and Maurice would have once stood. And Annie loved the feeling of living in history. She loved coming in here to the drawing room in the early morning to watch the sun rise over the rooftops of Paris, then dip and cast a golden glow in the evening. The tip of the Eiffel Tower twinkling, as if winking at her and welcoming her to her new home.

'I feel alive,' Annie told him, 'and that it's true what they say . . .'

'What do they say, *ma chérie*?' he asked.

'That's it's never too late to follow your dreams . . .'

And as Annie tilted her head sideways to kiss the man that she was falling in love with she gazed out through the open windows and up high into the cerulean blue, cloudless sky and across the beautiful City of Light. She smiled, feeling over the moon to have brought the sparkle back into her life, happy and excited as she thought about how her own postcard from Paris would now read . . .

Dear Reader,

I hope you have enjoyed reading *A Postcard from Paris* as much as I loved writing it. This year, more than ever, it was wonderful to transport myself to another time and place every day during lockdown as I wrote the book.

My first trip to Paris was in 2005 for a long weekend with my husband, then boyfriend. We travelled by train and arrived at Gare du Nord just as Annie does in *A Postcard from Paris*. From the very first moment I stepped into the bustling metropolis of Paris, joining the taxi queue and then asking the driver to take the scenic route past all the iconic highlights on the way to our hotel, I knew that I was going to adore the City of Light forevermore.

The sights and sounds that greeted us were incredible. I remember an elegant woman dressed from head to toe in Chanel, her hair in a chic, platinum chignon with a fluffy white Bichon Frise tucked under her arm, and a group of French men chatting animatedly, shrugging and gesticulating before hugging and going about their business. Both scenes are stored away in my memory and now immortalized in the pages of this book. There was accordion music, the scent of pomme frites drizzled in garlic butter, coffee and croissants, and creamy hot chocolate – or *chocolat chaud*, as they say in Paris – so deliciously dense you can stand a teaspoon up in the mug.

After checking in to our shabby chic boutique hotel in the Quartier de l'Opéra, we headed out to see the sights. Wandering along cobbled boulevards past red-canopied cafés and bistros and popping into covered markets – the Marché couvert de Passy with its original 1950s white façade – and admiring the pots of colourful flowers, the baguettes and Madeleine cakes piled up high. Climbing steep flights of steps for a glorious view in Montmartre, just as Annie and Etienne do when he wants her to see the Paris he loves. By night, we strolled the length of the Champs-Élysées, looking at the pretty lights in the shop windows before choosing a restaurant with a view of the Arc de Triomphe. We sat outside in the blissfully warm springtime breeze and ate the most delicious steaming pots of French onion soup with giant cheesy crouton caps, followed by the best *croque monsieur* I've ever tasted.

We explored some more, gasping at the illuminated, rose gold Eiffel Tower set against the starry night sky. The next day, we walked along the glittering Seine, past the many stalls to browse books and paintings before crossing the Pont des Arts bridge and onto the Louvre. We took in the gothic splendour of Notre

Dame, a moment of tranquillity in the gardens beside it. Onto the left bank, and I couldn't visit Paris without going into the world-famous Shakespeare and Company bookshop frequented by famous authors such as F. Scott Fitzgerald, Ernest Hemingway and T. S. Eliot. Dear reader, it was in the back of this bookshop amongst the first-edition romance classics that he asked me to marry him. Of course, I said yes. How could I not? In Paris, the most breathtakingly beautiful and romantic city in the world . . .

Alex x

Acknowledgements

Ooh, la la! Well, 2020 has been quite the year, hasn't it? I wouldn't have got through lockdown and all that it entailed, let alone written *A Postcard from Paris*, without the kindness, compassion and care packages of sweets from my brilliant editor and dear friend, Kate Bradley. My thanks also go to Kim Young, Charlotte Ledger, Jen Harlow, Lara Stevenson and all the incredibly hardworking team at HarperCollins. A special thanks to Andrew Davis for designing the most beautifully evocative cover for *A Postcard from Paris*, and instantly dispelling that old adage of 'never judge a book by its cover' – in this case I hope everyone absolutely does.

A very big thank you to my copy editor, Penny Isaac, for not only polishing up and putting the sparkle on my manuscripts for the last ten years but for sharing her invaluable knowledge gained from living in Paris too. My agent, Tim Bates, and the rights team at PF for getting my books into the hands of readers all around the world. To Kay Sharon for kindly getting involved and suggesting 'Joanie' when I asked my Facebook page community for character name ideas.

Caroline Smailes, as always, for being such a wonderfully kind, patient and generous friend. Thanks a million to my husband, Paul, aka Cheeks, for holding the fort while I procrastinated and then calming my panic when the deadlines were looming. An extra special thank you to my darling girl, QT, for giving me joy every day and offering a plethora of potential plot ideas and future book titles.

My biggest thanks go to all of you, my wonderful readers. I love chatting to you on social media and reading your emails and messages. I feel very grateful and humbled by the trust you place in me when you get in touch to share personal accounts of how my books have been a comfort or escape during a difficult time in your life, or when you've chosen one of my books to read in your precious holiday time. You mean the world to me and make it all worthwhile. Thank you so very much for loving my books as much as I love writing them for you.

Luck and love

Alex x

Keep in touch with

ALEX BROWN

Writes books...

For all the latest book news, exclusive content
and competitions, visit Alex's website
and sign up to her newsletter at

www.alexbrownauthor.com

When you sign up to the newsletter,
you'll be the first to hear about:

- New books

- Free extracts

- Giveaways and competitions

You will also receive my exclusive and free
short story, *The Beach Walk*.